MARIA FINN DOMINGUEZ

CUBA IN MIND

While teaching in the English Department at Hunter College of the City University of New York, Maria Finn Dominguez designed and taught an intersession writing course for CUNY students at Casa de las Américas in Havana, Cuba. She works as a freelance writer and has written for, among many others, *The New York Times*, *Audubon Magazine*, and the *Anchorage Daily News*, and she has been a commentator for Alaska Public Radio. She has an MFA in Creative Writing from Sarah Lawrence College and has published literary work in magazines such as *The Chicago Review*, *New Letters*, and *Exquisite Corpse*. She has lived and worked in Alaska, Guatemala, and Spain, and traveled extensively throughout Latin America. She and her husband, Rafael Dominguez, met in Havana, Cuba. They now live in Brooklyn, New York.

France in Mind, edited by Alice Leccese Powers

Ireland in Mind, edited by Alice Leccese Powers

Italy in Mind, edited by Alice Leccese Powers

Paris in Mind, edited by Jennifer Lee

CUBA IN MIND

CUBA IN MIND

AN ANTHOLOGY

Edited and with an Introduction by

Maria Finn Dominguez

Vintage Departures

VINTAGE BOOKS

A DIVISION OF RANDOM HOUSE, INC.

NEW YORK

A VINTAGE DEPARTURES ORIGINAL, JUNE 2004

"Declaration of Love" by Carilda Oliver Labra, from *Dust Disappears* (1991), published by
permission of Cross-Cultural Communication. Translated by Daniela Gioseffi
and Enildo A. Garcia.

Permissions can be found at the end of the book.

Library of Congress Cataloging-in-Publication Data
Cuba in mind : an anthology / edited and with an introduction by Maria Finn Dominguez.
p.   cm.—(Vintage departures)
ISBN 1-4000-7613-7 (trade paper)
1. Cuba—Literary collections. 2. Cuba—Description and travel. 3. American literature.
4. English literature. 5. Americans—Cuba. 6. British—Cuba. I. Dominguez, Maria Finn.
PS509.C82C823   2004
810.9'0327291—dc22   2003068898

Book design by JoAnne Metsch

www.vintagebooks.com

Printed in the United States of America
10 9 8 7 6 5 4 3 2 1

ACKNOWLEDGMENTS

I would like to thank my editor, Diana Secker Larson, for all her work on this book, as well as my agent, Jen Unter, for her continued support. I'd also like to express my appreciation to The Center for Puerto Rican Studies at the City University of New York, particularly Pedro Pedraza and Rossy Matos, who helped facilitate the research for this anthology. I am grateful to Britta Frahm and Alison Cornyn for helping me sort out the paperwork, and a special thanks to Brenda McCarthy for being an insightful reader of early drafts. Finally, I'd especially like to thank my parents, William and Beth Finn, for teaching me a love of reading and traveling.

CONTENTS

EXPATRIATES, REAL AND IMAGINED / 97

"People ask you why you live in Cuba and you say it is because
you like it. It is too complicated to explain. . . ."

—Ernest Hemingway

EXILES, IMMIGRANTS, AND THEIR OFFSPRING / 237

"My head buzzed with the sudden recognition of a place that held something for me beyond memory."

—Rosa Lowinger

INTRODUCTION

When Christopher Columbus arrived in Cuba in 1492, he wrote in his journal, "This country is the most beautiful that human eyes have ever seen." Since then, no other place on earth has evoked such passion, albeit as much for the politics as for the landscape. A contentious love-hate relationship has existed between the U.S. and Cuban governments for decades, and the economic embargo that prohibits Americans from traveling to Cuba has only served to fuel the rest of the world's interest. Even before these conflicts, Cuba had long been a popular destination for travelers, and writers who have visited over the years have left a record of their enthusiasm for this Caribbean island, whether they turned their gazes to the winding, coral streets of colonial Havana or the white sand beaches and sparkling blue seas.

Apart from the stunning architecture and natural beauty, it's the Cuban people who make the most profound impression: the Santería priests and priestesses, the *coco* taxi drivers, the cabaret dancers, the old women puffing cigars, the mambo drummers, the men and women who have fine-tuned seduction into an art form. A rhythm flows through Cuba, from the tapping of the *clave* in salsa music to the drumbeat of the rumba, from vibrant carnivals to political rallies, from the sea crashing over the Malecón to the wind blowing through the Royal Palms. A tropical undercurrent that pulses through both nightlife and nature, it is central to this country's gregarious people and their unique history. In Cuba, nothing is average; it is either heartbreaking or exhilarating.

For this anthology, I have chosen works by writers from differ-

ent time periods, places, and genres, so that the reader can get a
sense of the history and culture, but I also tried to choose pieces
that present this elusive rhythm and its seduction.

In the first of four sections, "Travelers," I have grouped the letters, journals, essays, and travel writing of visitors to Cuba span-
ning a century and a half, from Anthony Trollope to Robert
Stone, testimony to the enduring mix of bewilderment and fascination with which outsiders have always tried to understand the
island. The second section, "Expatriates, Real and Imagined,"
includes writing both by and about visitors who have come to stay
and therefore become more deeply entangled in the place, starting
with Ernest Hemingway, of course, and encompassing the fictional protagonists of Graham Greene and Elmore Leonard. The
third section, "Aficionados," presents essays, poems, and interviews by writers—usually repeat visitors—who have nurtured a
particular interest in or enthusiasm for Cuba. These range from a
reporter investigating Santería, to a naturalist recalling the island's
stunning wildlife, to a documentary filmmaker in search of the
spirit of Cuban women. Finally, "Exiles, Immigrants, and Their
Offspring" offers a range of poignant and often unsettling per-
spectives from those Americans—from Oscar Hijuelos to Cristina
García to Carlos Eire—who are bound to the island by the ties of
memory and love.

This collection of work has been greatly influenced by my own
experiences in Cuba. I recently taught a three-week writing course
at the Casa de las Américas in Havana for a group of New York
City undergraduate students, and I've created the anthology I
wish I had had when teaching the class. The course was in creative
nonfiction, and the students were to write memoirs, literary
essays, journalism, or travel writing. I encouraged them to follow
their interests, find their voices, and try to capture on paper a feel
for Cuba, but after reading their first drafts I realized how difficult
they found this. The students had certainly had vivid escapades,

and had been cajoled, swindled, charmed, and seduced by the Cubans. In class they were able to talk about their experiences—dancing all night at the feet of an enormous statue of Jesus that looms over the Havana harbor; the hip-hop clubs they found; the graveyards they went to, searching for their ancestors' names; the classic cars they rode in—but when it came time to write, they turned in drafts that could as easily have been written in a library in New York City. The lived experience of Cuba was missing from their writing.

So I had them read Langston Hughes, so they could absorb his description of music in Cuba: "The tap of claves, the rattle of gourds, the dong of iron bells, the deep steady roll of drums speak of the earth, life bursting warm from the earth, and earth and sun moving in the steady rhythms of procreation and joy." For those interested in Santería, I encouraged them to ignore the sensationalized accounts they came across and read an essay by Elizabeth Hanly that states: "Drumming in Cuba seems always to touch on desire. And every bit of the drumming, like the island's soul itself, is seeped in the sacred rhythms of Santería."

For the students interested in nature, *A Naturalist in Cuba* by Thomas Barbour was an absolute must, as he interweaves encounters with Cuban scientists and *guajiros* (the farmers or country people from the eastern provinces) and observations on culture and politics with amazing accounts of exploring the caves and forests of Cuba in the 1930s. For the Hemingway buffs, we visited his home, Finca Vigia, and read his explanation of why he chose to live in Cuba in the article "The Great Blue River."

I tried to teach that an essay should be about more than one thing, and I found a perfect example in the account of Rosa Lowinger visiting Cuba both as an art restorer and as a returning Cuban American: "For me, Cuba was a place left behind, a place of sadness and loss, a place once beautiful and full of promise that now languished in a rubble of despair."

Ultimately, their papers were wonderful, and the students' work in turn influenced this anthology. One student's visit to synagogues in Havana led me to seek out the short story by Ruth Behar about love, returning to Cuba, and her Jewish identity. Another student was searching for her Chinese grandfather who had left for Cuba never to be heard from again, so I looked for writings about the cultural contributions of the Chinese in Cuba, and to my delight found Ricardo Pau-Llosa's poem "Charada China." A paper on the Cuban chef and television personality Nitza Villapol led me to select an interview with her from the book *Trading with the Enemy* by Tom Miller. A student's tour through the sandlots of Havana brought to light the way baseball can serve as a metaphor for American-Cuban relations, and the short story "Batting Against Castro" by Jim Shepard couldn't illuminate the ironies any better.

The students and I left Cuba with heavy hearts, knowing it could be a long time before we would be allowed to return. Cubans are some of the friendliest, most accessible people in the world despite their authoritarian government; we had encountered unbounded generosity by Cubans in the face of crippling poverty, and, in the words of one of my students, "people who know how to have great fun while only earning seven dollars a month."

Compiling this collection has been an immense pleasure. Being steeped in writings about Cuba has been a salve for the sadness I've felt since leaving the island. Cuba changes people who visit, and when I left I felt as though the music that once surrounded me had stopped playing. So while researching this book, I searched for that rhythm and tried to find that music. I tried to capture as well the tropical beauty of the island, the warmth and humor of the Cuban people, and the volatile politics of this country.

It is my dream that the writers in this anthology will not long have to serve as eyes and ears for people who aren't allowed to go there, but instead as traveling companions. When that day comes, readers may be able to enjoy the tales told by Pico Iyer and Elmore Leonard, the ruminations of Allen Ginsberg, and the poetry of Jayne Cortez while the Caribbean sun drenches the horizon red, with a mojito in hand, *son* music playing in the distance, and good Cuban friends nearby.

CUBA IN MIND

Travelers

"Because most visitors have only the vaguest idea of Cuba's troubled history, I am going to review it as briefly as I can, and if you are not interested, you can skip to the part about cocktails."

—*Eleanor Early*

ANTHONY TROLLOPE
(1 8 1 5 – 1 8 8 2)

Intimate chronicler of Victorian life in England, Anthony Trollope published over forty novels, as well as short stories, travel books, and essays. While writing novels, Trollope also worked for Great Britain's postal service in Ireland. On post office business, Trollope traveled in Egypt (1858) and to the West Indies (1858–1859), and during this voyage he wrote a travel book titled *The West Indies and the Spanish Main*.

Trollope brings his novelistic descriptions and social commentary to his travelogue. The Spanish occupation of the island, the potential annexation of Cuba to the United States, and in particular, slavery, are topics of interest to him. By the eighteenth century, Cuba's prosperous economy was primarily based on sugar exports, and this period saw a rise in the importation of Africans sold into slavery to work the sugar plantations. By the nineteenth century Cuba was one of the richest colonies in the world. Trollope takes a keen interest in the moral and social implications of the slave trade. Slavery had been outlawed in England, and even the pre–Civil War United States had banned the importation of new slaves from Africa, and yet the Spanish still allowed the slave trade to take place in Cuba. Cuba did not officially ban slavery until 1886.

from THE WEST INDIES AND THE SPANISH MAIN

Cuba is the largest and the most westerly of the west Indian islands. It is in the shape of a half-moon, and with one of its horns nearly lies across the mouth of the Gulf of Mexico. It

belongs to the Spanish crown, of which it is by far the most splendid appendage. So much for facts—geographical and historical.

The journey from Kingston to Cien Fuegos, of which I have
said somewhat in my first chapter, was not completed under better auspices than those which witnessed its commencement. That
perfidious bark, built in the eclipse, was bad to the last, and my
voyage took nine days instead of three. My humble stock of provisions had long been all gone, and my patience was nearly at as
low an ebb. Then, as a finale, the Cuban pilot who took us in hand
as we entered the port ran us on shore just under the Spanish fort,
and there left us. From this position it was impossible to escape,
though the shore lay close to us, inasmuch as it is an offence of
the gravest nature to land in those ports without ceremony of a
visit from the medical officer; and no medical officer would come
to us there. And then two of our small crew had been taken sick,
and we had before us in our mind's eye all the pleasures of quar-
antine.

A man, and especially an author, is thankful for calamities if
they be of a tragic dye. It would be as good as a small fortune to
be left for three days without food or water, or to run for one's life
before a black storm on unknown seas in a small boat. But we had
no such luck as this. There was plenty of food, though it was not
very palatable; and the peril of our position cannot be insisted on,
as we might have thrown a baby on shore from the vessel, let
alone a biscuit. We did what we could to get up a catastrophe
among the sharks, by bathing off the ship's sides. But even this
was in vain. One small shark we did see. But in lieu of it eating us,
we ate it. In spite of the popular prejudice, I have to declare that it
was delicious.

But at last I did find myself in the hotel at Cien Fuegos. And
here I must say a word in praise of the civility of the Spanish
authorities of that town and, indeed, of those gentlemen generally wherever I chanced to meet them. They welcome you with
easy courtesy; offer you coffee or beer; assure you at parting that

their whole house is at your disposal; and then load you—at least they so loaded me—with cigars.

"My friend," said the captain of the port, holding in his hand a huge parcel of these articles, each about seven inches long—"I wish I could do you a service. It would make me happy for ever if I could truly serve you."

"Señor, the service you have done me is inestimable in allowing me to make the acquaintance of Don——."

"But at least accept these few cigars"; and then he pressed the bundle into my hand, and pressed his own hand over mine. "Smoke one daily after dinner; and when you procure any that are better, do a fastidious old smoker the great kindness to inform him where they are to be found."

This treasure to which his fancy alluded, but in the existence of which he will never believe, I have not yet discovered.

Cien Fuegos is a small new town on the southern coast of Cuba, created by the sugar trade, and devoted, of course, to commerce. It is clean, prosperous, and quickly increasing. Its streets are lighted with gas, while those in the Havana still depend upon oil-lamps. It has its opera, its governor's house, its alameda, its military and public hospital, its market-place, and railway station; and unless the engineers deceive themselves, it will in time have its well. It has also that institution which in the eyes of travellers ranks so much above all others, a good and clean inn.

My first object after landing was to see a slave sugar estate. I had been told in Jamaica that to effect this required some little management; that the owners of the slaves were not usually willing to allow strangers to see them at work; and that the manufacture of sugar in Cuba was as a rule kept sacred from profane eyes. But I found no such difficulty. I made my request to an English merchant at Cien Fuegos, and he gave me a letter of introduction to the proprietor of an estate some fifteen miles from the town; and by their joint courtesy I saw all that I wished.

On this property, which consisted altogether of eighteen hun-

dred acres—the greater portion of which was not yet under culti-
vation—there were six hundred acres of cane pieces. The average
year's produce was eighteen hundred hogsheads, or three hogsheads to the acre. The hogshead was intended to represent a ton
of sugar when it reached the market, but judging from all that I
could learn it usually fell short of it by more than a hundred-
weight. The value of such a hogshead at Cien Fuegos was about
twenty-five pounds. There were one hundred and fifty negro men
on the estate, the average cash value of each man being three hundred and fifty pounds; most of the men had their wives. In stating
this it must not be supposed that either I or my informant insist
much on the validity of their marriage ceremony; any such ceremony was probably of rare occurrence. During the crop time, at
which period my visit was made, and which lasts generally from
November till May, the negroes sleep during six hours out of the
twenty-four, have two for their meals, and work for sixteen! No
difference is made on Sunday. Their food is very plentiful, and of
a good and strong description. They are sleek and fat and large,
like well-preserved brewers' horses; and with reference to them,
as also with reference to the brewers' horses, it has probably been
ascertained what amount of work may be exacted so as to give
the greatest profit. During the remainder of the year the labour of
the negroes averages twelve hours a day, and one day of rest in the
week is usually allowed to them.

I was of course anxious to see what was the nature of the coer-
cive measures used with them. But in this respect my curiosity was
not indulged. I can only say that I saw none, and saw the mark and
signs of none. No doubt the whip is in use, but I did not see it.
The gentleman whose estate I visited had no notice of our coming, and there was no appearance of anything being hidden from
us. I could not, however, bring myself to inquire of him as to their
punishment.

The slaves throughout the island are always as a rule baptized.
Those who are employed in the town and as household servants

appear to be educated in compliance with, at any rate the outward doctrines of, the Roman Catholic church. But with the great mass of the negroes—those who work on the sugarcanes—all attention to religion ends with their baptism. They have the advantage, whatever it may be, of that ceremony in infancy; and from that time forth they are treated as the beasts of the stall.

From all that I could hear, as well as from what I could see, I have reason to think that, regarding them as beasts, they are well treated. Their hours of labour are certainly very long—so long as to appear almost impossible to a European workman. But under the system, such as it is, the men do not apparently lose their health, though, no doubt, they become prematurely old, and as a rule die early. The property is too valuable to be neglected or ill used. The object of course is to make that property pay; and therefore a present healthy condition is cared for, but long life is not regarded. It is exactly the same with horses in this country.

When all has been said that can be said in favour of the slave-owner in Cuba, it comes to this—that he treats his slaves as beasts of burden, and so treating them, does it skilfully and with prudence. The point which most shocks an Englishman is the absence of all religion, the ignoring of the black man's soul. But this, perhaps, may be taken as an excuse, that the white men here ignore their own souls also. The Roman Catholic worship seems to be at a lower ebb in Cuba than almost any country in which I have seen it.

It is singular that no priest should even make any effort on the subject with regard to the negroes; but I am assured that such is the fact. They do not wish to do so; nor will they allow of any one asking them to make the experiment. One would think that had there been any truth or any courage in them, they would have declared the inutility of baptism, and have proclaimed the negroes have no souls. But there is no truth in them; neither is there any courage.

The works at the Cuban sugar estate were very different from those I had seen at Jamaica. They were on a much larger scale, in much better order, overlooked by a larger proportion of white men, with a greater amount of skilled labour. The evidences of capital were very plain in Cuba; whereas, the want of it was frequently equally plain in our own island.

Not that the planters in Cuba are as a rule themselves very rich men. The estates are deeply mortgaged to the different merchants at the different ports, as are those in Jamaica to the merchants of Kingston. These merchants in Cuba are generally Americans, Englishmen, Germans, Spaniards from the American republics—anything but Cubans; and the slave-owners are but the go-betweens, who secure the profits of the slave-trade for the merchants.

My friend at the estate invited us to a late breakfast after having shown me what I came to see. "You have taken me so unawares," said he, "that we cannot offer you much except a welcome." Well, it was not much—for Cuba perhaps. A delicious soup, made partly of eggs, a bottle of excellent claret, a paté de foie gras, some game deliciously dressed, and half a dozen kinds of vegetables; that was all. I had seen nothing among the slaves which in any way interfered with my appetite, or with the cup of coffee and cigar which came after the little nothings above mentioned.

We then went down to the railway station. It was a peculiar station I was told, and the tickets could not be paid for till we reached Cien Fuegos. But, lo! on arriving at Cien Fuegos there was nothing more to pay. "It has all been done," said someone to me.

If one was but convinced that those sleek, fat, smiling bipeds were but two legged beasts of burden, and nothing more, all would have been well at the estate which we visited.

All Cuba was of course full of the late message from the President of the United States, which at the time of my visit was some two months old there. The purport of what Mr. Buchanan said regarding Cuba may perhaps be expressed as follows: "Circumstances and destiny absolutely require that the United States should be the masters of that island. That we should take it by filibustering or violence is not in accordance with our national genius. It will suit our character and honesty much better that we should obtain it by purchase. Let us therefore offer a fair price for it. If a fair price be refused, that of course will be a casus belli. Spain will then have injured us, and we may declare war. Under these circumstances we should probably obtain the place without purchase; but let us hope better things." This is what the President has said, either in plain words or by inference equally plain.

It may easily be conceived with what feeling such an announcement has been received by Spain and those who hold Spanish authority in Cuba. There is an outspoken insolence in the threat, which, by a first-class power, would itself have been considered a cause for war. But Spain is not a first-class power, and like the other weak ones of the earth must either perish or live by adhering to and obeying those who will protect her. Though too ignoble to be strong, she has been too proud to be obedient. And as a matter of course she will go to the wall.

A scrupulous man who feels that he would fain regulate his course in politics by the same line as that used for his ordinary life cannot but feel angry at the loud tone of America's audacious threat. But even such a one knows that that threat will sooner or later be carried out, and that humanity will benefit by its accomplishment. Perhaps it may be said that scrupulous men should have but little dealing in state policy.

The plea under which Mr. Buchanan proposes to quarrel with Spain, if she will not sell that which America wishes to buy, is the plea under which Ahab quarrelled with Naboth. A man is, individually, disgusted that a President of the United States should have made such an utterance. But looking at the question in a broader point of view, in one which regards future ages rather than the present time, one can hardly refrain from rejoicing at any event which will tend to bring about that which in itself is so desirable.

[…]

From such information as I could obtain, I am of opinion that the Cubans themselves would be glad enough to see the transfer well effected. How, indeed, can it be otherwise? At present they have no national privilege except that of undergoing taxation. Every office is held by a Spaniard. Every soldier in the island—and they say that there are twenty-five thousand—must be a Spaniard. The ships of war are commanded and manned by Spaniards. All that is shown before their eyes of brilliancy and power and high place is purely Spanish. No Cuban has any voice in his own country. He can never have the consolation of thinking that his tyrant is his countryman, or reflect that under altered circumstances it might possibly have been his fortune to tyrannize. What love can he have for Spain? He cannot even have the poor pride of being slave to a great lord. He is the lacquey of a reduced gentleman, and lives on the vails of those who despise his master. Of course the transfer would be grateful to him.

But no Cuban will himself do anything to bring it about. To wish is one thing; to act is another. A man standing behind his counter may feel that his hand is restricted on every side, and his taxes alone unrestricted; but he must have other than Hispano-Creole blood in his veins if he do more than stand and feel. Indeed, wishing is too strong a word to be fairly applicable to his state of mind. He would be glad that Cuba should be American; but he would prefer that he himself should lie in a dormant state while the dangerous transfer is going on.

I have ventured to say that humanity would certainly be benefited by such a transfer. We, when we think of Cuba, think of it almost entirely as a slave country. And, indeed, in this light, and in this light only, is it peculiar, being the solitary land into which slaves are now systematically imported out of Africa. Into that great question of guarding the slave coast it would be futile here to enter; but this I believe is acknowledged, that if the Cuban market be closed against the trade, the trade must perish of exhaustion. At present slaves are brought into Cuba in spite of us; and as we all know, can be brought in under the American stars and stripes. But no one accuses the American Government of systematically favouring an importation of Africans into their own States. When Cuba becomes one of them the trade will cease. The obstacle to that trade which is created by our vessels of war on the coast of Africa may, or may not, be worth the cost. But no man who looks into the subject will presume to say that we can be as efficacious there as the Americans would be if they were the owners of the present slave-market.

I do not know whether it be sufficiently understood in England, that though slavery is an institution of the United States, the slave-trade, as commonly understood under that denomination, is as illegal there as in England. That slavery itself would be continued in Cuba under the Americans—continued for a while—is of course certain. So is it in Louisiana and the Carolinas. But the horrors of the middle passage, the kidnapping of negroes, the African wars which are waged for the sake of prisoners, would of necessity come to an end.

But this slave-trade is as opposed to the laws of Spain and its colonies as it is to those of the United States or of Great Britain. This is true; and were the law carried out in Cuba as well as it is in the United States, an Englishman would feel disinclined to look on with calmness at the violent dismemberment of the Spanish empire. But in Cuba the law is broken systematically. The Captain-General in Cuba will allow no Africans to be imported into the island—except for a consideration. It is said that the present Captain-General receives only a gold doubloon, or about three pounds twelve shillings, on every head of wool so brought in; and he has therefore the reputation of being a very moderate man. O'Donnel required twice as large a bribe. Valdez would take nothing, and he is spoken of as the foolish Governor. Even he, though he would take no bribe, was not allowed to throw obstacles in the way of the slave-trade. That such a bribe is usually demanded, and as a matter of course paid, is as well known—ay, much better known, than any other of the island port duties. The fact is so notorious to all men that it is almost as absurd to insist on it as it would be to urge that the income of the Queen of England is paid from the taxes. It is known to every one, and among others is known to the government of Spain. Under these circumstances, who can feel sympathy with her, or wish that she should retain her colony? Does she not daily show that she is unfit to hold it?

There must be some stage in misgovernment which will justify the interference of bystanding nations, in the name of humanity. That rule in life which forbids a man to come between a husband and his wife is a good rule. But nevertheless, who can stand by quiescent and see a brute half murder the poor woman whom he should protect?

And in other ways, and through causes also, humanity would be benefited by such a transfer. We in England are not very fond of a republic. We would hardly exchange our throne for a president's chair, or even dispense at present with our House of Peers or our Bench of Bishops. But we can see that men thrive under the stars and stripes; whereas they pine beneath the red and yellow flag of Spain. This, it may be said, is attributable to the race of the men rather than to the government. But the race will be improved by the infusion of new blood. Let the world say what chance there is of such improvement in the Spanish government.

The trade of the country is falling into the hands of foreigners— into those principally of Americans from the States. The Havana will soon become as much American as New Orleans. It requires but little of the spirit of prophecy to foretell that the Spanish rule will not be long obeyed by such people.

WILLIAM CULLEN BRYANT
(1794-1878)

A precocious child prodigy, William Cullen Bryant published his first poem, a political satire on the Jeffersonian Party, in 1808 at the age of thirteen. By the age of eighteen, he had published the poem "Thanatopsis," which sealed his place in the American canon of poetry and earned him a reputation in England as well. Bryant went on to study and practice law, but that career did not last long, and he returned to writing poetry and took up journalism. Bryant traveled extensively in the United States, Europe, and Cuba. He sent reports of these places back to be published in the *Evening Post*. Eventually these letters were collected in book form and entitled *Letters of a Traveller*.

In Letter XLVIII, Bryant visits the town of Matanzas and the nearby valleys and mountainsides. From here he reports on the sugar industry and the process by which sugar was refined. Throughout the history of the island, Cuba's most important crop and primary export has been sugar. From the plantations that fueled the slave trade, the arrival of American landowners after the war of independence with Spain, and the recent collapse of Cuba's sugar industry, this crop has been intimately intertwined with Cuban history and culture.

※

LETTER XLVIII
from LETTERS OF A TRAVELLER
MATANZAS—VALLEY OF YUMURI

Los Guines, April 18, 1849

In the long circuit of railway which leads from Havana to Matanzas, I saw nothing remarkably different from what I observed on my excursion to San Antonio. There was the same smooth coun-

13

try, of great apparent fertility, sometimes varied with gentle undu-
lations, and sometimes rising, in the distance, into hills covered
with thickets. We swept by dark-green fields planted with the yuca,
an esculent root, of which the cassava bread is made, pale-green
fields of the cane, brown tracts of pasturage, partly formed of
abandoned coffee estates where the palms and scattered fruit-
trees were yet standing, and forests of shrubs and twining plants
growing for the most part among rocks. Some of these rocky
tracts have a peculiar appearance; they consist of rough projec-
tions of rock a foot or two in height, of irregular shape and full of
holes; these are called *diente de perro,* or dog's teeth. Here the trees
and creepers find openings filled with soil, by which they are
nourished. We passed two or three country cemeteries, where that
foulest of birds, the turkey-vulture, was seen sitting on the white
stuccoed walls, or hovering on his ragged wings in circles above
them.

In passing over the neighborhood of the town in which I am
now writing, I found myself on the black lands of the island. Here
the rich dark earth of the plain lies on a bed of chalk as white as
snow, as was apparent where the earth had been excavated to a little depth, on each side of the railway, to form the causey on which
it ran. Streams of clear water, diverted from a river to the left,
traversed the plain with a swift current, almost even with the surface of the soil, which they keep in perpetual freshness. As we
approached Matanzas, we saw more extensive tracts of cane clothing the broad slopes with their dense blades, as if the coarse sedge
of a river had been transplanted to the uplands.

At length the bay of Matanzas opened before us; a long tract of
water stretching to the northeast, into which several rivers empty
themselves. The town lay at the southwestern extremity, sheltered
by hills, where the San Juan and the Yumuri pour themselves into
the brine. It is a small but prosperous town, with a considerable
trade, as was indicated by the vessels at anchor in the harbor.

As we passed along the harbor I remarked an extensive, healthy-looking orchard of plantains growing on one of those tracts which they call *diente de perro*. I could see nothing but the jagged teeth of whitish rock, and the green swelling stems of the plantain, from ten to fifteen feet in height, and as large as a man's leg, or larger. The stalks of the plantain are juicy and herbaceous, and of so yielding a texture, that with a sickle you might entirely sever the largest of them at a single stroke. How such a multitude of succulent plants could find nourishment on what seemed to the eye little else than barren rock, I could not imagine.

The day after arriving at Matanzas we made an excursion on horseback to the summit of the hill, immediately overlooking the town, called the Cumbre. Light hardy horses of the country were brought us, with high pommels to the saddles, which are also raised behind in a manner making it difficult to throw the rider from his seat. A negro fitted a spur to my right heel, and mounting by the short stirrups, I crossed the river Yumuri with my companions, and began to climb the Cumbre. They boast at Matanzas of the perpetual coolness of temperature enjoyed upon the broad summit of this hill, where many of the opulent merchants of the town have their country houses, to which the mosquitoes and the intermittents that infest the town below, never come, and where, as one of them told me, you may play at billiards in August without any inconvenient perspiration.

From the Cumbre you behold the entire extent of the harbor; the town lies below you with its thicket of masts, and its dusty *paseo*, where rows of the Cuba pine stand rooted in the red soil. On the opposite shore your eye is attracted to a chasm between high rocks, where the river Canimar comes forth through banks of romantic beauty so they are described to me—and mingles with the sea. But the view to the west was much finer; there lay the valley of the Yumuri, and a sight of it is worth a voyage to the island. In regard to this my expectations suffered no disappointment.

Before me lay a deep valley, surrounded on all sides by hills and mountains, with the little river Yumuri twining at the bottom. Smooth round hillocks rose from the side next to me, covered with clusters of palms, and the steeps of the southeastern corner of the valley were clothed with a wood of intense green, where I could almost see the leaves glisten in the sunshine. The broad fields below were waving with cane and maize, and cottages of the *monteros* were scattered among them, each with its tuft of bamboos and its little grove of plantains. In some parts the cliffs almost seemed to impend over the valley; but to the west, in a soft golden haze, rose summit behind summit, and over them all, loftiest and most remote, towered the mountain called the *Pan de Matanzas*.

We stopped for a few moments at a country seat on the top of the Cumbre, where this beautiful view lay ever before the eye. Round it, in a garden, were cultivated the most showy plants of the tropics, but my attention was attracted to a little plantation of damask roses blooming profusely. They were scentless; the climate which supplies the orange blossom with intense odors exhausts the fragrance of the rose. At nightfall—the night falls suddenly in this latitude—we were again at our hotel.

We passed our Sunday on a sugar estate at the hospitable mansion of a planter from the United States about fifteen miles from Matanzas. The house stands on an eminence, once embowered in trees which the hurricanes have leveled, overlooking a broad valley, where palms were scattered in every direction; for the estate had formerly been a coffee plantation. In the huge buildings containing the machinery and other apparatus for making sugar, which stood at the foot of the eminence, the power of steam, which had been toiling all the week, was now at rest. As the hour of sunset approached, a smoke was seen rising from its chimney, presently puffs of vapor issued from the engine, its motion began to be heard, and the negroes, men and women, were summoned to begin the work of the week. Some fed the fire under the boiler with coal; others were seen rushing to the mill with their arms full of the stalks of cane, freshly cut, which they took from a huge pile near the building; others lighted fires under a row of huge cauldrons, with the dry stalks of cane from which the juice had been crushed by the mill. It was a spectacle of activity such as I had not seen in Cuba.

The sound of the engine was heard all night, for the work of grinding the cane, once begun, proceeds day and night, with the exception of Sundays and some other holidays. I was early next morning at the mill. A current of cane juice was flowing from the rollers in a long trunk to a vat in which it was clarified with lime; it was then made to pass successively from one seething cauldron to another, as it obtained a thicker consistence by boiling. The negroes, with huge ladles turning on pivots, swept it from cauldron to cauldron, and finally passed it into a trunk, which conveyed it to shallow tanks in another apartment, where it cooled into sugar. From these another set of workmen scooped it up in moist masses, carried it in buckets up a low flight of stairs, and poured it into rows of hogsheads pierced with holes at the bottom. These are placed over a large tank, into which the moisture dripping from the hogsheads is collected and forms molasses.

This is the method of making the sugar called Muscovado. It is drained a few days, and then the railways take it to Matanzas or to Havana. We visited afterward a plantation in the neighborhood, in which clayed sugar is made. Our host furnished us with horses to make the excursion, and we took a winding road, over hill and valley, by plantations and forests, till we stopped at the gate of an extensive pasture-ground. An old negro, whose hut was at hand, opened it for us, and bowed low as we passed. A ride of half a mile further brought us in sight of the cane-fields of the plantation called Saratoga, belonging to the house of Drake & Company, of Havana, and reputed one of the finest of the island. It had a different aspect from any plantation we had seen. Trees and shrubs there were none, but the canes, except where they had been newly cropped for the mill, clothed the slopes and hollows with their light-green blades, like the herbage of a prairie.

We were kindly received by the administrator of the estate, an intelligent Biscayan, who showed us the whole process of making clayed sugar. It does not differ from that of making the Muscovado, so far as concerns the grinding and boiling. When, however, the sugar is nearly cool, it is poured into iron vessels of conical shape, with the point downward, at which is an opening. The top of the sugar is then covered with a sort of black thick mud, which they call clay, and which is several times renewed as it becomes dry. The moisture from the clay passes through the sugar, carrying with it the cruder portions, which form molasses. In a few days the draining is complete.

We saw the work-people of the Saratoga estate preparing for the market the sugar thus cleansed, if we may apply the word to such a process. With a rude iron blade they cleft the large loaf of sugar just taken from the mould into three parts, called first, second and third quality, according to their whiteness. These are dried in the sun on separate platforms of wood with a raised edge; the women standing and walking over the fragments with their bare dirty feet, and beating them smaller with wooden mallets and clubs. The sugar of the first quality is then scraped up and put into boxes; that of the second and third, being moister, is handled a third time and carried into the drying-room, where it is exposed to the heat of a stove, and when sufficiently dry, is boxed up for market like the other.

The sight of these processes was not of a nature to make one think with much satisfaction of clayed sugar as an ingredient of food, but the inhabitants of the island are superior to such prejudices, and use it with as little scruple as they who do not know in what manner it is made.

In the afternoon we returned to the dwelling of our American host, and taking the train at *Caobas,* or Mahogany Trees—so called from the former growth of that tree on the spot—we were at Matanzas an hour afterward. The next morning the train brought us to this little town, situated half-way between Matanzas and Havana, but a considerable distance to the south of either.

WALTER D. WILCOX

(1 8 6 9 – 1 9 4 9)

While a student at Yale University, Walter Wilcox participated in an expedition in the Canadian Rockies that included several first ascents and spent much of the summer of 1893 camped on the shore of Lake Louise. This adventure led to his first book, *Camping in the Canadian Rockies,* which inspired many later climbers to visit the region. Wilcox went on to explore and chronicle many other places, including Cuba, and he reported for *National Geographic* on his investigation of the forests and swamps of Cochinos Bay, near the city of Cienfuegos. In the article, Wilcox describes the Caribbean colors and tropical flora and fauna, along with sketches of the region's history, with the fresh eyes of a traveler and the seasoned experience of a naturalist.

AMONG THE MAHOGANY FORESTS OF CUBA

The Bay of Cochinos, on the south coast of Cuba, is about forty miles west of Cienfuegos. It is the largest protected bay in Cuba, with a length of over 15 miles and an average breadth of about four miles, great depth of water, and very fair protection from the sea, and it is surprising at the first glance not to find a thriving port town located here. On the contrary, this is one of the wildest and most sparsely populated parts of Cuba.

Until within a few years this bay was said to be the resort of brigands and bad characters of all kinds; the waters were supposedly infested with sharks and other dangerous fish and the shores with crocodiles, while the swampy interior was the reputed breeding place of innumerable mosquitoes. The days of piracy are past, and while crocodiles and sharks do abound, no fatalities have ever occurred.

The isolation of this region, to which may be attributed the vagueness of these evil reports, is due to the fact that this entire coast is hemmed in by a line of almost impassable swamps more than fifty miles in length, called the Cienaga de Zapata, which cut off communication with the interior. Then, too, the comparatively new city of Cienfuegos, situated on this beautiful land-locked bay, which Humboldt pronounced one of the most magnificent harbors in the world, has served as an outlet for the adjoining region.

In connection with the purchase of a timber tract on this bay, I had abundant opportunities to learn many interesting facts about the region. On the first visit a small boat was engaged to sail from Cienfuegos. Under the influence of a fresh land breeze, the forty miles westward along the rocky coast were run in the night, and early the following morning the boat was well within the Bay of Cochinos and approaching a low, flat shore covered by a uniform expanse of green forest. Above the tree-tops the sky was a rosy red in the early dawn. It was a typical midwinter day in the tropics— the bay smooth as a mirror; the cool air laden with forest odors and the perfume of flowers, while the chattering of wild parrots could be heard from the shore. Our captain entered a small river or inlet and poled the boat to a convenient landing place.

A year later, at this same spot, a landing was made with a force of carpenters and laborers and a cargo of lumber and tools. A place was cleared in the forest for a house, docks were built, gardens laid out, wells dug, and eventually a permanent home made, comfortable enough to house my family during the succeeding eighteen months.

In all that time we were not molested by the natives, and no case of illness occurred in any member of the household. It seems that malaria and yellow fever are unknown among the natives of this entire region.

HERONS, WHITE EGRETS AND CROCODILES

The encircling shores of Cochinos Bay are low and flat. The west shore is a sandy beach four or five feet above the water. This coast is often a mere strip of dry land separating the bay from swampy tracts and lagoons full of mangrove trees. Herons and various wading birds, including the white egret, sought for its feathers, abound here in great numbers. Hunters shoot the latter bird by the hundreds, unfortunately in the breeding season, because the feathers are then at their best, and only the inaccessible nature of these lonely lagoons and the plague of insect life prevent their total extinction.

Crocodiles likewise abound, and in the night-time may be heard catching birds near the water's edge. During the last two years some eight or ten men have been constantly employed killing crocodiles in the depths of the swamps and carrying on a profitable business selling their hides. In the remote parts of the swamp, where the great reptiles have never been disturbed, they are easily killed. An old hat is placed on the end of a short stick, which is held in the left hand and waved over the water. The crocodile rushes blindly at the hat and is struck a sharp blow behind the head with a machete.

Sharks infest these shores and often swim in the water so shallow as to become half stranded on the sandy shoals. Natives say that in the old days this bay was a resort for pirates and slave traders, and that the sharks were originally attracted by the large numbers of dead and dying slaves thrown overboard.

IN THE MAHOGANY FOREST

The east shore is entirely different, totally devoid of sand beaches or swampy tracts, and is a rocky plain from five to ten feet above sea-level, covered by a heavy forest, which extends eastward three or four miles to the edge of the swamps.

The number of species of trees is very great, and, while including such splendid varieties as mahogany, sabicu, ebony, and Spanish cedar, there are many other hardwoods, probably 150 in number, some of which are very rare or quite unknown to experts in tropical timbers. Some of these trees have a wood harder than ebony, and the best steel axes are frequently broken in felling them. Many are fine-grained and beautifully banded and veined with two or more colors, and are susceptible of a high polish.

The mahogany and cedar are imposing trees, the latter sometimes reaching a diameter of seven feet. Their massive branches, hung with purple and yellow orchids, bromeliads, ferns, and other parasitic plants, are the resort of parrots and other birds of brilliant plumage. In contrast, the silent swamps present a different aspect. The forest is interrupted by stretches of open prairie, by slow-flowing streams of great depth and clumps of heavy trees hung with long shrouds of gray Spanish moss or over-run by climbing cactus, mistletoe, and orchids, which in early spring make a gay display of white, yellow, and purple blossoms. The royal palm here reaches its maximum size, the stately trunks, symmetrical as Grecian columns, rising more than a hundred feet to spread their crowns of foliage in the glistening sunshine above the dark sombre forest.

The swamp water, having general currents toward the sea and eventually escaping by underground channels, is clear and perfectly wholesome, with, however, a slight taste and color of vegetable matter. Many of these lagoons are very picturesque, especially where long vistas open up in the forest and display the overhanging foliage dipping down to the water surface. These black pools are occasionally disturbed by the splash of a crocodile or the rising of the "sevalo," a kind of fish that comes from the sea through subterranean passages and rivers which drain the swamps.

The general land surface, while perfectly level, is rocky and the soil is very scanty, being apparently washed down into the numerous cracks and joints in the rocks. It seems remarkable that trees of great size can and do grow on such little soil, and one often sees their long roots spreading over the ground for twenty yards or more in search of some hole or crevice to descend. The soil, however, is remarkably fertile, and such plants as reach down deep enough to be independent of surface conditions of moisture and drought succeed admirably. Bananas, limes, and oranges of delicious flavor and quality are raised in several places near the bay. Vegetables and small fruits succeed only when sufficiently watered, as the light, porous soil dries out very quickly. The rocks are entirely of coral formation, very hard and rough on the exposed surface, but underneath turning to a soft, yellow stone made up of shell fragments and corals similar to existing beaches on the western shore of the bay.

Outside of two or three poisonous plants, these forests contain very few dangers of any kind. The poisonous manzanillo tree spreads its picturesque branches out over the rocky shores and drops its green apples into the sea. Certain fish eat these apples, and in some cases, when caught at the critical time, have caused fatal cases of poisoning. The milky juice is feared by every Cuban axeman, who will never under any circumstances fell one of these trees, a single drop in the eye being sufficient to cause total blindness. Snakes are abundant, but universally harmless, while the sting of Cuban scorpions and centipedes is little worse than that of honey-bees. One native nearly ninety years old has spent forty-five years on his clearing in these woods and is still strong enough to do all his work.

THE CHANGE OF SEASONS

At the close of winter, in March and April, the forest loses a great part of its foliage, while some varieties of trees shed their leaves altogether. This period marks the close of the dry season. The entire forest when seen from a distance is suffused with a reddish glow, as the old leaves fall and the new ones burst from their buds. This is in many respects the finest part of the year in Cuba, an uninterrupted succession of bright sunshiny days, with an ideal temperature both day and night. The forest revels in a profusion of flowers, one kind of tree succeeding another in its time of blossoming, and the air is sweet with the scent of countless blossoms. The majagua tree, famous for its green wood and fibrous bark, from which the strongest ropes are plaited, is brilliant with tulip-like blossoms of fiery red color; the baria is hung with masses of white, and the roble, the so-called Cuban oak, is adorned with clusters of delicate pink and white flowers, resembling the mountain rhododendron. The dull hum of honey-bees tells of the harvest of nectar, and at this season the natives are kept busy pressing honey and melting wax.

The variety of birds is very great at this period, as the Florida species, driven south by the cold of winter, have not as yet returned to the north, and the native birds are singing and mating. The Cuban crows call one another with a great variety of peculiar sounds and modulations, which one could easily fancy to be a kind of conversation among themselves, and the parrots come in noisy flocks of several hundreds and drive away by their loud chattering all thought of sleep after the earliest trace of dawn.

Emerald-colored humming birds dart from flower to flower on the gaudy hibiscus bushes or poise in midair amid the pink clusters of the coral vine. Many of the wild birds are sociable, and I have seen four or five different kinds at one time on or near the verandas of the house.

MISERABLE POVERTY OF THE FEW NATIVES

The natives of this region are a mixed race, rather dark in color and with a probable mixture of considerable negro blood. They live in miserable houses thatched with palm leaves, generally without windows or other protection from insects and weather. They

are excellent woodsmen, handling the axe and machete with great
skill. They think nothing of walking ten or fifteen miles on the
most trifling errand. Many have small clearings where they raise
bananas, yucca, and a kind of sweet potato. These fruits and vegetables, together with their live stock and beehives, eked out by the
results of hunting and fishing, give them an uncertain and miserable diet. When they are fortunate enough to get work, they buy
provisions; but a little stock in the cupboard is a temptation to quit
working at once. It would be difficult to find a lower standard of
diet and general living outside of savage tribes.

From lack of care and cleanliness, the teeth of these people
decay and fall out before middle age, and their monotonous diet
causes suffering from digestive troubles. Like all Cubans, they are
very fond of pets, and it is no uncommon thing to see all the ordinary animals of the barn yard—goats, pigs, turkeys, chickens,
etc.—wandering at will inside their houses. On an iron hoop sus-
pended from a rafter a tame parrot may usually be seen, while
many houses have a kind of rat-like animal, called the "jutia,"
which lives in the forest trees, tied up as a half wild and treacher-
ous pet. Naked children sprawl about on the floor and many dogs,
in a state of extreme emaciation from continued starvation, howl
at every passer-by and add to the general misery. Were it not for
the balmy temperature and the continued sunshine and general
cheerfulness of the Cuban climate, these people would rapidly
become extinct. In such hovels, abounding in filth and squalor,
one meets with evidences of genuine hospitality in marked contrast to the surroundings. The stranger is invited to enter, offered
the best chair, and coffee is prepared at once. Cuban coffee is
roasted in small quantities and ground just before making. A cloth
bag holds the ground coffee while hot water is filtered through it
several times. The resulting coffee, while strong and excessively
roasted, has a very fine aroma and flavor. Rather than be deprived
of his coffee and cigarettes, a Cuban would prefer to go several
days with little or no food.

In the huts of these humble people, great formality, an inheritance from the Spanish, is observed on arriving and departing. Withal there is general ignorance, few being able to read or write, and their life is woefully monotonous, though they seem light-hearted and happy, prattling for hours about the most trifling events in their daily life. They observe frequent holidays in connection with church festivals, birthdays, etc., and delight in dancing and music, the latter being barbaric and showing strong evidence of African origin. They believe that the moon has a great effect on the planted seed, and sometimes one sees an umbrella carried at night to ward off the evil effects of moonlight.

WONDERS OF TROPICAL MARINE LIFE

Among the beautiful shells of the west-coast sand beaches were pieces of spongy volcanic rock, purple and green in color, which may have had their origin in the eruptions in Martinique.

As may be imagined, the water in this deep bay is of the utmost purity and clearness. The color is blue, rivaling that of the Mediterranean, and the bottom may be clearly seen in forty or fifty feet of water. The abundant tropical marine life affords a never-ending source of delightful study. On bright, calm mornings one can look down through fathoms of crystal water and see the sunlight sparkling on snow-white beds of coral sand. Among branching corals, Neptune's cups, sponges, and purple sea-fans, fish of many strange forms and colors may be seen gliding to and fro, apparently within grasp of the hand—the blue llora, the red and green parrot-fish, the red-snapper, and the spotted cherna. On moonlight nights, moving rapidly through the water in a launch, one feels as though sailing over an enchanted sea of crystal, where every ripple is faintly outlined with phosphorescent fire.

The bay is a fisherman's paradise. The rapacious and dangerous picua is caught by trolling from rapidly moving sailing craft, but still fishing in deep water gives better results. Sharks often bite fish off the hooks before they can be landed, unless the line is taken in rapidly. Sea turtles of several varieties and the shell-bearing tortoise abound, the Cuban tortoise-shell being the most beautifully variegated and high-priced in the world. Sometimes the water surface for an acre in extent may be seen disturbed by a violent commotion of terrified and struggling fish when pursued by some larger enemies. Hundreds of sea-gulls add to the confusion, darting down on the water and catching the fish in midair.

HURRICANES

Hurricanes are most frequent in September and October. The last hurricane occurred October 17, 1906, the center passing not far west of the Bay of Cochinos. After a slow fall of the barometer for five days previous, the morning of the 17th was heavily overcast, with the wind southeast and occasional squalls of rain. About sunset the barometer began to fall rapidly and alarmingly. Five or six schooners took shelter within the Caleta, their captains wisely suspecting foul weather. The wind increased in force, till at nine o'clock the crash of broken branches and falling trees could be heard above the roar of surf on the bay, which was a mass of phosphorescent foam in the darkness. The barometer foretold an approaching climax, and though the house was very low and surrounded by forests, it seemed best, about midnight, to put out all lights and seek shelter among some rocks near the Caleta.

Fortunately the rain had ceased, it being a "dry" cyclone, which the natives had told us were the most severe, and the only danger was from flying branches and falling trees. Meanwhile the gusts came in ever-increasing fury, the forest roared in a subdued monotone and the trees were dancing wildly, waving their branches like angry demons in the fury of the gale. About one o'clock the barometer suddenly began to rise, a few stars appeared amid wisps of flying scud, and we knew that the center of the storm had passed, but nearly a hundred trees were uprooted around my house. This hurricane did the most damage in Havana and at Batabano, where it drove sixty schooners and steamers on shore. Such severe cyclonic disturbances are less frequent in Cuba than in other islands of the West Indies and are only expected once in five or six years.

ELEANOR EARLY
(? - 1 9 6 9)

Eleanor Early wrote several travel books with such titles as *And this is Boston!*, *And this is Cape Cod!*, *And this is Washington!* Despite the breeziness of these titles, Early is an observant, reliable travel writer, and her writing on Cuba, excerpted from her 1937 book *Ports of the Sun,* provides an entertainingly quirky overview of Cuban history as told through the stories of the places she visited in Havana. Along with history, she takes the readers through the beaches and hotels, the orphanages and harbors, reviewing popular foods and drinks in a place still not yet transformed for travelers into the playground of glittering mob-run casinos and live sex shows that it would soon become.

from PORTS OF THE SUN

Because most visitors have only the vaguest idea of Cuba's troubled history, I am going to review it as briefly as I can, and if you are not interested, you can skip to the part about cocktails.

Spanish rule was notorious for immorality and prodigal wastefulness. Corrupt administrations had imposed heavy taxes and military repression. And selfish exploitation had brought about a grave economic condition, which led finally to the Ten Years' War (1868–1878).

Spanish governors were cruel, but now the rebels burned and killed. "Butcher" Weyler came from Spain, and resorted to inconceivable horrors to wipe out the revolutionists. Conditions were such that intervention by the United States seemed probable, but did not happen. And then at last there was peace.

But Spain did not live up to her agreements, and there was more trouble. President McKinley opposed recognition of the rebels, but affirmed the possibility of intervention. Spain resented our attitude . . . and in February of 1898 the battleship *Maine* was blown up in Havana Harbor. Many have maintained that the explosion was internal and the disaster accidental, but it furnished the excuse for us to declare war on Spain—a war that cost many American lives and many millions of dollars.

Eight months later peace was declared, and Spain "relinquished" Cuba to the United States, in trust for its inhabitants. For three years we maintained a military rule, and during this time we achieved reforms of administration, sanitation, public works, and education. But the greatest thing we did for Cuba was to eradicate yellow fever, which had plagued the island for centuries.

Since our withdrawal there have been frequent insurrections. Elections have been fraudulent and unjust, and there have been constant charges of maladministration. Under President Machado, there was execution without civil trial, and finally rebellion led by Fulgencio Batista, a top-sergeant, part white, part Negro, and part Indian. Machado had made the sergeant a member of the general staff, and so he became acquainted with the curious subterranean passages of Cuban politics.

Army officers loyal to the Government barricaded themselves in the Hotel National. And it was Fulgencio Batista who led the assault against them. Within a day the officers capitulated, and of a sudden Sergeant Batista became the strong man of Cuba. This was in 1933.

As virtual dictator, he made officers of the non-commissioned men, and began the erection of a military city de luxe, which is one of the things you should see. It will help you understand why the Cuban army likes its job.

Thousands of tourists never get any farther than Sloppy Joe's, which is funny, because we have lots of bars at home. Personally I prefer the Orphanage, but unless you are interested in institutions or in child education, it might bore you.

You should see Morro Castle, of course, and La Cabaña
Fortress. The old Convent of Santa Clara is interesting, if they
will let you in. It is the building of Public Works now. You should
certainly visit the beaches and some of the night clubs, and see a
native dance. *Las Fritas* is best, where the Negroes do the *rhumba*
and the *son,* but it may have been exploited and spoiled by the time
you get there. *Las Fritas* means "The Frieds," which is like calling
a Bowery dance-hall The Hotdog. You should visit the Plaza de
Armas, and some of the old distilleries where meals are served.
The Bacardi bar is very smart, and the free drinks are grand. The
cigar factories are rather interesting, and many people like the
sugar and rum factories.

Probably more tourists visit the Cathedral than any other
place—Columbus Cathedral, they call it, because they think that
Columbus is—or was—buried there. As a matter of fact, he never
was. He died in Spain and was buried in Valladolid in 1508. Later
his body was taken to Seville, and still later to Santo Domingo,
where the casket was placed in the Cathedral. In 1795, when the
French captured Santo Domingo, the retreating Spaniards removed
some bones which they thought were those of Columbus, and
carried them to Havana, where they were reburied beside the altar
with all kinds of pomp and ceremony. A hundred years later (following the Spanish-American War), they were taken to Spain and
placed in the Cathedral of Seville. Spanish authorities maintained
then, and still do, that they are the true remains.

But here is the other side of the story. In 1877, when workmen
were making repairs in the Cathedral at Santo Domingo, they
uncovered a casket that said on it, as plain as day, that the contents
were the remains of "The Illustrious Cristobal Colon, Discoverer
of America." So that the evidence is pretty strong that the remains
of Columbus rest, not in Seville (where you may have paid them
homage), but in Santo Domingo, where they were deposited centuries ago.

The Cathedral does not appeal to me. All its treasures are locked up, and it seems a dreary place. But if you go there and the sacristan unlocks the cabinets for you, be sure to see the gigantic silver statue of Saint Christopher. Christopher is the patron saint of Havana, and legend says that he was so big and tall that he used a palm tree for a staff. One day he saw a little child trying to cross a river, whom he lifted to his shoulder. And the giant Christopher was crushed by the terrific weight of the Child, and fell upon his knees and adored Him, who was Jesus, Son of God.

In former times, on Saint Christopher's Day (November 19), all business places were closed, and everybody went to church. But now the day is observed principally by good little girls. The Templete, where the first Mass was said, is thrown open, and any girl who wishes a favor from Saint Christopher must visit the Templete, and also go to the Cathedral to pray to Christopher. And all day long she must be silent, because if she speaks a single word, her prayer will not be heard.

The church I like best in Havana is the Church of Our Lady of Mercy, where there is a fabulously lovely altar. If you could see it blazing with candles—on Saint Joseph's Day, perhaps—when the chancel is filled with tube roses, I think you could never forget either the beauty or the swooning sweetness.

Another interesting church is the Holy Christ of the Good Voyage, probably the first parish church in Havana. The Dons used to pray there for a safe voyage when they had need to cross the sea, and the old custom persists. I know a Villa Nova man who goes there to pray every time he goes up in a plane.

Beneficencia Convent where the Sisters of Charity make a thousand children happy is a lovely place—and I hate institutions, especially orphanages. It was founded in 1778 by Bishop Valdes to care for illegitimate children. The Bishop decreed that the orphans all should take his name, and that is why there are so many Valdeses in Cuba today.

He provided a basket in which unmarried mothers might place the babies for which they could not provide. Nuns, keeping vigilance, took charge of the little ones. And before long the nuns had so many children they didn't know what to do.

Then the Bishop said that when mothers abandoned their children, they should lose them forever. As soon as a child enters the convent, marks of identification are destroyed. And if a woman comes to ask for her child, she is told that no one knows which is hers.

There are cases in the Convent filled with coins and medals from which small pieces have been cut away. These coins and medals were placed about the necks of the abandoned babies, the mothers keeping the bit that would fit the mutilated disk. There are Bibles from which a single page is torn, and letters torn in halves, so that, in later years, if mother and child should meet, they might know one another. It seems sad that no records are kept by which such identification might be made, but Bishop Valdes said it would lead to all sorts of complications, and of course it might.

The basket of long ago has been replaced by a revolving contraption in which the baby is placed from the street. Then the mother rings a bell, and the thing whisks about and deposits the child in a bedroom where two nuns are sleeping. The bell awakens them, and they take the child and bathe and change it, and put it in an adorable bassinet. The bassinet is of blue, all ruffled and shirred, and there are pink linen sheets on it, hand-hemmed and embroidered! In this room there are toys and beautiful dolls.

Newcomers are isolated for observation, and are usually in need of hospitalization. In the infirmary are babies' wards, and wards for older children.

The dormitories are prettier than any boarding-school dormitories you ever saw. The girls' is pink, with flowers and birds painted on the walls, and the floors are pink marble. The little beds are pink, and they have fine linen on them that is changed *every day*—and the orphans don't work in the laundry either. The boys' dormitory is blue, and almost as pretty. The dining-rooms have small marble-topped tables with fresh flowers on them. And the chairs are every color of the rainbow. And the walls have Mother Goose pictures on them. The nurseries and kindergartens have decorated walls, and tiled floors rich in color. There are club-rooms, and a library with story books.

But the most extraordinary thing about this lovely orphanage is the clothes the orphans have. Every little girl has *twelve* dresses—with hair ribbons and socks to match! And every little boy has twelve suits. The clothes are made by the older girls from the prettiest of patterns, and they are exactly like the dresses of French voiles and handkerchief linens that sell in the States for eight and ten dollars. I know this sounds absurd, but it is true. On Sundays and holy days the orphans wear their best clothes, and the babies are dressed in embroidered frocks, with frilly bonnets and hand-knit sweaters.

There are toys for everyone, and such beautiful toys! Small boys have roller skates, and little girls have jump ropes. And big boys play Jai Alai on fine modern courts.

There are nearly a thousand boys and girls in Beneficencia, and they range in age from one day to twenty-one years. For a long time the sisters had charge of everything, but now there are professional athletic instructors. And when they ordered shorts for the girls, and had the boys strip to the waist for sports, the nuns almost fainted.

Little girls have a shower every morning. And little boys have one in the morning and one after gym, which is probably a world's record for an orphanage. Children of four and five take their own baths, and I have seen them under child-size showers, soaping themselves from head to foot, and loving it.

Twice a week there are outdoor movies, and the children present plays and give musicals. One waif became a great musician, but most of them are artisans. Parents of legitimate children, jealous of the practical training given orphans, petitioned for the privilege of sending their youngsters to Beneficencia. And now, for ten dollars a month, many legitimate children share the good fortune of abandoned waifs.

Across from the Convent is a fine monument to Maceo, Cuba's great mulatto general. And a bit up the Malecón, almost in front of the National, is another that commemorates the *Maine*—this, I think, is the finest monument in Cuba.

If I were you, I should get a guide for the historic places. Sightseeing buses used to be one of my particular hates, but now I rather like them. It is rather jolly riding around with a flock of funny people—most tourists, you know, *are* funny. It's only you and I and a few others who really *appreciate* things. But if you prefer, you can hire your own car, and a guide. Cuban drivers generally are dumb in history and deficient in English, so pick your guide with care. The alternative to this is three tours, which will cost (all told) about eight dollars.

There is the City Tour which covers the city's high lights, and will give you a chance to see the places in which you can browse later by yourself. You will probably plan to return to the Plaza de Armas. The Templete is here (you remember I told you how the girls go there on Saint Christopher's Day). Probably you know that when the Spaniards made a settlement, the first thing they did was have a Mass said. After that they started building—and sometimes they killed a few Indians.

Beside the Templete is La Fuerza, the oldest building in the city. It does not look much like it now, but it was a fort once, and it was built by Ferdinand de Soto. The moat has been filled with earth. The drawbridge is replaced by a walk, and the old observation towers are gone. But in de Soto's time it was the strongest fort in the New World. Here the explorer said good-bye to his girl-wife, Doña Isabel, and went off to Arkansas. (That sounds odd, doesn't it?)

I remember how the story of de Soto was drilled into my reluctant brain. His picture was in the history book—one of those make-believe persons with a pointed beard and a suit of armor, who left Spain (a quite mythical country) to help Pizarro (another funny man in armor) in a place called Peru. The incomprehensible de Soto played an important part in the conquest of the Incas (it was twenty years before I knew or cared who the Incas were). He started for Florida (a place on the map) looking for gold, and discovered the Mississippi, which didn't make sense. Returning to Cuba (a land of which he was Governor), he died. And he was buried in the river he discovered, a very difficult river to spell.

Until I saw La Fuerza, de Soto was a plague of my childhood, and nothing more. But when you look up at those massive walls, and picture Doña Isabel at the window, watching and waiting for her husband—then, at last, de Soto lives. He was gone four years, and all that time Doña Isabel waited—waited and prayed—as women do. She had golden hair, and blue eyes that were red with weeping when half of her husband's expedition came home without him. They told her of how he died, and how they buried him at night in the waters of the river. And she held her golden head high, and tried to be brave as became the wife of a hero. But in three days she was dead of a broken heart, and they said a Mass, for her soul and his, in the Plaza de Armas where the ceiba grows.

For centuries afterward La Fuerza was not only a fortress, but a treasure house for gold and precious gems from Peru and Mexico awaiting convoy to Spain, safe here from even Drake and Morgan.

Near-by is the old Presidential Palace, built in the days of the American Revolution. The President lives uptown now in a modern palace, and this one is nothing but an office-building.

You should see the funny bath-houses where the proud Dons and their ladies bathed in 1520; and the village slaughter-house. Architects will be interested in a gorgeous ceiling in the old Santa Clara Convent, and in the hand-carved cedar woodwork. And you must not miss the clubs. Havana is the greatest club city in the world. Nearly half of the people belong to clubs, and this is not a general statement but an actual fact. One club—the Gallego—has

fifty thousand members, and the Asturiano has almost as many.
There are clubs for everyone, from wealthy sugar barons to poor
street-cleaners, and the clubs go back to the very beginning of
Cuba. Spanish pioneers, in order to meet and fraternize, organized into societies. Spaniards from Gallego founded the Gallego,
and those from Asturias the Asturiano. Even the clerks have a
club of their own, and a million-dollar clubhouse! Each club
maintains its own staff of medical men, dentists, legal advisers,
and each supports a hospital, libraries, schools, gymnasiums, and
asylums. For monthly dues of about $1.50, a Cuban clubman gets
practically everything for nothing, including a funeral.

I have said that Havana is an expensive place, but I was thinking of it from a visitor's viewpoint. Natives can live well on very
little money. Newspaper people in Cuba are notoriously under-
paid, but they can be beautiful hosts, and the best times I have had
in Havana have been with my friends the reporters. Armando
Maribona introduced me to El Orbe—across from Sloppy Joe's—
where reporters, actors, and musicians go. The food is so good
that the management had to raise prices to keep the crowds out—
three courses and coffee for forty cents, and be sure you have
guava and cheeses for dessert. José Caminero knows I like sea
food, so he took me to La Zaragozana, and the mayonnaise on the
filet of sole was so good that we went to the kitchen to watch the
chef make it.

Spanish mayonnaise is supposed to be the best in the world,
and all the chef did was put three egg yolks in a bowl with the
juice of three limes and a pinch of salt. Then his assistant added
slowly a fifth of a gallon of Spanish olive oil, while the chef beat
madly with a wire whisk. The secret of the thing, I think, was the
whisk—an eggbeater is not so good. They said either French oil
or Italian would do, but that Cubans prefer the Spanish. Sometimes the chef adds a bit of garlic and dry mustard. And at the
end, he dashes in a bit of cold water to tone down the color. And
then he beats some more. To measure a fifth of a gallon, use a

liquor bottle. And you do not have to add the oil drop by drop, like cooking school. The whole business does not take five minutes.

I start to tell about tours, and go meandering off on mayon-naise—well, sooner or later everyone goes to Morro Castle and La Cabaña. You take a boat across the bay, and pick up a guide—an imaginative fellow, if you are lucky, who will tell you blood-curdling tales about Spaniards and sharks.

Morro was completed twenty-five years before the Pilgrims landed at Plymouth Rock, but Cabaña was not built until a hun-dred and seventy-five years later. In Morro there are cells cut from solid rock below sea level, and there is a chute that leads through thick walls to the sea. Prisoners—both living and dead—were thrown through this chute into the shark-infested sea. And this is not ancient history, but modern. In Cabaña there is a dry moat where condemned men were forced to kneel while a Spanish firing-squad riddled them with bullets. And if you do not like such stories, you can enjoy the view of the city while your guide regales the rest of your party with horrors.

The third tour I suggested is called the Country Trip, and it will take you through the lovely Tropical Gardens to the famous Brew-ery. The management served free beer once, and all you could drink. But downtown bars protested, and they had to stop. On this trip you see the Havana Country Club with its magnificent golf course (Cubans say it is the finest in the world), the Casinos, the Beach Clubs, and many of the dazzling night clubs.

Another pleasant country trip is to Rio Cristal, a tavern that was once a convent. A specialty of the house is filet of sole with almonds and black beans, and there is a cocktail called *Rio Cristal* that is incomparable.

Enrique Berenguer, the host, and his charming friend, Antonio Martin, had a competition once to see which could mix the finest cocktail, and I was the judge. Señor Martin called his *Nito Cupes* (Never Mind), and it was pretty fussy, but worth it. Here is the way he mixed it for the three of us:

For every cocktail, one part pineapple juice, one part white Bacardi, and the juice of a Cuban lime.

For every two cocktails, one teaspoon of grenadine and one teaspoon of Bénédictine.

For every three cocktails, the white of an egg.

Señor Berenguer submitted his standby, *Rio Cristal*. And now all
you have to do is find a passion fruit. Crush the pulpy part around
the seeds and strain. Add one part passion fruit, two parts white
Bacardi, a bit of lime peel, and honey in the comb to sweeten.

Hardly anyone knows how to mix a proper Bacardi cocktail, so
I asked Señor Rafael Valiente, who is host at the famous bar, and
he told me that you should take the juice of half a lime, half a teaspoon of granulated sugar, one and a half ounces of white Bacardi, mix thoroughly, and shake well with ice.

If you do not care about cocktails, maybe you had rather hear
about flying home from Havana. The flight to Florida was brief
and lovely. Plenty of what is known as the illimitable blue, and tea
in the clouds.

CONSUELO HERMER AND
MARJORIE MAY

Rather than list hotels and recommend beaches, explain the island's history or describe tourist sites, Consuelo Hermer and Marjorie May set out to create a travel guide to Cuba that educated readers on the social customs of Cubans in the 1930s. While a tremendous amount of change has taken place in Cuba since that time, the humor and irony of Cubans, the musicality of the place, the belief in luck and magic, and the gregarious nature and romantic leanings of Cubans that modern writers still touch upon can be found in this light-hearted account of Cuba and the Cubans.

from HAVANA MAÑANA: A GUIDE TO CUBA AND THE CUBANS

So much has been written about Cuba's sugar mills and tobacco plantations that most people haven't an inkling of the country's most flourishing national industry. It is charm! Even Dale Carnegie would be baffled by the scale on which it is produced. The Cubans could teach him a thing or two, for all of them, male or female, young or old, rich or poor, have so much charm that one can be lenient about their faults. Yes, charm is the national industry, all right. To be *simpático* is as natural and as necessary to a Cuban as breathing.

What is this charm? It is a blend of many qualities. An intense appreciation of the aesthetic is one of the chief elements. Cubans have a deep-rooted and genuine feeling for the beautiful. Everything from the dimple in a baby's elbow to a glorious sunset thrills them. A beautiful woman will be twice as beautiful in Havana, where loveliness is so audibly and enthusiastically acknowledged. Especially are the Cubans moved by the beauties of Nature. They speak with feeling of the luxuriant countryside, the white brightness of the moon, the exquisite scent of the flowers.

The poetic impulse is reflected again in the picturesque phrases of everyday talk. Children are called "smiles of God," a negligee is a "jump-out-of-bed," popcorn blooms as "roses of corn," a station-wagon becomes a "step-and-run," and there are many such vocabulary inventions. Even the names of the shops show imagination at work. The main department store calls itself "The Enchantment"; "The Cuban Rose" romanticizes a dingy little grocery; a certain hardware store staggers along as "The Sun of America."

When Cubans utter endearments, they are endlessly resourceful. You can be called anything from *bandolera,* "little bandit," to *Santa de ojos bellos,* "Saint with beautiful eyes." Unlike Americans who do everything possible to hide a poetic strain, these people proudly indulge their love of imagery, and constantly make use of romance and oratory. Once, we were introduced to a muscular young sportsman. There we stood in a crowded lobby. He bowed over our hands, then straightened up. "Margarita! You said the name was Margarita!" he exclaimed delightedly. The one of us who was a Margarita nodded. "Margarita!" he beamed. *"Dios!"* And then he launched into a poem about *margaritas* (daisies); the recitation lasted a full five minutes, complete with gestures. Finally, he bowed and walked away with no more self-consciousness than if he had muttered a perfunctory "howyababe."

As deep as his poetic streak is the Cuban's love for music. All day long, Havana echoes with song. In the morning you are awakened by the melodic cries of the chicken seller, the vegetable hawker, the peddlers of coat hangers and the knife sharpeners. Each has his distinctive trade chant. In every café, no matter how small, there are a guitarist and singer; at night, on every corner, strolling musicians. Cubans are lyric-minded and their voices naturally have a cantabile quality. Their conversation runs in ripples and rills, and after a while, you will find the same cadence creeping into yours. When you call for the chamberman at the hotel, you don't say *Camarero;* you sing it. Cubans will burst into song at the slightest provocation, without a trace of bashfulness. They are surprised when you confess you can't warble a note. Once we even got a bitter complaint from our escorts: that we never sang to them on the way home. There is rhythm in their chromosomes; a rhythm that shows in everything, from the way the women walk to the way a little errand boy pats out *conga* beats on the box he is delivering.

Indeed, they are aesthetic. But the other side of the picture is earthy, robust, out-and-out Rabelaisian. Pick up a newspaper, and you will see what we mean. The woman in that political cartoon may have nothing to do with the point of the story, but she will be drawn *female* in no uncertain terms. Nothing subtle or understated is good for a laugh; jokes are full-blown. There is the famous story of the pint-sized nobleman whose prankish friends stripped him down to his BVD's, stuck a big black cigar in his mouth and left him in the Benificencia [orphanage] turnstile one night, when he was far gone in his cups. Never a dull moment for the little Count! He inspired many of Havana's most elaborate practical jokes; in fact, we understand they even buried him once.

Humor of this type is what keeps the natives chuckling, which is interesting in view of the fact that the Cubans in so many other respects have attained a degree of sophistication that virtually borders on decadence. Cuban women make us seem like Girl Scouts; Cuban men make ours seem rather bucolic. They are a suave and worldly race; the girls are grown at twelve, married at sixteen. A young *caballero* starts maintaining his bachelor apartment as early in his teens as he can afford it.

Habaneros are walking contradictions. Perhaps that is what makes them so attractive. Interwoven with everyday common sense are superstition and a morbid interest in the mystic. Sensible women warn you sincerely against the evils of night air or relate the incomprehensible things that can happen under a full moon. Even hardheaded businessmen will avoid appointments on days not considered propitious. And as for luck, lucky numbers are as vital a part of Havana life as the daily newspaper. Friends meeting you at the pier may follow an effervescent greeting with "What was your stateroom number?" and then painstakingly comb the city to buy a lottery ticket including that number. To complicate matters even further, there is a double chance to be lucky; each number has its own related symbol; so that you have a good-luck insignia as well as a lucky number. Thus, if you dream of a death, you will play number eight, but if it should be an important death, say that of a statesman, then you will play number sixty-four, the number for the "big death" symbol. As in all places, including our own South, where there were African slaves, voodoo is prevalent and taken for granted among the Negroes, though the more sensational side of the *ñáñigo* cults was long ago subdued by the Government. One girl we know found a little wooden arrow with a black tip jabbed through the lid of her hat-box when she went to pack on her last night in Havana. But her apprehension dwindled when she discovered it to be white magic, a *ñáñigo* goodwill gesture from her hostess' cook, who wished her a return trip swift as an arrow.

Nobody can deny that love of gambling is an outstanding national trait, innate and important in the Cuban nature. Everybody buys lottery tickets; everybody plays the *Bolita,* known in the States as the numbers racket; and everybody plays roulette or chemin de fer at the night clubs and private spots. Everybody gambles at the races. If a Cuban taxi driver can't afford to buy a two-dollar ticket on a horse, he'll scout around until he finds nine others; then each will play as little as twenty cents to make up the bet. Just as they bet so much more on sports, so, when they go in for games, it is the gambling aspect of a game that attracts them, rather than the chance to excel in skill. Dominoes, regarded as a fairly innocuous game in our country, here is a complicated part-nership affair, involving betting for every play. Each small café you pass at night has its faithful clique of regular patrons grouped around a table, fighting fiercely over their game, with kibitzers *Cubanos* playing an even more active role. Cubans will bet on any-thing. The big electric sign overlooking Parque Central has dice that change each time the lights flicker on and off, inspiring fast and furious wagers along the sidewalk stands. There is a green-with-age saying about women being like street-cars, one along every minute. In Havana, it is Lady Luck who comes along every minute; natives bet hotly on whether the next trolley car will be red or green.

ROBERT STONE

(1 9 3 7 –   )

Robert Stone is no stranger to the darker side of life; his novels *Children of Light, Dog Soldiers, A Flag For Sunrise,* and *Outerbridge Reach* explore the underbelly of, respectively, Hollywood filmmaking, the jungles of Vietnam, the dirty politics of Central America, and the challenge of solitude on the seas. His texts are political, ironic, and masterfully written, and he brings these traits to his essay "Havana Then and Now." The essay was inspired by a visit to the Hotel Inglaterra just after the fall of the communist bloc in Europe. While Stone remarks on the strangeness of this anachronistic replication of bleak Soviet-style communism in a place of sun and color, he is moved to recall the first time he saw the once-glamorous city, in 1955, when he was a young man in the U.S. Navy moored in the Havana harbor, and the Hotel Inglaterra was a very different sort of icon.

HAVANA THEN AND NOW
REVISITING A CITY ONCE AGAIN IN
HISTORY'S STRAITS

Late one sad Thursday night in October, two Americans retired to the bar of the old Hotel Inglaterra in Havana. We had spent the evening in a suburban apartment, watching a speech of Fidel Castro's on television. At the Inglaterra, among the tiles and potted palms, an orchestra in Cuban costumes from a forties MGM musical, faded and shiny with too much dry cleaning, was playing "Siboney." Three young Germans were cuddling with some local lovelies in spangles and mascara. A lone, gaunt Irishman sat taking pictures of the band. The light was yellow and smoky, the streets outside unlit and sinister. A man in dark glasses sat by the entrance door.

One day there may be a market for Soviet block nostalgia; movies will delight audiences by reproducing the hotel lobbies of late-twentieth-century Communist capitals. At the Inglaterra that night everything was in place—the bored tourists, the hookers, the hokey native orchestra, the watcher at the door. Also the hustlers and black-marketeers in the blacked-out adjoining streets. All that was missing were the official Gypsies and the Arab thugs chain-smoking under fringed lampshades.

In terms of the big picture, of course, a lot was missing: namely, the Communist bloc, of which the Inglaterra lobby had become a melancholy souvenir. It was a rather obvious irony. While Eastern Europe whirled between the future and Bram Stoker's Baedeker, Havana, Cuba, of all places, was imperfectly replicating Warsaw or Bucharest in the age of Brezhnev.

There were a few local touches. *Granma,* the Communist Party daily, was the only newspaper available at the hotel kiosk that evening. It had a tiny item on the Clarence Thomas affair. The item informed readers that Judge Thomas had displayed his sexual organ to Anita Hill. *Granma* had subtly improved on events to underline the contradictions of bourgeois society and, perhaps, to make the whole thing comprehensible to Cuban readers.

If the walls of the Inglaterra could bear witness, they would attest to countless journalistic misrepresentations, slight liberties with the facts, colorful invocations of reality. During the 1890s, when the American yellow press was hounding the Spanish rulers of Cuba into an unequal war, Hearst's and Pulitzer's star reporters pioneered the Ramos gin fizz at the Inglaterra while calling on heaven to witness Spain's supposed atrocities. And from the hotel the Hearst artist Frederic Remington, lacking the verbal resources of his colleagues, sent the famous complaint to his boss: Everything was quiet, Remington told Hearst, and there would be no war. More American schoolboys today probably know Hearst's celebrated reply—that if Remington furnished the pictures, he would furnish the war—than know who said, "Don't give up the ship."

"No man's life, no man's property is safe," wrote the *New York World*'s James Creelman, a frequent Inglaterra guest at that time. "American citizens are imprisoned and slain without cause. . . . Blood on the roadsides, blood in the fields, blood on the doorsteps, blood, blood, blood!" In the face of these conditions, American reporters could be seen daily on the hotel's terrace, composing their dispatches, having their shoes shined.

The Inglaterra was always the stuff of dreams, celebrated for its formal elegance and its misunderstandings. Insults in the lobby led to duels, wars were conceived, American misconceptions and gaucheries gave way to more exotic ones, Russian or Chinese.

From my own room at the Inglaterra later that night, I could look out on the spires of the Teatro Nacional next door. It took me back. I had been in Havana once before, more than thirty-five years earlier, in another world. The theater's preposterously heroic mass still towered over the old city. There are no white skyscrapers in Havana. That Havana rose elsewhere, in exile across the Straits of Florida. Seeing all that stone heraldry of the theater in the tropical moonlight, Castro's Victor Hugo–like cadences still sounding in my brain, I felt absurdly complicit in Cuba's fortunes.

Havana was my first liberty port, my first foreign city. It was 1955 and I was seventeen, a radio operator with an amphibious assault force in the U.S. Navy. For most of a month we had been engaged in war games off the Puerto Rican island of Vieques. On moonless nights we would pretend to sneak ashore and kill enemies and then guide in aircraft that shot up the island at dawn. The World War II Navy wanted the Pacific war, in which it had performed so well, never to end.

Sunday afternoons on Vieques we got to go swimming. The blue-green water and the palm trees were wonderfully exotic to me, like Treasure Island. On the other hand, there were sand fleas and barbed wire, so it was pleasant and exciting when the operations were over and we were told that we would have liberty nights in Havana.

One of my mentors in those days was our chief radioman, Schultz. I asked him what Havana was like.

"In Havana," Schultz told me, "you can get an around-the-world for a dollar."

My sensual horizons were still rather limited. On long weekend passes from the base in Norfolk I would go up to New York City and date my girlfriend in Yorkville. To avoid brawls, I would not wear my uniform and we would go to the tenement apartment she shared with her parents and neck to Frank Sinatra records. Each week she would attend confession and the priest would tell her not to do it anymore. On my next leave, we would have to murmurously negotiate the whole thing over again. I suppose we enjoyed ourselves.

Anyway, I had trouble picturing myself suavely handing over a dollar for an around-the-world. Essentially, I had no idea what an around-the-world was, although the phrase sort of made a picture. I wasn't about to tell that to Schultz.

"As a city, though," I persisted. "What's it like?"

"Like all of them down here," Schultz said. "Crummy. Fucked up."

I remember that as we steamed past the ramparts of El Morro Castle, into Havana Bay, an elderly Cuban couple stood applauding on the opposite shore of the narrows, in the park around the Castillo de San Salvador. I reported the incident to Schultz.

"They must own a whorehouse," he said.

They hadn't looked to me like the sort of people who owned a whorehouse. Neither then nor since could I altogether reason out a political position that would lead citizens of Havana to applaud the visit of a U.S. Navy transport. It seemed to auger well, though.

The USS *Chilton* was not an attractive vessel and the Navy did not offer it for display. We tied up at one of the docks at the south end of Habana Vieja, Old Havana, not far from the railroad station and the old city walls. Walking out of the shadows of the covered wharf and into the bright sunlight of the street, I took my first step into that problematic otherness that would so tax our country's moral speculation: the un-American world.

Touts were everywhere and the streets smelled weird. Led by the old hands, a bunch of us made our way to the Seven Brothers bar. The Seven Brothers was an old-time waterfront saloon with a big square bar, a jukebox, and a fat Central European bartender whom I later liked to imagine was actually B. Traven. It had everything but women. After a great many Cuba libres, it was decided to go to the Barrio Chino, Chinatown, for more serious action.

On the way to the Barrio Chino, we stopped at the Bacardi distillery and drank free daiquiris. I looked younger than anyone else in the outfit. I probably was younger; in any case, I had the role of comedy virgin thrust on me.

I still recall the name of the cabdriver who took us to the brothel in the Barrio Chino; it was Rudy Bradshaw, and he was a Jamaican immigrant and spoke English like us. The place was called the Blue Moon. It had a curving wall of translucent glass bricks and a bar with a travel-poster photo of the Havana skyline. Young women came out to be bought drinks and taken upstairs. One of them approached me. I have many recollections of that day, but I can recall neither the woman's face nor her name nor the details of our encounter. I do recall there was a certain amount of laughing it up and pretending affection and also that there was paying. The bill came to quite a lot of money. I presume I was cheated in some way, but everyone was nice.

Afterward we went out into the streets of the Barrio Chino. The Barrio Chino in those days was large, and thousands of Chinese must have lived there. (Today, all that remains of the Barrio Chino are a few worn pagoda roofs and sun-faded signs offering phantom *comidas chinas y criollas*.) Many had settled in Havana after working as plantation laborers, and some of them no doubt hoped to slip into the United States, smuggled over by characters like Hemingway's Harry Morgan. There were many good Chinese Cuban restaurants and curio shops and Chinese markets, but what the world knew best about Havana's Barrio Chino was the Teatro Shanghai. The Shanghai was a blue-movie parlor and burlesque house that was home to the Superman Show, the hemisphere's paramount *exhibición*.

Viewers of *Godfather II* will have some idea of what the staging of the Superman Show was like, since part of the act is briefly reproduced in that film. One of the performers was always a nearly naked blonde whose deportment was meant to suggest wholesomeness, refinement, and alarm, as though she had just been spirited unawares from a harp recital at the public library. What on earth, she seemed to be asking the heartless, brutal crowd, am I doing onstage in a Havana pork palace? Another performer was always a large muscular black man who astonished the crowd and sent the blonde into a trembling swoon by revealing the dimensions of his endowment. There were other performers as well, principally a dog and a burro. Suffice it to say that the show at the Teatro Shanghai was a melancholy demonstration that sexism, racism, and speciesism thrived in prerevolutionary Havana. I hasten to add that during much of the time this vileness unfolded I was blessedly asleep, having drunk myself into a state of what might be described as American innocence.

At the end of the show, we all staggered into the night and got into taxis and hence home to the battleship-gray womb of our mother fleet. When I woke up the next day my mood was penitential. At the commencement of liberty I joined forces with my best buddy, a bookish electronics technician who had the kind of reverence for Ray Bradbury that I had for Hemingway. Abandoning our role as boozing, wenching buccaneers, we resumed exis-

tence as high school dropout teenage savants. Instead of carrying
on in the red-light district and having our pictures taken with parrots, we were determined to behave like proper expatriates. We
would go and do some of the cool foreign-type things experienced world travelers did, like drinking black coffee very slowly
from very small cups. At dusk we set out for the Paseo del Prado,
the grand boulevard that runs between the seafront and the Parque Central.

In memory it is probably too good to be true—the crowds
ragged, elegant, ebullient, restrained; the graceful women vari-
ously haughty or laughingly unselfconscious; the men in *guayaberas*
and straw hats, gesturing with cigars, greeting one another and
parting with quick handshakes and *abrazos*. The coffee in small
cups was fine, the air was sensuous and fragrant. The park was full
of almond trees and poincianas. There was music everywhere;
conga bands filled the street with metal syncopation and the flat-
ted wail of African flutes. There were fortune-telling parakeets.
A delicious breeze rustled through the foliage from the seafront.
At the time I noted also the beggars blind with untended cataracts
or crippled by polio, squatting in doorways. (Unless something
unforgettably bad happens, better memories always prevail.)

For me, in 1955, this Havana served as an introduction to the
older, unreformed world. In fact, things were changing ruthlessly
in the midfifties. A line of towering new hotels stood in the
Vedado section of the city, a couple of miles west along the seafront from the end of the Paseo del Prado. An extension of the
Florida Gold Coast, the Vedado casinos went a long way toward
financing the mob's expansion on the mainland. In 1955 they represented someone's bright dream of the future. Reflected in the
silver surf, they twinkled at night like the Playboy Philosophy
itself. George Raft actually ran the casino at the Capri. Howard
Hughes would have been at home atop any one of them.

For the most part, sailors stayed out of the Vedado, where their troublesome, penniless presence was unwelcome. At the time, I was struck less by the frivolity of Havana than by its unashamed seriousness. It was then that I first saw the facade of the Hotel Inglaterra. Its formal elegance and polite luxury embodied something I had never quite experienced outside of books. Beside the Inglaterra stood the overdone but monumental Teatro Nacional, a structure besotted with its own aspirations toward high culture, fearlessly risking absurdity, all trumpets, angels, and muses. It was a setting whose pleasure required a dark side—drama, heroism, sacrifice. All this Spanish tragedy, leavened with Creole sensuality, made Havana irresistible. Whether or not I got it right, I have used the film of its memory ever since in turning real cities into imaginary ones.

Literature had always pursued this Havana, and literary perceptions of the many-layered city at that time centered on the work of two English-speaking foreigners, Ernest Hemingway and Graham Greene. Somewhat puerile sophisticates, already insulated by their superstardom, they were the great exploiters of Cuba's conduciveness to melodrama and its aspect of "playground." Romantics, erstwhile Catholics and pro-Communists, both found in Cuba an ambiance to reflect the minor-key stoicism and sadomasochistic violence they employed in fiction.

Hemingway dominated the world's sense of Havana then, less through his work than through his much publicized presence in the suburb of San Francisco de Paula. Neither of his Cuban settings—the early pages of *To Have and Have Not* and *The Old Man and the Sea*—actually invoke Havana. But it was not necessary to be bookish in the midfifties to be aware that "Don Ernesto" was in town. His bearded, bare-chested figure was part of the pop iconography of the period. Magazine pictures sometimes showed him with his wife, entertaining U.S. servicemen at his house, the Finca Vigia. There—in our imaginations—he dwelled, chief of all worldly American expats, hanging out with bullfighters, jai alai players, and ex–Spanish Loyalist guerrillas, awash in drink and worldly women, fishing by day, partying by night, writing the whole time.

Compañero Graham Greene was a higher-class act. In the Summer 1991 issue of *Cuba Update,* a quarterly published by the Center for Cuban Studies in New York City, the travel writer Tom Miller describes his contemporary quest for Greene's city of the 1950s, celebrated so memorably in *Our Man in Havana.* "His life," Miller writes of Greene, "held an intoxicating mix of literature, espionage, revolution and sex; all of these he found in the final years of the Batista regime." This is a fine advertisement for a life, if not for a regime, and it sounds almost as perfect as Hemingway's. One of Greene's favorite haunts, according to Miller, was the aforesaid Teatro Shanghai; there he "enjoyed what he called the louche atmosphere." If the Shanghai, with its live animal act, was Graham Greene's idea of ambiguity, it's hard to imagine what he might have considered down and dirty. It's even harder to imagine how he could have endured the sweaty proximity of all us loud Americans, ruining the louche with our snores and braying. It must have been enough to drive a sensitive traveler to Russian roulette.

In *Our Man in Havana,* Greene describes a dive called the Wonder Bar, a saloon where all manner of depravity is catered to. Apparently the place was purely fictional, despite the fact that a number of Cubans in Havana today claim to remember it. Such is the power of legend, especially the cinematic-cum-existentialistic legend of Hemingway-Greene, two macho coxcombs who had so much trouble staying at the right end of their own firearms. Both were elaborately proclaimed Hispanophiles, famous for their Latin friendships. Hemingway favored *toreros* and waiters. Greene, in his later years as nemesis of the American Century, became a junketeer and rosy ornament to the *cuadrilla* of Omar Torrijos, in whose translated conversation he professed to detect profundities.

"Both of them spoke exactly two hundred words of Spanish," the Cuban émigré novelist Guillermo Cabrera Infante told me once, speaking of Hemingway and Greene. Cabrera Infante had been a Cuban diplomat during the early years of the Castro regime; today he is an opponent of Fidelismo. "But Greene and Hemingway could never have conversed," he went on to say. "Each knew two hundred different words."

The Cuban novelist Antonio Benítez-Rojo, who during the seventies and eighties ran the publishing division of the state-run cultural center, Casa de las Américas, remembers Greene's hobnobbing visits with Castro in Havana; he recalls, too, how Greene and other distinguished foreign guests were referred to ungenerously as *come mierdas*.

Returning to Havana late in 1991, I'd felt by the end of my first day in the city like a petty harbinger, a terminal gringo whose marginal appearance augured the ungood. Standing on the Malecón at dusk, looking toward the lights of Vedado, it was incredible to think that so much time was lost to me, or at least had gone by. Somewhere out on the Gulf of Mexico, Hurricane Fabian was scattering the flying fish, and a vast tower of white cloud, trailing dark wisps like telltales, had appeared to attend the sunset. Breaking waves lashed the seawall, drenching loiterers, splashing the windshields of passing cars. The Vedado lights were fewer and dimmer than the ones I remembered, sacrificed, like so much else, to shortages. It seemed I would miss out on the good times again.

A rush hour of sorts was under way. In the evening's strange storm light, the promiscuous whirl of odd contraptions rattling past the proud street's crumbling arcades had the aspect of a dream. There were Plymouths with Looney Tune curves and fanged, finned De Sotos, not to mention Soviet-made Ladas and the largest number of motorcycle sidecar combos assembled since the Blitzkrieg. The defiant posters in front of the old American embassy were exercises in socialist realism, but magical realism seemed more appropriate to the frame. Everything in the early evening's landscape appeared fantastic. The painted slogans above the crumbling buildings were like artifacts from the past.

Havana was an exercise in willpower, a dream state being grimly and desperately prolonged.

Earlier that day I had seen Hemingway's house for the first time. Surrounded by ceiba, fig, and flamboyant trees, it was a ghastly sight, moldering indecently in full view like an open grave. In the living room, ancient bottles of rye from long-defunct distilleries had gone cloudy white. Newspapers and old magazines were piled in hideous yellowing stacks: *Look* magazine, *Collier's*, and, at the top of the stack, *Soviet Life,* as if it had been Papa's special reading treat. Then there were the animal heads, absurd and obscene, looking less like trophies of the field than something a mafioso would send his least favorite Hollywood producer. That had been the first vertiginous moment, seeing the room imperfectly embalmed in the past yet seeing it with the eyes of the present: realizing that the front ends of twelve antelope pasted to a single wall no longer look the way they did in the fifties, when such a sight suggested virile jollity and Old Grandad.

The most cheerful thing about the house was the neat line of cats' graves outside, each with its cute name; it was reassuring to witness decent interment. The scariest was the presence of pale Cuban maidens who sat presiding in each and every room, as even-featured, silent, and unsmiling as cemetery angels. I would like to think I imagined them, although I know full well why they were there. Their supervisor was a middle-aged lady who had been one of the Hemingway household's young servants. Brisk and officious, the sort of ladies' maid turned martinet who appears in the wake of revolution, she was thoroughly in charge, supervising the tentative visitors, issuing observations and commands. She spoke of her late employer with a certain suppressed humor and without affection.

It seemed both ironic and fitting that this regiment of women represent Hemingway's persona in custody of the revolution. He who played at causes has one imposed upon his memory. The severity of the maidens also suggested the ambiguous relationship between Castro's Cuba and the Hemingway myth. He was, *en fin,* just another rich American who came to fish and drink. It is unlikely he would have thought well of present-day Cuba. Plainly, the Cubans, without quite letting on, understand this.

I spent a week, often accompanied by an American supporter of Fidel who lives part of every year in Cuba, listening to the residents of Havana. In a Vedado apartment, an old Spanish Loyalist refugee expressed determined devotion to Castro and the regime. A writer's wife reverently showed us a photograph she owned of Che Guevara, taken while he was ill in the mountains, looking Christlike and sacrificial. Another woman, the wife of an official, showed me a picture she had taken of Fidel at rest displaying it with moving, motherly affection. Many of those I spoke with were artists and professionals whose attachment to the government ranged from enthusiasm to sympathy to resigned acceptance. In a comfortable farmhouse outside the city I talked with members of a family whose large landholding had been taken over by the state and who had seen numerous relatives flee to the United States. It was clear they felt that the revolution had given them more than it had taken away. The same seemed true of another family I was introduced to in the old slum of the Barrio Chino. Many of the enthusiasts were people of principle who resembled not at all the cynical apparatchiks I used to encounter on visits to Eastern Europe.

Still the mood of the city seemed forlorn and surly. In the downtown streets youths hassled tourists for dollars. Prostitutes were out in numbers near the Vedado hotels, and there were endless lines in front of the ubiquitous "pizzerias" in which scorched cheese concoctions were dispensed, uninteresting but filling meals to augment the rationed goods available in state groceries. In one of those consumer crises that bedevil socialist economies there was an absence of soap in the city, eroding morale among the fastidious Habaneros, forcing people to wash their clothes, their dishes, and themselves in Chinese toothpaste. A surprising number of young people, encountered casually on the street, denounced the government in bitter and obscene terms. Many of these youths were poor and of color—the very people who, in theory, benefited most from the revolution. A story was making the rounds. A little boy stands on the Paseo del Prado watching the tourists comfortably sightseeing. Whatever he wants, he finds, is on sale only for dollars, to foreigners. Asked what he wants to be when he grows up, the boy replies: "A foreigner."

One aspect of the situation in Havana was brought home about the middle of the week, after I had dinner with two other Americans in town, a man and woman about my age, at Hemingway's old haunt in Habana Vieja, the Floridita. Lobster was on the menu at thirty-five dollars a claw. There were daiquiris. Musicians played "Guantanamera." Outside, we started walking the streets of Habana Vieja, as romantic a collection of Spanish colonial buildings as the hemisphere affords but, in present circumstances, crumbling and run-down. About two blocks from the Floridita, on the picturesque Calle Obispo, we were jumped and knocked to the pavement by four or five youths who grabbed the woman's bag and disappeared down the cobblestone streets.

It was a fairly noisy business, with shouts and curses and laughter from the kids who had the bag. Police state or not, no cops were forthcoming. If the Calle Obispo had a branch of the feared Committee for the Defense of the Revolution, the committee was either in recess or had decided to exclude yanqui visitors from its protection. The few cautious citizens who appeared were curious but fearful. They conveyed a sense of not really requiring our presence and expecting the same. Back at the Floridita, a bartender poured free drinks. Someone called the police, who eventually arrived.

Walking into the old Spanish fortress that serves as headquarters for the city police in Habana Vieja, it occurred to me that no tour of the twentieth century could be complete without a visit to a Communist police station. This one was the traditional precinct green. Behind the desk was a sergeant who looked for all the world like a New York Irish cop, complete with jug ears and an attitude. He was smoking a cigarette under a sign that said NO FUMAR. A few locals were standing against the walls, looking as though they foresaw some unhappy outcome.

One of us pointed out to the serge that his smoking was a violation. He grinned at this piquant demonstration of North American political correctness and explained that the sign was for people in front of the desk, not for him. There was a second sign behind him that read PROHIBIDO ENFADARSE, "It is forbidden to get mad." Presumably this was also directed to the public.

As Che Guevara, Frantz Fanon, and Lenin himself would have agreed, there's nothing like a little violence to define the propositions—the mugging was trivial, a sign of discontent in terms of human nature. But there were others in Havana during my visit whose discontent and opposition to the status quo were as principled as anything I heard from Fidel's supporters.

José Lorenzo-Fuentes is a novelist and journalist who fought with Che Guevara in the Escambray Mountains at the time of the revolution. In May 1991 Lorenzo-Fuentes, together with nine other Cuban writers, signed a declaration in the form of a petition to the government. It reads, "We, Cuban intellectuals, profoundly worried about the dangerous situation in which the country finds itself, have decided to try to promote a reasonable and moderate attitude in all sectors of our society in order to avoid amongst all of us the approaching economic, social, political and cultural catastrophe."

The declaration goes on to ask for "a national debate without exclusions" on Cuba's future, democratic procedures, a liberalized economic system, and freedom for "prisoners of conscience." As

a result of his signing, Lorenzo-Fuentes was subjected to harass-
ment by rapid-response brigades, organized mobs of official agi-
tators. He counts himself lucky so far, since other signers have
been arrested or harassed in more extreme ways. Lorenzo-
Fuente's opinions have gotten him in trouble before: In 1968 he
was arrested as the result of his friendship with a Mexican diplomat accused of being a CIA agent. He served three years in prison
and was unable to publish for many years.

"A young girl came to my door," Lorenzo-Fuentes explained
when I spoke with him one afternoon in Vedado. He is a slight,
formal man, who appears older than his years. That particular day
he seemed resigned and weary. His wife looked on with a nervous
smile. "I read the petition," Lorenzo-Fuentes went on to say, "and
it seemed reasonable. I thought it was the right thing to sign. I
accept the role that the writer has always had in the country." His
wife permitted herself the observation that the mix of literature
and politics in Cuba might be difficult for outsiders to understand.

The "young girl" at Lorenzo-Fuentes's door could well have
been the poet María Elena Cruz Varela. Formerly an avid Marxist-
Leninist, Cruz Varela is the spark of a dissident group known as
Alternative Criterion. Only a week before my arrival in Havana,
her Alternative Criterion and a number of other human rights
groups that are joined together in a coalition known as the Cuban
Democratic Convergence met at the house of Elizardo Sánchez,
another veteran of the revolution. The Convergence called upon
the Fourth Congress of the Party "to initiate constitutional reforms
and to take other steps to protect human rights and establish democratic institutions in Cuba."

Within a week of the meeting, the Convergence and the signers
of the May petition had the government's reply. Speaking to the
Fourth Congress in Santiago, Castro gave them what amounted to
a summary answer. "Reactionaries have no role in Cuba," he said
in a speech carried live on Cuban television. "They have nothing
to do here." Castro went on to offer the Congress swashbuckling

intransigence; blood, sweat, and tears; shortages and labor: a continuance of the revolution in defiance not only of the United States but of the times.

"Tendremos otro Baragua," he told the crowd in Santiago. "We will have another Baragua." The reference was to the stand of the revolutionary general Antonio Maceo during Cuba's war of independence with Spain. Surrounded, offered terms of surrender, Maceo defied his enemies. Fidel was announcing his intention to do the same.

Not long after, he sent a less rhetorical message to the human rights activists of the Convergence. Fourteen of them were arrested in the early-morning hours of October 9 and 10. Three of them were tried on October 16, charged with "illegal association," "clandestine printing," and "incitement to commit crime." Each was given a prison term. The signers of the May petition were accused of "treason" in *Granma*. Cruz Varela was denounced for "betraying her country" and being "in league with the CIA." On November 27 Cruz Varela and three others associated with Alternative Criterion were sentenced to prison terms of between one and two years on charges of holding illegal meetings, printing clandestine documents, and defaming state institutions.

Here is one of Cruz Varela's underground poems, as translated in *The Miami Herald*. May it be among the last to represent that uniquely twentieth-century form, samizdat.

> *Because I know nothing. Because if I ever knew,*
> *torn among the thistles I have forgotten.*
> *Here the thorns hurt. Here the brambles hurt.*
> *Here I leave my smell. The smell of the*
> *persecuted. . . .*
>
> *Because I know nothing*
> *Because I can hardly touch my knee and I*
> *don't know anything else. And I am*

this crumbling city. And I am
this country of shipwrecked fools.

Left adrift
aboard their ship.

Downstairs the band played "Siboney," the old stones of the city were bathed in moonlight, the scented air was full of tragedy, heroism, intransigence, sacrifice. The terminal gringos at the Inglaterra were getting it all wrong. "Literature, espionage, revolution, and sex." "Blood, blood, blood!"

Ninety miles away, visible on clear nights from the Tupolevs beginning their descent toward José Martí Airport, twinkled the lights of the Florida Keys. It was all different over there: They had plenty of soap; the talk was of real estate, drugs, and T-shirt shops, and you could say what you liked. God in His mercy only knew how many Cubans were out paddling in the darkness between El Morro and Twelve Mile Reef, thirsty, salt-poisoned, shark-stalked, in search of the less heroic life.

The aspect of militant Spanish Revenger represents only one side of Cuba's personality. In spite of "Baragua!" and *"Socialismo o muerte,"* Cuba is not an apocalyptic culture. There is another slogan of sorts, a bit of folk poetry the slaves recited to keep themselves going. *"Lo que hay que hacer es no morirse."* "What you gotta do is, you gotta not die." Socialism or death? Why not socialism or somewhat less socialism? Why not socialism or regulated private enterprise? Death?

But among the ghosts of the Inglaterra, it is not hard to sympathize with Cuba's refusal of her assigned role in the American Century. A hundred years ago, in the fullness of our gilded age, we came weeping at our own propaganda, the particularly American variation on crocodile tears, reflecting the pity of the eagle for the forsaken lamb. (During the Vietnam era, I heard somebody remark that you could always tell the objects of American benevolence by the hunted look in their eyes.) Fair-haired Protestant heroes, descendants of Drake, we dashed the whip from the cruel Spaniard's hand, banished the sneering inquisitor. We announced the imminence of order, commerce, and light. But, of course, Cuba as a chaotic and materially backward country was useful to us in a variety of ways.

Descendants of Drake, it turned out, and equally of Blackbeard and Henry Morgan. What happened next is well known, and even if we were not at the root of Cuba's problems our proximity and involvement never represented a solution to them. At best we offered Cubans an opportunity to emulate our own pragmatism, optimism, and common sense. At the same time, we offered our worst, a prolonged insult, a dehumanizing, sometimes racist condescension. Such attitudes are hard to forgive. People take them personally.*

We ought not to be surprised that, led by embittered middle-class Spanish Cubans such as Castro, Cuba took an opportunity to decline our halfhearted offer of middle-class progress. In doing so she was being true to the aesthetic and aristocratic foundations of her culture, embracing faith and heroism, declining mediocrity. Thus the enthusiasm of Compañero Greene, who hated all vulgarity but his own, a self-indulgent mandarin who, in truth, hated democracy as well and rejoiced in Castro's regime as in the Church of Rome.

Neither Cubans nor Americans much love irony, but the ironies of the Hotel Inglaterra abound. It is unlikely that Castro, in spite of what he has since said, set out to make Cuba a formal member of the Soviet bloc. He was, as he claimed, a follower of José Martí and thus an opponent of American domination. A great dreamer, he saw himself as a hemispheric figure, a successor to Bolívar. He

*Any reader wishing to sample some American attitudes toward Cuba from the early years of the century is advised to consult a period travel guide. On the subject of commercial relations, Thomas P. McCann's history of United Fruit, *An American Company,* also makes lively, mortifying reading.

came to power in the post-Bandung world of Sukarno, Nkrumah, Nasser, Tito. No doubt he entertained the notion that in some Siberian vault a college of wise Marxist gnomes had it all figured out, economically speaking. He himself was a soldier, a knight of faith. He may have been the only Marxist head of state on earth who actually believed in the doctrine. For that he probably deserves to be left holding the bag.

History loves ambiguity as well as irony. Castro's regime has caused great suffering for countless Cubans. At the same time it has destroyed much of the old political pathology in which Cuba was bound. For centuries the Caribbean crescent labored under a curse concealed beneath its loveliness. Like much of America, its conception had a dark aspect, the shadow of genocide and slavery. What it offered to the world was not nourishment but the things of appetite. The Spaniards who came for spices tortured the Indians for gold. When the gold was gone there came tobacco, sugar, coffee, cocaine, emeralds, marijuana, the very names of which suggest violence and greed, Latin tyranny and Yankee filibustering. Graham Greene might have called them louche.

Under Castro ordinary Cubans grew healthier; many learned to read and write. However passively, Castro involved the mass of people in the political process. This may not justify his regime, but it is true all the same. Perhaps it is philistine to hope for happy endings in Cuba, a place so steeped in short-term gaiety and long-term tragedy. It is possible, however, to hope for new beginnings. The final drama of Fidel Castro's Cuba may be that he has prepared a future for his country in which he and his ideologues serve no purpose, have no place.

At the same time, while Fidel and the Communists were trying to reshape Cuba, a second Havana was rising in Miami. The Cuban Americans there are often presented as an intransigent monolith committed to violence, a mirror image of the present Cuban government. Reality has proved more complex. Last spring, Liz Balmaseda in *The Miami Herald* described increased cultural contacts between the two centers: "Quietly, history is being made beneath our noses. The cream of Havana's cultural crop is flocking to Miami. Most go back but some defect. More importantly they are talking, sparking the sort of contact some Cuban Americans have always feared. Neither Miami nor Havana will ever be the same."

In the same piece Balmaseda describes the reaction of a visiting Cuban artist to the general *cubanía* he encountered in Miami—the Spanish billboards, the huge Cuban-owned shopping centers and banks: "[But] all I kept thinking as I rode through the city was, why couldn't we do this in Cuba?"

On irony's head, more irony. The speaker was Tomás Esson, a black Cuban of peasant origin. It may have been only the Castro revolution that enabled a man like Esson to study and become an artist. Enfranchised, he was able to see American shops and banks as something belonging to his world, as achievements in which he shared. Thus Esson remains in Miami, where he has the freedom, denied him in Cuba, to paint as he wishes.

At the end of my stay I got tired of the bar at the Inglaterra so I walked down the Prado to the Wonder Bar for a final daiquiri. As Graham Greene reported in *Our Man in Havana,* all the appetites of the Antilles are catered to there. You can get anything, nothing is changed. Errol Flynn is the bartender. Remember him? He claims Hemingway still comes in. And George Raft, too, he says. The music's great, and Havana's just the way I remember.

It's a very romantic place, the Wonder Bar, though louche as can be. It's where Cubans and North Americans meet. Everybody gets what they like but nobody gets what they deserve. The Cubans are always talking about the United States and the Americans talk about Cuba. Everyone's an expert and gets everything right. People's eyes are bright with dreams. Everybody's beautiful.

Some people say the Wonder Bar doesn't exist, but don't believe it. They say the same thing about God and the Dialectic, without which any kind of coherent history would be impossible.

You have to have things like those, especially in the Spanish-speaking world where it verges on the United States.

They're going to open a place like the Wonder Bar in Miami one day soon, with the music and the dreams. There has to be one. I wonder if it will ever be the same.

ALMA GUILLERMOPRIETO
(1 9 4 9 –   )

Since the arrival of Christopher Columbus, Catholicism has played a central role in the history of Cuba. It was the official religion of the country, until Castro's government seized the Catholic schools and expelled over a hundred priests in 1961. By 1962, Cuba was declared officially atheist, and in 1969, the government canceled Christmas as an official holiday, banning the display of Christmas trees and nativity scenes. Government officials claimed it would interfere with the sugarcane harvest. The visit of Pope John Paul II to Cuba in 1998 was a watershed occasion—one that broke the international blockade against Cuba and brought the country back into the Catholic fold with other Latin American nations. Slowly, church services and holidays have come back to Cuba. Alma Guillermoprieto, a native of Mexico City who covers the culture and politics of Latin America for *The New Yorker*, was on hand to report on this momentous event. This essay is from her third book, *Looking for History: Dispatches from Latin America*. Her two prior books are *Samba* and *The Heart That Bleeds*.

from LOOKING FOR HISTORY: DISPATCHES FROM LATIN AMERICA

January 25: Sunrise again, and I have been walking briskly through the cool, expectant dawn, headed for the Plaza de la Revolución, where today's mass, the central act we have all been waiting for, will take place. The pilgrims and foreign priests at the hotel left for the plaza in chartered buses hours ago, and I am afraid that I have already missed something, that a river of people has already flowed into the plaza and left me behind. In a characteristic tactical masterstroke, Fidel has gone on television a few days earlier to exhort everyone—Catholics and Fidelistas—to show up at the plaza today, and to greet the pope warmly, and to refrain from any sign of disrespect, such as whistling at bits of the homily they might not like or shouting revolutionary slogans. Even when set against John Paul II, Fidel is no mean politician: After this broadcast appeal, the large contingent of Cuban exiles who are making their pilgrimage to the Plaza will look foolish, or worse, if they try to turn the mass into a political rally. And no one will be able to say whether the crowds in the plaza are the pope's or Fidel's. No one will be able to claim that the *acto* was an act of defiance against the regime. In effect, Fidel has offered his faithful on loan to the pope for the day, like the splendid host he is reputed to be.

But it seems that his faithful are staying away. There are people out on the streets, certainly, but very few of them are going in my direction (even though the ever-vigilant neighborhood Comités de Defensa de la Revolución have been reminding people that they are expected at the event). It is only in the vicinity of the plaza, where the loudspeakers broadcasting an *animador's*—emcee's—enthusiastic chanting can already be heard, that the odd cluster of people I see here and there, carrying missals or rosaries and little plastic flags in the Vatican's yellow and white colors, start to form into a crowd. These are the pope's faithful.

It is not quite 7 A.M. when I reach the Plaza de la Revolución, and it is already more than half full of people who have obviously been here for hours, looking as if they are about to levitate from sheer joy. Hymns are being sung with the kind of full-throated enthusiasm I remember was voiced for the Revolution back in the seventies. The crowd, I conclude, is overwhelmingly Catholic and not, as Fidelistas claim about Catholics, overwhelmingly elderly, although it is, as is also alleged, predominantly white. A bizarre visual displacement has taken place: on the front of the National Library, where large portraits of Marx, Lenin, or the like usually hang, there is a gigantic mural of the Sacred Heart of Jesus. A slogan underneath it reads JESUS CHRIST, IN YOU I TRUST. The emotional epicenter of the plaza is no longer the podium that is always set up for revolutionary *actos* at the foot of a horrid statue of José Martí erected by Batista, but a graceful white canopy set at right angles to it, which shelters the altar where the mass will take place.

Because the altar is not set very high, it will be almost hidden from view by 9 A.M., when the plaza has filled and the mass is about to begin. Police barriers divide the crowd in half and define a pathway along which the Virgin of Charity, Patroness of Santiago and indeed of Cuba, is now carried in procession to the altar. Unexpectedly, the Popemobile is suddenly visible along this pathway too, and there are screams and a flurry of enthusiasm as the crowd catches sight of John Paul II. It is still early and the skies are gray; no one can be suffering from heatstroke or dehydration, but the Red Cross volunteers posted throughout the plaza are kept busy ferrying people on stretchers to the first-aid tents—elderly women, mostly, who may have fainted from sheer emotion. Has Fidel arrived? Where is he? I ask over and over again. No one seems to know, or care.

And now it is the mass, set to beautiful Cuban music specially composed for this occasion. The *clave de son*—the distinct Afro-Cuban one-two-three, one-two beat clicked out with wooden sticks as a convocation to the dance—fills the sound system. Everywhere, people are waving yellow-and-white flags. They sing along, tentatively and then more forcefully, guided by booklets that have been handed out. "He who sows love harvests love," they sing. I come from a long Mexican anticlerical tradition, but these sentiments are a refreshing change from the intransigent chants of the Revolution ("Whoever pops his head up, hit him hard, Fidel!"). Throughout the mass, crowds continue to enter the plaza. Oddly, though, throngs are also leaving it. One possible explanation is that these are the non-Catholics who have come here out of curiosity or because Fidel said they should, and who, having seen enough, depart.

I leave too, because no one can tell me if Fidel is here and I cannot bear to miss the spectacle I have come all this way to witness. In search of a television, I wander around a poor neighborhood behind the plaza until I hear the mass blaring from a television set. The sound comes from the front room of a tiny house whose front porch holds a couple of rusty bicycles and a decrepit lawn chair. Inside is more dilapidated furniture, the television, and a pleasant-looking woman who is peeling garlic in a creaky aluminum rocker in front of the set and who immediately offers me her seat. She brings me a glass of cool water, and then a tiny cup of sweet, dark coffee, keeping up a running commentary all the while on the mass. The pope is handing Bibles to a group of Church activists, including an elderly woman whom he draws to him for an embrace. "See that!" my hostess exclaims. "That little old lady must feel like we do when we get our Party card!" Her mood changes when the camera cuts away to the row of chairs immediately in front of the altar to show, at last, the sight I have been waiting for: Fidel Castro, attending mass in the Plaza de la Revolución. Behind the altar, facing where he sits, is the mural of the Sacred Heart of Jesus. I remark that this is a sight I never expected to see. "And neither did I," my hostess says, not smiling. "Neither did I."

My hostess is a lifelong Party militant in her midthirties. She and her eight-year-old son sleep in one of the two bedrooms in the little house. The other is occupied by her former husband, who in the seven years since the couple divorced has been unable to get the officials in charge of these things to authorize new living quarters for him. There will be meat for Sunday dinner today because a friend has brought her a cut of pork, but even though the food situation has improved greatly and she says she no longer goes hungry, as she did during the lean 1990–1994 years, the shelves in her kitchen are nearly bare. She offers me a present—a commemorative issue of *Granma* on the anniversary of Che's death.

Later she will insist on giving me a farewell present as well—a color photograph of Fidel—before walking with me to the main avenue, from which we can see the Sacred Heart of Jesus. The day she came upon the mural as she was walking to work will remain in her memory forever, she says. "I remember all the years that we would evaluate our coworkers in our work centers, and we had *compañeras* who were hardworking, and skillful, and punctual, and loyal, and comradely, and when it came time to evaluate them for promotion or grant them the right to new living quarters, we would always say no, because they were Catholic. And now here is this mural in the place where we usually put our heroes. Was this what we held back our Catholic *compañeras* for?" she asks in a sudden outburst. "I accept what I am told to accept, because I am loyal. But I do not understand."

I wonder what Fidel makes of this strange new position he finds himself in. I wonder if his admiration for John Paul II is increasing as he watches him play a crowd with a skill few men other than Fidel himself have ever shown. The pope's most important sermon addresses the question of the embargo and the evils of neoliberalism, "which subordinates the human person to blind market forces and conditions the development of peoples to those forces." The interesting thing is that the crowd I take to be overwhelmingly Catholic, and therefore, perhaps, conservative, cheers and claps with rising enthusiasm during this impassioned denunciation. "Do you think people are supposed to clap during mass?" my hostess wonders, and at that point the pope interrupts his discourse, jokingly, to address that very question. "The pope likes it when you applaud," he says, each word an effort. "Because when you do so, he can rest a little bit." The camera shows us that Fidel is laughing with the crowd.

Although the pope is speaking more clearly than he has throughout the trip, his voice is nearly gone, his facial muscles are so deteriorated that a smile is almost impossible, and still he manages to convey irony, humor, and a bantering tenderness in his improvised remarks that have the crowd in a frenzy of delight. When the cheering stops, he continues with the prepared text. "At times unsustainable economic programs are imposed on nations as a condition for further assistance," he reads, and by now my hostess is with the crowd in its enthusiasm. "Did you hear that!" she yells. "That man is going to be a Party militant by the time he leaves this island!"

In the plaza the roaring approval goes on for so long that the pope holds up a hand. "Thou art a very active audience," he admonishes, again with that bantering intimacy. "But now we must continue." He holds the pause a beat. "It's only one more page." And now, while the orchestra plays a lilting Creole melody, it's time for the kiss of peace, the moment in modern Catholic ritual when people turn to each other and embrace while wishing each other peace. The screen shows members of the Communist Party Central Committee exchanging hugs with nuns, cardinals wishing peace to Fidel. One of the young priests serving as acolytes for this liturgy is in tears. The mass is over.

Something extraordinary has taken place. Later, I will ask a wise and wily priest just what it was that occurred. "None of us knows," he answers. "And the first thing we have to do now, all of us, is sit down and reflect on what we saw. One thing is certain: it has been proved that all Cubans—Cubans from the island and Cubans from Miami, nonbelievers and Catholics—can gather joyfully and in peace, for a good cause. And if this happened once, it can happen again, with the right conditions."

I comment on the general perception that Fidel was entranced by the pope, and on my perception that the pope was not necessarily entranced back. "The pope is entranced by no one," the priest says dryly. "The pope is entranced by his God."

Perhaps, I suggest, this is because his need was nowhere as great as Fidel's. After all, what could Cuba offer the pope in exchange for the Vatican's stand against the blockade? Rather sharply, I am told that for the pope there was never any question of an exchange. "The pope has a different sense of time, he is Polish, and he likes to point out that for two hundred years Poland did not exist as a nation, until at long last, because there were always Poles who took care to keep alive the language and the culture and the idea of the fatherland, Poland reemerged among the world of nations. And so the pope says," says the priest, "that if we cannot know if our acts will have consequences a hundred years from now, or two, or five hundred, all one can do is what one feels is right at any given moment, without expecting results."

ANDREI CODRESCU
(1 9 4 6 –)

Andrei Codrescu, born in Sibiu, Romania, came to the United States in 1966. Having come of age under a Communist regime, Codrescu cast a critical eye on Castro's government as a National Public Radio correspondent reporting from Cuba. The book that resulted from his journey, *Ay, Cuba!*, is a thoughtful and witty read that showcases Codrescu's other talents and interests—poetry, humorous musings, and an eye for the erotic.

In Cuba, the term *jinetera* literally means "jockey" but it's used to refer to the young men and women who "ride the tourists"—that is, date and/or sleep with them, sometimes for American dollars but sometimes just for a night out in restaurants or clubs that would be prohibitively expensive to most Cubans or ordinarily forbidden to them. Codrescu navigates this sex trade, which is a ubiquitous part of the tourist experience in a country short on almost everything but tattered ideals and beautiful youths.

from AY, CUBA!

HAVANA STREETS

The *jineteros* and *jineteras* jammed in front of the hotel entrance swarmed around us like a happy flock of hummingbirds. *Jinetero* is Cuban for "hustler," and it can mean anything from prostitute to self-appointed tour guide or penniless dance lover. The women were bare-legged, dressed in short skirts or body-hugging Lycra, and spanned the color spectrum from Mediterranean white to lustrous ebony. The sounds of salsa from the disco next door had them on the move, hips wiggling, torsos shimmying, hands playing invisible maracas. The boys gave off the same signals, though they were not as overtly sexual as the girls, and offered themselves as tour guides. The girls offered, well, everything.

Most of them were young, barely sixteen, but they were unmistakably women, self-possessed and most aware of the effect their surging bodies had on men. There were no *jineteras* over eighteen. After that age they must have married and led normal lives. Hustling was some kind of initiation. David said: "Where do they keep the older women?"

"There aren't any," Art said. "It's a country of young girls."

Ariel's presence deterred them only briefly, though the girls did approach her first, asking where she was from and trying to ascertain what her relationship to us was. This was their way of asking permission to capture us. It was an open and friendly exchange. Ariel explained that it would never occur to any Cuban woman to deny a *jinetera*'s right to a tourist, unless she was married to the man. The assumption that all foreigners were there to help Cubans from starving was deeply held. Ariel, honest to a fault, answered the *jinetera*'s questions earnestly. She treated them with dignity and interest, without a trace of condescension, an attitude for which they were grateful. In fact, nearly every stranger who came into contact with us for whatever reason conceived instant respect and sympathy for Ariel, whose entire being seemed to communicate an unassuming simplicity. Ariel made no big deal of her position with us—she was, after all, a translator, someone who made good money—and generally let us fend for ourselves in situations involving the locals, figuring (not always rightly) that we were big boys who could take care of ourselves.

Two of the beauties with the most insistent eyes draped themselves like clusters of grapes on my arms and fired off questions in snippets of Italian, German, Russian, and English. When they discovered that we were from the United States their enthusiasm became boundless. My left side said: "My aunt and my cousins are in Miami. You know them? Beautiful girls! You go dance with them, okay?" My right rejoined: "My father is in Detroit. I hate him." They were not making this up. Everything about them, including their intentions, was transparent. They were candid and fearless.

"You don't believe me," said my right. "Why would I lie to you? All I want is for you to take me dance. Maybe we drink a Coca."

Ariel confirmed that most of these girls were not prostitutes. Many of them were college girls or young professionals out for a night on the town. There were even some doctors among the *jineteras*. At Cuban salaries of ten to fifteen dollars a month, none of them could afford the discos' entrance fees. They were not averse to having a meal bought for them, and for a small present, they would gladly go to bed with their date. Cuban girls, Ariel said, were sexually experienced from a very young age.

Art and David were doing their best to fend off other teenagers who undulated about them in their platform sandals, making multilingual siren sounds.

"I am religious," David protested. "I only love the Virgin." The schoolgirl in her polka-dot blouse and miniskirt who leaned against him like a steady sweetheart assumed an angelic expression and, placing her hand loosely on her thigh, exclaimed, "I am a virgin. Can't you tell?"

The half block between the Capri and the National Hotels in Havana was awash in adolescent concupiscence and cheap perfume. We negotiated it with the utmost difficulty and were abandoned with regret only at the entrance to the National, where the *jineteras* were forbidden to enter. A tourist confined to this area would get an image of joyous, sensual Afro-Cubans, an image as clichéd as "happy pickaninnies." The irony, if that's what it was, was that the Revolution had professed to free Cuban blacks from just such clichés.

The National was both grander and more conspicuously policed than the Capri. We had to show our *tarjetas* and explain to a distinctly hostile civilian that Ariel was our translator. He directed us to get film festival badges as soon as possible, and waved us in.

The grandeur that was once Lucky Luciano's embraced us with its columns, fanciful lighting, grand stairway, wall frescoes, and terraces. Music wafted from discreetly placed ensembles near bars hidden in tropical foliage and blooms. The scents of bougainvillea and jasmine mingled with the perfume on the necks and arms of evening-gowned beauties with jet-black hair, dancing in the arms of dashing young film stars. The opening party of the film festival was in full swing. Miraculously, we found seats on a rattan couch before a low table and lowered ourselves into the pure fantasy of an exotic night that gave no hint of being shared with the groaning masses of socialist Cuba. That is, it would have given no hint if I had not begun listening to the song which the black-clad singer of the band by the bar belted out with all the passion of his Afro-Cuban heart: "Your beloved presence, Che Guevara, Comandante Che Guevara, Querido Comandante . . ." It was the Che Guevara song, a romantic tribute to the Revolutionary hero, a song whose melody began to haunt us all through our stay in Cuba until one night, at the Hotel Grande in Santiago de Cuba, I made a desperate bet that we would hear it twelve more times before we left the island in two days. David bet six times. Ariel, five. Art, two. I won. But that evening, the song sounded profoundly beautiful. The two impeccably dressed couples at the table next to ours applauded wildly and, while tipping the band, requested them to play another Communist Top-Ten hit, "Mañana Compañeros."

Art rose to tip the band, too, and discovered they were selling a tape that included the Che Guevara song. "How many pesos?" he asked. "Pesos?" replied the indignant singer. "Ten dollars. Dollars."

"There is something here Che wouldn't be too happy about," Art said when he came back.

David bought a fat cigar, and we ordered, at Ariel's suggestion, Planter's Punch, which our waitress pronounced "Poonch." It was a lemonady concoction of dark rum, lemons, and a sprig of mint, that produced an instant beneficial surge.

At this point, Ariel made her exit, pleased, I think, with our gang. Not long after, Art did the same, claiming that one Poonch was enough to rob him of reason. Knowing him as I did, I knew that he had been practically wild. This was the longest time I ever remember Art enjoying the mindless pleasure of a drink, without taping the sounds of the ice cubes or something.

David and I stayed on, valiant knights, and ordered more Poonch.

I had just become absorbed by the sinuous grace of a Hispanic beauty who wore a white flower in her hair and was dancing with a midget producer, when I felt the merest touch on my shoulder, the feathery brush of an angel's wing.

"Do you have a light?" sang a husky but girlish voice. I looked up into a mess of curly black hair.

"Can we sit here with you?" Julie asked, and before I could say anything, Julie and Ysemina floated onto the rattan opposite from us and trained the reflectors of their eyes on the two Yankees.

"He looks like John Travolta," Ysemina told Julie.

Julie studied David for a long second. "Definitely," she said.

I translated this for David, who looked impassive, and then I asked, "Who do I look like?"

Julie picked up my empty Poonch glass and stared intently at the ice cubes and the sprig of mint stuck there. "Sting," she said.

I leave this to my readers to judge.

"Do you read ice cubes and mint?"

"Like a hand," said Julie. "Cubans read everything. Tea, coffee, hands, cracks . . ."

"Cracks?"

"Yes. Cracks in the street, in the walls, in the ceiling. In Cuba everything is cracked." She started laughing helplessly, like a schoolgirl. Ysemina cracked up, too.

"What are they laughing about?" asked David.

"You," I said. "They think you're cracked."

"Why do Cubans read everything?"

Julie leaned over, nearly touching my face, and whispered. "To find out about the future. See when the Crazy One dies, nobody knows what will happen. Do you want me to read your hand?"

That was pretty daring of Julie, but as I would find out in the coming days, waiting for the "Crazy One" to die was a common Cuban pastime.

"Sure, go ahead." Julie took my hand and looked carefully at the paths carved there by the Fates. "A lot of girls," she said. "One of them is me. Wait, I'll write over these other girls. Do you have a pen?"

I gave her my felt-tip pen. She wrote her name, address, and telephone number on my palm.

Tropical breeze, beautiful girls, flowers, the smell of the sea, big stars above, the proximity of the equator, black, liquid woman's eyes . . . Another Planter's Poonch would have put me under the spell of romance. I was aware that all harbors are hypnotic, like the insides of flowers, and that Havana was the first harbor of the New World. With some difficulty, and only after promising to call next day, we took our leave of the two young women.

"How do you suppose they got into the hotel?" asked David, as we shook our heads no to the seductive entreaties of the girls on the street.

I suspected that Cuba, like Romania, was in that stage of its development when everything could be had for one dollar.

THE POWER OF PRAYER

I looked at my watch before I took it off. It was two A.M., the bed was lumpy, and I felt charged with energy. I wrote in my notebook, trying to capture in words Julie's vanilla scent, the silky air, the paunch of the fat man mouthing the Che song, the cigar smoke. A sickle moon was plastered against the window. When I finally lay down, I drifted off immediately. Not for long. From behind the partition separating my room from the one next to it, came a deep man's voice, charged with dramatic emotion:

"THANK YOU, LORD! THANK YOU, LORD, FOR YOUR SPECIAL CREATION, FOR THIS BLESSED PEOPLE AND THEIR MUSIC! YOU FILL ME WITH JOY AND ETERNAL PLEASURE!"

This powerful appeal to the Lord was followed by a weak woman's voice, whispering in accented English: "Thank you, Lord!"

"LOUDER, DAUGHTER! LOUDER! HE CAN'T HEAR YOU IF YOU WHISPER! THANK YOU, LORD! GRACIAS, SEÑOR! I SEE THE LIGHT! THANK YOU, LORD!"

I stood bolt upright in my bed, not sure if I'd died and gone to Texas. The man's accent was definitely Texan, and it belonged in a country church. We were in Cuba, for Chrissakes! What the hell was going on?

I banged on the partition. "Excuse me, good Christians, but what do you think you're doing yelling in the middle of the night!"

"Pardon us sinners!" came the preacher's booming voice, addressed to, I'm not sure, either me or the Lord. "I've been bringing another soul to the Lord!"

"Fine," I said, "Just do it quietly."

The racket ceased and I lay back down on the bed. Soon there was some fervent whispering, and then some rustling and heavy motion like a body being pummelled, and I heard the girl weep. I stood bolt upright. Had the preacher murdered the girl? I picked up the phone to call the front desk, but then I remembered: I was in Cuba. Besides, there was no dial tone. I had to take care of business myself. There was some walking back and forth behind the partition, then some whispering, then what sounded like the counting of money. By this time, I'd dressed quietly and was holding my camera like a rock, fully prepared to slam the Texas fellow and liberate the crying woman. I heard the door swing open next door, and close.

Presumably alone, the preacher lapsed heavily onto his soggy bed whose springs creaked, and sighed with what I could have sworn was a drunken slur, "Blessed be the meek. . . ."

Next morning, I rose from a troubled sleep, put on a clean shirt, and, without bothering to shave, went out. Just outside my door, wafting on a cloud of Old Spice, was my old acquaintance and next-room neighbor, Bill Huxley, sports evangelist. He looked hearty, hale, and freshly shaven, and he had a music case on his back.

"Reverend Huxley," I said, "was that a sports star in your room last night?"

He laughed uproariously. "Why, not at all, that was a *jinetera*!"

I must have looked angry, because he hastened to explain. He told me that in addition to sports evangelism, which was pretty slim pickings, his mandate also called for driving hustlers away from sin and to the Lord. What he did was pay the girls the money they'd have gotten by spending the night in sin, and then preach to them about Christ instead, by using examples drawn from his own life, particularly the joys of fidelity and marriage.

Recalling all the odd noises of his sermonizing, I asked him what that was about. "Sounded more like a beating than praying, to be quite honest, Rev."

"At the end, when they accept Christ, I lay hands on them and we pray together. We pray out loud, and the girls sometimes cry and let loose some awful spirits. Sometimes I break down myself, but because you demanded your sleep, we prayed quietly."

Well, if that was quiet, I hated to think what loud was. I thanked him nonetheless for his consideration, but the vision of this beefy, gray-pompadoured fellow laying his big, sweaty hands on the bare chocolate shoulders of a poor *jinetera* like Julie gave me the creeps. In their place, I'd much rather perform the furtive but thankfully brief motions of paid sex.

I asked Reverend Huxley what the instrument on his back was for.

"I play the trumpet," he said, "on the street, at the train station, at the airport. Folks come and join me in song. Sometimes they bring their own instruments. I then lay down the trumpet and tell them what I know about the things that changed my life."

Playing music on the street had been forbidden until the late 1980s. Then the Soviets kicked the bucket, and the musicians took over. Geraldo Piloto, the composer for the salsa band Klimax, said, "Cubans live on music the way others live on bread and water." That was the literal truth.

We rode the elevator down in silence. At the bottom, Huxley was joined by a white-haired fellow I'd never seen, and two of the other sports evangelists from the plane. They were all carrying music cases. It was soul-collecting time at the train station in Havana. Blow that trumpet, Gabriel!

But if Yankee religious trumpeting was safe, some Cuban music was not. The popular group Charanga Habanera had been banned for playing for six months for singing "Hey green mango, now that you're ripe, why haven't you fallen yet?" Everyone knows that for the past thirty-five years the big mango in Cuba has worn green fatigues.

I met Art and David for breakfast at the hotel restaurant and told them about my night. Our sojourn was beginning in proper surrealist order. The breakfast buffet was surprisingly good: papaya, grapefruit juice, eggs, fresh rolls, sausage, and—one mango. This was no communist repast. The mango was ripe.

KIMI EISELE

(1 9 7 1 -)

Kimi Eisele has written about Cuba and other Latin American countries for the Pacific News Service, *Orion,* and *Fourth Genre,* among others. While earning a master's degree in geography at the University of Arizona, she founded *you are here: the journal of creative geography.* Currently she works as the managing editor and lead writing mentor for *110 Degrees,* a magazine produced by teenagers in Tucson, Arizona.

Eisele's experience in Cuba echoes that of many young people, backpacking illegally to a place not yet on the radar of chain stores and fast-food restaurants. There, she is not only confronted with the reality of Cuban's lives, but must face her own identity as a North American in a place that considers the U.S. government its enemy while welcoming its citizens with open arms. Eisele also develops a crush on the long-dead Che Guevara, arguably the world's most handsome revolutionary, whose image is not just ubiquitous in Cuba everywhere you look, but appears on T-shirts and coffee mugs worldwide. Eisele's fascination with Che is heightened by the fact that she arrives in Cuba just as his bones, having been recovered in Bolivia three decades after his death, are being returned to a hero's welcome in Cuba.

THE FLESH, THE BONES, AND THE BEATING HEART

The remains of Che Guevara landed in Cuba on a sweaty day in July, thirty years after his death. They were carried from the plane in a small boxy coffin. The pallbearers walked down a long band of red carpet past a line of stiff military salutes. Fidel declared it a day of national mourning.

I arrived that same day, wearing flimsy pants and a tank top, a small backpack slung across my shoulder. The Havana airport was crowded and sticky, and I stood in a long line under yellow lights before handing my passport to the customs official. I heard three distinct thumps and feared he was stamping my actual passport, not the special visa *volante* I had folded inside of it. It is still against U.S. law for its citizens to visit Cuba without special permission. A stamped passport would have, in essence, incriminated me in my own country, but I was spared. The official smiled and ushered me through the gate. My own red carpet of sorts. Though still affiliated with the *yanqui* enemy, I, a mere tourist with green in her pockets, was now fully welcome on the island.

Within days of my arrival, the fragments of Che's skeleton were finally laid to rest in the town of Santa Clara. But his image I saw everywhere—in cigar factories, in living rooms, in shop windows, along the highway, leaning large against the side of a building in Havana's Plaza de la Revolución. They nearly swept me off of my feet.

I'm not usually one to gawk at attractive men held up as idols, pinups, luminaries. My jaw doesn't drop often, and I don't willingly enter illusions, particularly when I'm certain that the thicker the gloss, the more truth and imperfection fade. But I couldn't help it. I gaped at the sight of the broad eyebrows, heart-shaped face, thick lips. I dizzied at the thought of being caught up in the arms of that romantic, rebellious man.

Che first went to Cuba in the mid-1950s after meeting Fidel in Mexico City. He joined the revolutionary force that invaded the country in 1956 and eventually overthrew President Fulgencio Batista. After that, he cut cane, pushed wheelbarrows, opined on national policy, and served as head of the country's Ministry of Industry.

I went to Cuba in the late 1990s after meeting Pepe, my colleague at a school in Quito, Ecuador, where I taught geography and English to middle-school children for two years. Pepe spent

the better part of a year teaching my effervescent eighth graders
how to play baseball. He traveled home to Cuba for the summer
to be with his wife and twelve-year-old son. He was hoping to
convince them to join him in Ecuador, where he was paid well for
what he did—coaching baseball, giving massages, playing bongos,
and teaching salsa lessons.

I joined Pepe for a two-week visit to the island. My timing was
impeccable—that day in July, a Messiah returned.

"This is an important day for Cuba," said Pepe's sister-in-law,
Evania, on the evening of my arrival. We were sitting on a pink
sofa in her living room in a crumbling building of Havana Vieja
watching television replays of the solemn parade for Che's remains.
Cuba, she intimated, had been waiting thirty years for Che's body.

After nine years in Cuba, Che left the island to carry the revolution to the Congo, and then to Bolivia, and then, he hoped, to all
of Latin America. At dawn, on October 9, 1967, long before his
work was done, he was assassinated in Bolivia. His remains had
been discovered and excavated there, decades after the fact, by a
team of archaeologists and historians.

That first night, I explained to Evania how growing up watching the fleets of flimsy rafts reach the Florida coast during the
Cold War taught me to think of Cuba as an ugly, repressive, backward place. She laughed. "Some here think the same about your
government," she said. "But we don't hold it against you."

I tried to distinguish myself from other Americans by telling
her about my life in Ecuador. I told her how living in Latin America had overturned my notions of wealth and control, power and
trade. How in the face of so many contradictions, I had been left,
at times, cowering with embarrassment at my patrimony. While in
Ecuador, I began to rethink the word "Cuba" in a place where
T-shirts with Che's face were all over the marketplace, where the
Cuban revolution was both the capital letter at the start and the
exclamation point at the end of conversations about everything
from contemporary literature to the devaluation of local currency

to the arrival of a new McDonald's in Ecuador's capital city. These conversations were what made me want to see Cuba, to understand another system, to go where the grip of my own country, years ago, had been severed.

I arrived in Cuba ready to flirt with what for so long had been deemed illicit. That first night, giddy with excitement, I observed Evania as she watched the television. She seemed relaxed and content, as if she had just found something missing for a long time. I sat, sticking to the sofa, a visitor—novel and living and whole. On the screen, Che—heroic and fragmented and dead—was carried off the plane. As the scenes played over and over again, I felt the seconds, minutes, hours, years, decades unravel.

Most afternoons, I wandered through Havana with two American companions marveling at the colorful bulk of 1950s American automobiles, the sorry decay of colonial buildings, the zigzag of rusty bicycles, the absence of Coca-Cola, and the presence of people *everywhere* in the street—sitting, squatting, standing, playing, cleaning, conversing, watching. We bought watery ice cream for three cents, and watched long-legged *mulatas* in Lycra pants and backless halter tops make conversation with their hands.

We stopped in front of the ubiquitous photos and paintings of Che behind glass windows. People saw him every time they looked up from their cigars, every time they turned the corner, every time they sat on their sofa. Such a reiterated face, I thought, could either fatigue or comfort or thrill.

In front of every image, we stared and commented on his handsome, rugged face. We felt like schoolgirls, gazing and giggling. Inside one shop, we sifted through a stack of old photos of Che. One of us lifted up one of him with a broken arm in a cast and cried out in sympathy. "Sweetie," said the other, "he's *dead*." "I *know*," she whined. Laughing at the extent of our infatuation, we considered the tales of Che the womanizer, thought about the maids and sister revolutionaries and *guajiras* he surely seduced. Men with a mission easily tempt women who want one of their own. My travel mates and I knew how easy it was to be wooed by Latin men, as we had each in our turn fallen for one. Che represented another charismatic romantic. Besides, it was easy to forgive departed heroes, safe to ogle at the dead.

Before he became "Che," Ernesto Guevara from Argentina was like a lot of people I know. He didn't know exactly what he wanted except to see life and be tough. Then he traveled around Latin America on a motorcycle and saw life and got tough. He grew a wiry beard. He smoked. He was equally shaken by the magnificence of the Inca's ancient cities and by the misery of the continent's hungry and ill. He suffered from chronic asthma and decided to learn medicine to help the lepers. He was the kind of man I admired. While fawning over his image, my obsession oscillated between wishing to be *liked* by him and wishing to *be* like him.

In the absence of possibility, I began to look for connections, conjunctions that might let me share, at the very least, something with him. *I* had clung haphazardly to someone's waist on the back of a motorcycle and flown through tiny villages of at least one Latin American country on the equator; *I* had been shaken by what some claim to be the lost city of Incan goddesses; *I* had wandered, depressed and overwhelmed, through shantytowns in cities south of the border. *I* suffer from asthma.

In my stretch of shared sentences, though, I left out the larger context, one that certainly did not fit in the same paragraph. The point of origin. The nation where I come from is, by most standards, the world's most powerful. This is either a great fortune or a major handicap, depending on whom you ask. In Cuba, the United States is either the root of all evil or the Promised Land. For me, it was a piece of heavy luggage. I wavered between wanting to clutch it tightly or to throw it down and run.

* * *

In Varadero, where we went to see the beautiful beaches, I imagined the days of the American mafia, and white women with large sunglasses in high heels and bikinis, and U.S. diplomats with cigars and white pants and pointy shoes and ice clinking in their glasses. Almost fifty years later, only government-owned hotels lined the coast. They were not yet gigantic and tasteless high-rises like those along other Caribbean beaches, but it was still hard to find an open stretch of sand. When we did, we spent hours up to our waists, fifty meters out, in clear blue water. We were modest travelers by most standards, but we had dollar bills. We drank rum and cola all day, listened to live salsa music, and felt like we could be anywhere but Cuba.

Eventually we befriended the members of the salsa band and spent the rest of the afternoon and evening with them, despite the hotel's warnings to its employees to not mingle with guests. The bass player told me the band members each made the equivalent of fifty cents a gig. He cursed the hotel. Then he talked about being poor and about how work in tourism was the only way to make anything of a living. "If Che were here," he said, the return of the bones likely on his mind, "we wouldn't be living like this."

The only heroes in America, I told them, were movie stars and dead rock stars. "What about John F. Kennedy?" the bass player asked. Yes, well, John F. Kennedy, too. But nobody wears him on a T-shirt. And no one is really waiting for him to come back. Why not? Probably because people watched his death over and over on television.

If it hadn't been clear before, by the end of that afternoon it was apparent to me that the work ethic Che had preached was no longer something people in Cuba could hold on to. The bass player quietly mourned its absence, indicating the growing distinction between high government officials and the masses. He cursed the system, but like almost everyone I would meet in Cuba, had figured ways around it—if you can hustle dollar bills you can buy what you need.

I would see the kind of desperation he spoke about all over the island. It would stretch out from the *bodegas,* where people lined up to get their rations of staple food items—eggs, bread, rice, beans. It would punctuate the incessant invitations from hustlers in Havana, in Varadero, in Trinidad, to stay at this guesthouse, eat in this *paladar,* or private dining room. Many blamed the U.S. embargo of trade with Cuba for this desperation. People used to buy, on special days, the latest style of shoes. Now women slept with foreign men to buy clothes; others longed for soap, shampoo, cooking oil, T-shirts.

We sat with the musicians for a long time, with that famous and luscious stripe of white beach behind us. After a while, the sun went away and the wind stirred up. Suddenly everything on the ground was brighter than the whole sky. We turned around to watch the storm move in. The dark gray reach of clouds clashed with the turquoise expanse of sea. If I squinted hard enough, I thought, I might see the coast of Florida off in the distance.

In the town of Trinidad, the sun lit up the colored colonial walls late in the afternoon and a boy wearing shorts and no T-shirt started trailing us. We thought he was another hustler, but he introduced himself as "a friend to all foreign visitors." He was eleven years old and his name was Ernesto Camilo, from Ernesto Guevara and Camilo Cienfuegos, two of Fidel's right-hand men. Camilo chewed a wad of pink gum he told us he bought with his own money. He had a toothy smile, round brown eyes, and a crew cut. He asked us lots of questions and took turns holding each of our hands. He toted around my handheld tape recorder and had no reservations about stopping people on the street to interview them. Just before sunset, we bought him a big bowl of ice cream.

Camilo invited us home to meet his mother. She sat in a rocking chair and told us she wanted to buy a television for her son. "He loves to read, but he should learn English," she said. Camilo blurted out "cool" and "beautiful" to his mother, boasting the words he learned from us. He pulled out a small blue flannel bag and from it unloaded a thick bundle of envelopes. They were letters from France, Italy, Venezuela, all from tourists like us he had met in town. Camilo got excited as he splayed out the letters before us. Someday, he said, maybe he'd get to go visit some of those places.

For Camilo, the world beyond Cuba spanned out wide and round. It came back to him only in the handwriting of strangers. The name of the only town he'd ever known, Trinidad, means the Trinity in English, a holy order of three. Yesterday, today, and tomorrow. To him, yesterday was probably incomprehensible. Though he shared Che's name, I doubted that this young Ernesto fully understood how the *comandante*'s first landing in Cuba had altered the course of history. Nor was it likely that he understood the full implications of Che's return, in pieces, just days earlier. This Ernesto was more interested in the arrival of people like me, foreign tourists with stories of other lands and lots of shiny coins. Today was for chewing gum, ice cream, and whatever else he could hustle without really becoming a hustler. Tomorrow would be everything. If his world were to open up, he would leap into it fully.

If she could have, the seventy-one-year-old woman who lived across the hall from Evania would have leapt fully into the past, or maybe the imperfect preterit. Dolores worked as a custodian in a dark, and nearly empty, department store where I met with her one afternoon a few days before I left Cuba.

In 1959, Dolores told me, her house served as one of the rebel headquarters. She worked with Che in the cane fields and she loved him. And she loved Fidel. "My love for both of them was pure and clean and so untainted," she said. "If I had to do everything I did over again, I would do it with the same spirit."

Dolores lit up a cigar and puffed gusts of smoke into the dim room. The smell of the tobacco was heady and thick. "I retired from that part of the revolution," she said wistfully. "But not from another. I still carry guns in my hands."

I fast-forwarded her to the future.

"We'll have problems because of the empire that suffocates us," she said. "We are a very little country. It's like a lion with a cat. The cat has to be smart, because the lion is very big and powerful."

Everything Dolores said made me believe she was still a believer. Sitting there, I tried to imagine her young and agile, with muscles in her arms and hands that could easily grip whatever they reached for. But Dolores was no longer a robust young woman. How long before she would tire, I wondered, before something, something as big as a lion, knocked the guns from her hands?

Dolores was kind to me, almost grandmotherly. As we said good-bye, she advised me to take hold of the future and to fight for what I believed in. I was stirred by her words, but secretly I wondered why I did not offend more. How did the reality of me and scores like me, American tourists in Cuba, fit into her ideal? Why didn't she see my presence as a frightening compromise?

The night before I left Cuba, my friend Pepe and his family treated us to a night at the opera, where tickets cost less than twenty-five cents for Cubans. Havana's Grand Theatre was ornate the way a theater should be: old but still luminous, with bulky gold molding, heavy wooden beams, fluted columns, and blood-colored curtains.

The show was *Madame Butterfly*. I was moved by the weight of the maiden's sorrow, the shrill magnificence of her voice. At the intermission, Evania pointed out the rococo design of the theater. I was amazed that it was virtually free to sit in there and watch the national opera company perform. Why? Because the arts thrive in front of an audience, Evania told me, and should therefore be accessible to everyone.

But among the things that were changing in Cuba, said Pepe's wife, Alina, was arts appreciation. "People are too busy making money now. But they can't earn anything here. They want dollars, so they drive taxis. They don't read as much anymore."

Pepe chimed in, "If it weren't for the economic situation, I would be here in Cuba."

Alina said she didn't want to join her husband in Ecuador. She was happy on the island, she said, and she wanted Pepe to come home for good.

Evania sympathized with her sister. Her husband left Cuba for Spain several years ago. Their marriage, she assumed, was over. She hadn't wanted to leave. "I feel like a person here, a human being," she said. "As long as I can laugh, dance, fall in love, sit in the park, go to the movies," she told me, "I'll stay here."

I did not see in Evania the kind of desperation I saw in Madame Butterfly. She did not walk the *malecón* at night watching for the hulk of her lover's ship to curve over the horizon. "Yes, there are difficulties here," she told me, "but there's a little light."

On our last stroll through the streets of Havana, my American companions and I posed again to take photos next to Che. We puckered our lips up to the image and giggled. There were moments of rationality, of course, when I recognized the impossibility of my desire, ridiculous in its dependence on a mere two-dimensional facade, a cheap image plastered across T-shirts and billboards. Still, when I stared at Che's image, I was lured by the possibilities. Not by the possibility of being *with* Che (I knew this was a forever unrequited love), but by the possibility that good things could and would still happen. That equality wasn't some kind of tarnished dream, that the privilege of knowing places in the world beyond one's own was in itself a kind of emancipation, that someday my country might recognize that there were more important evils to battle than those that supposedly lingered among the dark halls of Communism.

Isn't this what falling in love is meant to do? Inspire within us arousal, prospect, hope? Perhaps it was Che's image—painted and pasted on the sides of buildings, in cigar factories, in living rooms—that for so many years remained as the reminder of a promise for Cuba. Perhaps that reminder was Evania's little light.

But what did it mean, then, for me to be there with a camera dangling around my neck gazing at it? Standing in front of that handsome image, I felt the glossy past buck under the reality of the coming future, one likely to shine down on the island and its people erratically and unevenly.

The Cuba that Che returned to that clammy day in July was, of course, an entirely different Cuba from the one he had first discovered and helped to transform forty years earlier. Things had slipped. The decades of Soviet support, that cargo of goods and legitimacy, had certainly commanded compromises, but compared to now, compared to the mysterious future, even they seemed preferable. America and its inextricable notions of democracy and capitalism had skulked back into the ring, a strong and powerful lion. The U.S. embargo labored on. The people of Cuba were hungry.

And all those new dollar bills moving around the island seemed crisp, desirable, necessary. And so it seemed quite possible that together with the twenty-one-gun salute, the scarlet carpet, the national day of mourning for Che, Cuba was also celebrating *me*—an American visitor with a special floppy visa, and the swarms of others just like me.

Since the day Che left the island, his image had communicated what it was supposed to. It was flat enough to smother his flaws (among them, severe hatred for his enemies and a reported facility for bumping off "traitors" in his own ranks) and stout enough to drum up the past and inspire invincibility. But it is one thing to gawk at posters and paintings and imagine the ideal, invisible but immortal, springing back to life. It is entirely something else to contend with the inanimate reality of a corpse.

There is, in the archives of the history of the Americas, another notable image of Che. This one is a photograph of his bones— fleshless, brittle, brown, and old—arranged neatly into a skeleton. They are bare bones, ugly bones, anyone's bones. More important, they are *real* bones. Their existence, much like the repeated footage of John F. Kennedy's slow-moving convertible passing the grassy knoll, erase the possibility that the man might someday return, bearded and bereted, virile and fervent, to life and to Cuba.

How and in whom, then, is the future to be imagined? Who can arrive to deliver Cuba from temptation?

In the now, people wait for smaller things—for letters ornamented with colorful stamps, for tips, for houseguests, and for foreign men with plentiful lust and deep pockets. Or big things: "All the Cubans want to go to the United States," one woman told me. "It's the golden dream." As the streams of tourists, now Americans, begin to flow into the airports, ferry south across the thin band of ocean from Florida, who can really afford to idealize the past, fantasize the future? Who doesn't long to get their hands on the dollar bills?

At the end of Puccini's opera, Lieutenant Pinkerton, the American for whom Madame Butterfly has waited three years, returns to the Japanese harbor, his new American wife in tow. Betrayed and overcome with grief, Butterfly stabs herself with a thick shiny dagger and the curtains close.

There are, I hope, endings less tragic.

After the opera, once outside the theater, we heard a thunderous rumble, the pop and wallop of drums. We followed the sound up a wide marble staircase and into an auditorium on the second floor of the opera house, where a dozen or more dancers dressed in brightly colored costumes formed a convulsing semicircle on-stage. The drums were full and emphatic, and the sounds bounced around the entire room. One of the dancers wore red and black and a strange scary mask.

"Changó," Pepe leaned in to tell me, naming one of the Yoruban orishas, deities worshipped first by African slaves on the island and now, in some form or another, by most everyone. "The god of drums, thunder, masculinity."

As the boom of the drums got louder, the dancer thrust his arms forward and back and jumped high off the ground. The movement was astounding, charged, full. The sound crescendoed, the moment expanded into something gigantic and powerful. Changó leapt into it perfectly and brilliantly.

Then the folkloric dancers in the upstairs auditorium of the Grand Theatre of Havana invited members of the audience to the stage. I heeded the call. I wound myself around and around and lost myself in the thunder of drums.

Later, outside on the street, the night air still warm and viscous, I reeled from the pulse and ardor of Cuba. I walked through the thick of it, letting myself imagine a scene in which the coming of the future, unimaginable and cryptic, fails to fully disintegrate what has already passed. Letting myself imagine a scene in which even I get to kiss that heroic, sturdy, unshaven face.

Expatriates, Real and Imagined

"People ask you why you live in Cuba and you say it is because you like it. It is too complicated to explain. . . ."

—*Ernest Hemingway*

ELMORE LEONARD

(1 9 2 5 –   )

Elmore Leonard, a prolific writer of westerns, crime noir novels, and short stories, is noted for his ear for dialogue and lean prose, and many of his works
have been popularized by film adaptations, including *Get Shorty, Jackie
Brown,* and *Out of Sight.* Leonard has named Hemingway as his biggest
influence (he once said, "I saw *For Whom the Bell Tolls* as a western, studied
closely how he wrote action sequences as well as dialogue"), and like Hemingway, Leonard has been drawn to Cuba as a subject. In his 1998 novel,
Cuba Libre, he brings his trademark mix of gritty realism, cowboy heroes, and
fearless women to bear on the Cuban revolution and the explosion of the
battleship *Maine* in 1898. Leonard mines this historical event for a swashbuckling adventure where cattle rustlers take on sugar plantation owners and
join guerrilla fighters in the battle for Cuba's independence from Spain. In the
following excerpt, a young American woman, Amelia, has met a wealthy
sugar baron named Boudreaux in New Orleans, and has traveled to Cuba to
live with him. There, she befriends Boudreaux's employee Victor Fuentes,
who lures her into helping the cause of independence.

Ironically, while Leonard has brought Cuban history to American readers,
his work has also had an enduring impact on Cuba's image of the United
States. The 1957 Glenn Ford film based on Elmore Leonard's story *3:10 to
Yuma* proved to be very popular in Cuba, and the word *Yuma,* with its evocation of the American Wild West, has become a slang term in Cuba for the
United States and people from there.

from CUBA LIBRE

They came through rolling hills aboard the sugar train to Matanzas, Boudreaux telling Amelia there were more sugar estates here than in any province in Cuba. "How many, Victor? Four hundred and seventy-eight, if I'm not mistaken?"

"Not anymore," Fuentes said. "Maybe three hundred something. Many of them in the past year burn down, or the owner has enough—wake up in the morning and see black smoke in the sky, over his fields."

"I ask you a question," Boudreaux said, "I like a simple answer, whatever is the fact, not your opinion."

"You want to know exactly how many burn down?"

"That's enough, Victor."

The train was creeping through the outskirts of the city, pale stone and steeples and red tile roofs, and now Boudreaux was pointing out to Amelia the villas of the wealthy, the old cathedral, the domed railway station, the ornate bridge that linked the city to the fortress of San Severino on the bay. "The second largest city in Cuba," Boudreaux said, "and some say the most beautiful."

"It's true," Fuentes said, "even though the word *matanzas* means slaughtering place."

"That's enough," Boudreaux said. He turned, shaking his head, to give Amelia a weary look.

"For the slaughter of livestock," Fuentes said, "cows to make *biftec* for here and for Havana. I don't mean the slaughter of Indians who lived here—"

"Victor?"

"Or the twenty-three thousand last year, the *reconcentrados* who were made to starve to death, kept in filthy sheds along the Punta Gorda."

"I said that's enough," Boudreaux said. "Are you becoming

restless, Victor, you want to move on?" He said to Amelia, "Victor, at one time, was a reader in a cigar factory. Which one was it, Victor?"

"La Corona."

"Victor read to the employees while they rolled cigars. He'd read every word of the newspaper including the advertisements while they sat there rolling away. He even read a book once. Wasn't it Martí, Victor, the poet who's become you-all's hero?"

"They wouldn't let me read Martí."

"I can understand why. But Victor did read a book by Martí. *A book.* Beware, Amelia, of anyone who's read a book and, hence, believes he knows everything."

Amelia watched Fuentes, the way he stood stoop-shouldered, swaying on his feet, as he gazed out the window of this private parlor car, the man not appearing bothered by Boudreaux's remarks. Fuentes even seemed to smile as he shrugged and said to Amelia, "Maybe you like to read Martí sometime. He say a country with only a few rich men is not rich."

"You see," Boudreaux said to her, sounding weary of it, "what I have to put up with?"

He told Amelia they were coming to a village called Varadero and showed her on a map how his rail line went past Matanzas, circled the east side of the harbor and ran along the shore to a peninsula, a finger of land pointing into the Gulf, the Bay of Matanzas on one side, the Bay of Cárdenas on the other. Varadero was situated at the neck of the peninsula, where Boudreaux's rail line ended and he kept a stable of horses and a squad of his private army he called Boudreaux's Guerrillas—a name, he told Amelia, he'd thought of himself, Boudreaux's Guerrillas—to patrol the finger of land and protect his summer house, about six miles from Varadero. Several homes along the beach, he said, had been destroyed by insurgents. And for no reason, perfectly good summer homes burned to the ground.

At Varadero the horses were brought to them as they stepped from the train into afternoon sunlight. Amelia found Victor staying close to her while Boudreaux rode off at the head of his guerrilla column with Novis Crowe—the bodyguard holding on to the saddle horn with both hands—and the officer in charge of the squad. "A young man by the name of Rafi Vasquez," Fuentes told Amelia, "a wealthy *peninsulare* from Havana."

He said, "*Peninsulares* are the Spaniards living here. All the rest of us, no matter our color, are Cuban. We go to war with the Spanish government and thousands of *peninsulares* take up arms against us, calling themselves Volunteers. And I can tell you, the Volunteers are as barbaric as the Guardia, or even worse. Thirty years ago in Havana—January 22, 1869, I know, because I was there—they surround a theatre, the Villanueva, and while the audience is watching the play, the Volunteers fire into them, killing dozens of men, women and children. Only weeks later, Easter Sunday, the assassins perform the same criminal act at the Café del Louvre, again killing unarm people. You want to hear about the Volunteers, I can tell you. There was a captain-general name Valmaseda who turned their foul passions loose on the countryside, allowing them to kill whoever they want, without fear of punishment. The Butcher Weyler, during this Ten Years' War, was a student of the Butcher Valmaseda. Weyler went home last fall and the new captain-general, Blanco, the loyalists consider a joke. What else do you want to know? Listen, in a military trial thirty-eight students, young boys, were accused of defacing a Spaniard's grave; they wrote something on the stone. Eight were executed and the rest sent to prison for life. You know what the Volunteers say? 'Suffer the little children to come unto me that I may strangle their precious young lives.' What else? I keep in my head a list of indiscriminate mass murders, rapes, molestations of all kinds and obscene mutilations.

"These men," Fuentes said, indicating Boudreaux's column, his private army, "are known as guerrillas, but they come from the Volunteers. Just as Tavalera the Guardia is a peasant by birth, the son of a prison guard, Rafi Vasquez the Volunteer is a gentleman, the son of wealth. And both are criminal assassins.

"Now then, on the side of liberty," Fuentes said, "the revolutionists are insurgents or *insurrectos,* or you heard them called *mambís* or *mambises.*"

"Rollie," Amelia said, "calls them that sometimes."

"Yes, because he believes he knows everything. He says it's an African word brought here from the Congo by slaves and is from the word *mambíli.* I tell him, well, I was a slave at one time and use the word, but it didn't come from Africa."

"Really? You were a slave?"

"Until I was sixteen and became a *cimarrón,* what you call a runaway. Before that, part of me was Masungo, related by blood to the Bantu. Now I'm Cuban. I tell Mr. Boudreaux the word *mambí* came from Santo Domingo. Fifty years ago the people there fighting for their independence had a leader called Eutimio Mambí. So the Spanish soldiers called them the men of Mambí. Then when they came here the Spanish began to call Cuban revolutionists *mambís* and *mambises.* I tell Mr. Boudreaux some of this history; he doesn't listen. I ask him has he read the words of José Martí, patriot and martyr, first president of the Cuban Revolutionary Party? No, of course not. I leave the essays of Martí in English where Mr. Boudreaux can find them, learn something about human rights. He throws them in the fire. What is right to him is the way things are."

"I believe it," Amelia said.

"Mr. Boudreaux looks at me. . . . What do I know of anything?"

They kept to high ground along the finger of land, following a road cut through dense thickets, a road that looked down on mangrove and lagoons, a stretch of white sand, a chimney rising out of brick and stone rubble. Fuentes pointed.

"You think they burn it down for no reason? Your Mr. Boudreaux, his head up there in a cloud, he think so."

"When did he become my Mr. Boudreaux?"

"Anytime you want him, he's yours."

"Why would I, because he's rich?"

"That's a good reason."

"Give me a better one."

"You meet famous people with him."

"On a sugar estate?"

"Sure, or here. You know who came to this house where we going? General Weyler himself, the man who made the twenty-three thousand people he sent to Matanzas starve to death. The Butcher came here to visit on someone's yacht. He meets you, he want to come back. Sure, you meet generals and admirals and envoys from Spain, the most important people. Also you hear Mr. Boudreaux talk to his friends, all those rich men who want to invest money with him. You see what they're doing, what the Spanish are doing. . . ."

She could hear the horses ahead of them and the clink of metal. She said, "You're asking me to spy for the *mambís*."

Fuentes turned his head to look at her. "You like that name?"

"Aren't you?"

"I see you not very busy, so I wonder, what is the point of you?"

A good question.

"I haven't yet decided." And then right away she said, "You stay close to Rollie. You hear him talking to people, don't you?"

"I don't get as close as you."

"But you talk about the crimes of the Spanish—you annoy him with it. Isn't he suspicious?"

"Perhaps in a way he is, yes, but it doesn't worry him. He believe he smarter than I am. He believe he smarter than everybody, and I think is important he continue to believe it."

Fuentes looked off at the Gulf and said, "Do you see that ship, what's left of it? A wreck now, but it was once a coastal vessel from Nueva Gerona, on the Isle of Pines, a ship with two masts and two sails, big ones. They carry yucca and tobacco from the Isle of Pines to Havana and sometime to Matanzas and Cárdenas, so they know the coast and places to hide. Oh, they smuggle goods too. But on this day two years ago they came from Key West, the ship full of rifles and cases of bullets and they get caught in the open by a gunboat that chase the ship and it run aground and break up on that sandbar. You can't see it, but is there. Two years ago to this day, March the seventeenth, 1895. There was seven of them aboard. And now come a company of Volunteers to wait for them on the sand. The men of the ship have no choice but to wade ashore and surrender. When they do this, half the Volunteers continue to aim their Mausers at them, while the others draw machetes and hack the unarmed men to death. Rafi Vasquez was the officer, the one who order it to happen. Your Mr. Boudreaux was also here, to watch."

"And you were here," Amelia said.

"Yes, I was here. And you see two men shot in the head. You see how easy it is for the Guardia to do it. I watched you. You don't close your eyes or turn your head to look away. You don't say oh, how can they do that. You accept what you see with your own eyes and you think about it. A crime is committed, the execution without giving it a thought of two innocent men. You don't say oh, no, is none of your business. You see they don't care, they can kill anybody they want, and you begin to wonder is there something you can do about it."

For several minutes they rode in silence, until Fuentes said, "How do you think about that?"

"Last year," Amelia said, "or was it the year before, it doesn't matter, I took work to help the sisters in a home for lepers."

As she spoke, Fuentes turned in his saddle, stirred. He said,

"There is a leper home in Las Villas, San Lázaro," and gestured, "that way, in Santa Clara, the next province east of here. I was there once to visit a woman I know and I see the devotion of the people working there, the most dedicated people in the world to do that. And you are one of those people?"

"I didn't do much," Amelia said. "I wrote letters for them, I played checkers, I gave them their medicine, two hundred drops of chaulmoogra oil a day. For fever we gave them Fowler's solution. Powdered mangrove bark was given for something, I don't remember what."

"For nausea," Fuentes said, "sure, mangrove. Look at it down there, in the swamp. So, you know how to prepare it as medicine."

"I lasted five days," Amelia said, "less than a week among the lepers and I ran out of dedication. What it means is, I can believe in something, I can want to throw myself into a cause and see myself tireless in my devotion—look at her, a saint—but it turns out I don't have enough of a sense of . . . I don't know."

Fuentes said, "Duty?"

"Yes, I suppose, duty or a sense of purpose. Five days and I gave up."

"No, I think the reason you left there," Fuentes said, "is because if you stay at the leper home then you don't come here. You understand? Then this would not become what you want to do most. But it must be what you want to do because you came here, didn't you?"

"Is it that simple?"

"What, to know what you want to do? Go by what you feel and don't think so much."

"It takes energy," Amelia said, "and a strong will."

"Yes, of course."

"And hatred."

"Hating can help, but it isn't necessary."

"You asked me, 'What is the point of you?' " Amelia said, and smiled a little hearing herself. "Tell me what's the point of you,

Victor. Are you an anarchist, a communist of some kind, a collectivist?"

His face brightened as he said, "More of you comes out. You prepare yourself for this."

"At the knees of my maid," Amelia said. "Are you one of those, an anarchist?"

"It's enough at this time," Fuentes said, "to be Cuban."

STEPHEN CRANE
(1 8 7 1 – 1 9 0 0)

During the Cuban Revolution against Spain, most journalists from the United States reported from hotel bars in Havana and never entered the fields nor witnessed any of the sights they wrote about in their accounts for the papers back home. Stephen Crane was an exception to this, and traveled the battle-fields alongside U.S. and Cuban troops. Willa Cather pointed out that Crane's Cuban stories were unmarred by "the much tainted war correspondent journalism of the time." Crane is often credited with introducing realism to American literature, and it was largely on the basis of his remarkable depiction of warfare in his Civil War novel, *The Red Badge of Courage,* that he was sent to cover the conflict in Cuba as a foreign correspondent. His short stories about Cuba fictionalize many of his journalistic experiences and show the historical clash of nation with nation in human terms.

THE CLAN OF NO-NAME

> *Unwind my riddle.*
> *Cruel as hawks the hours fly,*
> *Wounded men seldom come home to die,*
> *The hard waves see an arm flung high,*
> *Scorn hits strong because of a lie,*
> *Yet there exists a mystic tie.*
> *Unwind my riddle.*

I

She was out in the garden. Her mother came to her rapidly. "Margharita! Margharita, Mr. Smith is here! Come!" Her mother was fat and commercially excited. Mr. Smith was a matter of some importance to all Tampa people, and since he was really in love with Margharita he was distinctly of more importance to this particular household.

Palm trees tossed their sprays over the fence toward the rutted sand of the street. A little foolish fish-pond in the centre of the garden emitted a sound of red-fins flipping, flipping. "No, mamma," said the girl, "let Mr. Smith wait. I like the garden in the moonlight."

Her mother threw herself into that state of virtuous astonishment which is the weapon of her kind. "Margharita!"

The girl evidently considered herself to be a privileged belle, for she answered quite carelessly: "Oh, let him wait."

The mother threw abroad her arms with a semblance of great high-minded suffering and withdrew. Margharita walked alone in the moonlit garden. Also an electric light threw its shivering gleam over part of her parade.

There was peace for a time. Then suddenly through the faint brown palings was stuck an envelope, white and square. Margharita approached this envelope with an indifferent stride. She hummed a silly air, she bore herself casually, but there was something that made her grasp it hard, a peculiar muscular exhibition, not discernible to indifferent eyes. She did not clutch it, but she took it— simply took it in a way that meant everything, and to measure it by vision it was a picture of the most complete disregard.

She stood straight for a moment. Then she drew from her bosom a photograph and thrust it through the palings. She walked rapidly into the house.

II

A man in garb of blue and white—something relating to what we call bed-ticking—was seated in a curious little cupola on the top of a Spanish blockhouse. The blockhouse sided a white military road that curved away from the man's sight into a blur of trees. On all sides of him were fields of tall grass studded with palms and lined with fences of barbed wire. The sun beat aslant through the trees and the man sped his eyes deep into the dark tropical shadows that seemed velvet with coolness. These tranquil vistas resembled painted scenery in a theatre, and, moreover, a hot, heavy silence lay upon the land.

The soldier in the watching place leaned an unclean Mauser rifle in a corner and, reaching down, took a glowing coal on a bit of palm bark handed up to him by a comrade. The men below were mainly asleep. The sergeant in command drowsed near the open door, the arm above his head showing his long keen-angled chevrons attached carelessly with safety-pins. The sentry lit his cigarette and puffed languorously.

Suddenly he heard from the air around him the querulous, deadly-swift spit of rifle bullets and an instant later the poppety-pop of a small volley sounded in his face close, as if it were fired only ten feet away. Involuntarily he threw back his head quickly as if he were protecting his nose from a falling tile. He screamed an alarm and fell into the blockhouse. In the gloom of it men with their breaths coming sharply between their teeth were tumbling wildly for positions at the loop-holes. The door had been slammed, but the sergeant lay just within, propped up as when he drowsed, but now with blood flowing steadily over the hand that he pressed flatly to his chest. His face was in stark yellow agony. He chokingly repeated: "Fuego! Por Dios, hombres!"

The men's ill-conditioned weapons were jammed through the loop-holes and they began to fire from all four sides of the block-house from the simple data apparently that the enemy were in the vicinity. The fumes of burnt powder grew stronger and stronger in the little square fortress. The rattling of the magazine locks was incessant, and the interior might have been that of a gloomy man-ufactory if it were not for the sergeant down under the feet of the men, coughing out: "Por Dios, hombres! Por Dios! Fuego!"

III

A string of five Cubans in linen that had turned earthy brown in color slid through the woods at a pace that was neither a walk nor a run. It was a kind of a rack. In fact the whole manner of the men as they thus moved bore a rather comic resemblance to the American pacing horse. But they had come many miles since sun-up over mountainous and half-marked paths, and were plainly still fresh. The men were all practicos—guides. They made no sound in their swift travel, but moved their half-shod feet with the skill of cats. The woods lay around them in a deep silence such as one might find at the bottom of a lake.

Suddenly the leading practico raised his hand. The others pulled up short and dropped the butts of their weapons calmly and noiselessly to the ground. The leader whistled a low note, and immediately another practico appeared from the bushes. He moved close to the leader without a word, and then they spoke in whispers.

"There are twenty men and a sergeant in the blockhouse."

"And the road?"

"One company of cavalry passed to the east this morning at seven o'clock. They were escorting four carts. An hour later one horseman rode swiftly to the westward. About noon ten infantry soldiers with a corporal were taken from the big fort and put in the first blockhouse to the east of the fort. There were already twelve men there. We saw a Spanish column moving off toward Mariel."

"No more?"

"No more."

"Good. But the cavalry?"

"It is all right. They were going on a long march."

"The expedition is half a league behind. Go and tell the General."

The scout disappeared. The five other men lifted their guns and resumed their rapid and noiseless progress. A moment later no sound broke the stillness save the thump of a mango as it dropped lazily from its tree to the grass. So strange had been the apparition of these men, their dress had been so allied in color to the soil, their passing had so little disturbed the solemn rumination of the forest, and their going had been so like a spectral dissolution, that a witness could have wondered if he dreamed.

IV

A small expedition had landed with arms from the United States and had now come out of the hills and to the edge of a wood. Before them was a long-grassed rolling prairie marked with palms. A half-mile away was the military road and they could see the top of a blockhouse. The insurgent scouts were moving somewhere off in the grass. The General sat comfortably under a tree, while his staff of three young officers stood about him chatting. Their linen clothing was notable from being distinctly whiter than those of the men who, one hundred and fifty in number, lay on the ground in a long brown fringe, ragged—indeed, bare in many places—but singularly reposeful, unworried, veteran-like.

The General, however, was thoughtful. He pulled continually at his little thin mustache. As far as the heavily patrolled and guarded military road was concerned, the insurgents had been in the habit of dashing across it in small bodies whenever they pleased, but to safely scoot over it with a valuable convoy of arms was decidedly a more important thing. So the General awaited the return of his practicos with anxiety. The still pampas betrayed no sign of their existence.

The General gave some orders and an officer counted off twenty men to go with him and delay any attempt of the troop of cavalry to return from the eastward. It was not an easy task, but it was a familiar task—checking the advance of a greatly superior force by a very hard fire from concealment. A few rifles had often bayed a strong column for sufficient length of time for all strategic purposes. The twenty men pulled themselves together tranquilly. They looked quite indifferent. Indeed, they had the supremely casual manner of old soldiers, hardened to battle as a condition of existence.

Thirty men were then told off whose function it was to worry and rag at the blockhouse and check any advance from the westward. A hundred men carrying precious burdens—besides their own equipment—were to pass in as much of a rush as possible between these two wings, cross the road and skip for the hills, their retreat being covered by a combination of the two firing parties. It was a trick that needed both luck and neat arrangement. Spanish columns were for ever prowling through this province in all directions and at all times. Insurgent bands—the lightest of light infantry—were kept on the jump even when they were not incommoded by fifty boxes, each one large enough for the coffin of a little man and heavier than if the little man were in it, and fifty small but formidable boxes of ammunition.

The carriers stood to their boxes and the firing parties leaned on their rifles. The General arose and strolled to and fro, his hands behind him. Two of his staff were jesting at the third, a young man with a face less bronzed and with very new accoutrements. On the strap of his cartouche were a gold star and a silver star placed in a horizontal line, denoting that he was a second lieutenant. He seemed very happy; he laughed at all their jests although his eye roved continually over the sunny grass-lands where was going to happen his first fight. One of his stars was bright, like his hopes; the other was pale, like death.

Two practicos came racking out of the grass. They spoke rapidly to the General; he turned and nodded to his officers. The two firing parties filed out and diverged toward their positions. The General watched them through his glasses. It was strange to note how soon they were dim to the unaided eye. The little patches of brown in the green grass did not look like men at all.

Practicos continually ambled up to the General. Finally he

turned and made a sign to the bearers. The first twenty men in line picked up their boxes, and this movement rapidly spread to the tail of the line. The weighted procession moved painfully out upon the sunny prairie. The General, marching at the head of it, glanced continually back as if he were compelled to drag behind him some ponderous iron chain. Besides the obvious mental worry, his face bore an expression of intense physical strain, and he even bent his shoulders, unconsciously tugging at the chain to hurry it through this enemy-crowded valley.

V

The fight was opened by eight men who, snuggling in the grass within three hundred yards of the blockhouse, suddenly blazed away at the bed-ticking figure in the cupola and at the open door where they could see vague outlines. Then they laughed and yelled insulting language, for they knew that as far as the Spaniards were concerned the surprise was as much as having a diamond bracelet turn to soap. It was this volley that smote the sergeant and caused the man in the cupola to scream and tumble from his perch.

The eight men, as well as all other insurgents within fair range, had chosen good positions for lying close, and for a time they let the blockhouse rage, although the soldiers therein could occasionally hear above the clamor of their weapons shrill and almost wolfish calls coming from men whose lips were laid against the ground. But it is not in the nature of them of Spanish blood and armed with rifles to long endure the sight of anything so tangible as an enemy's blockhouse without shooting at it—other conditions being partly favorable. Presently the steaming soldiers in the little fort could hear the sping and shiver of bullets striking the wood that guarded their bodies.

A perfectly white smoke floated up over each firing Cuban, the penalty of the Remington rifle, but about the blockhouse there was only the lightest gossamer of blue. The blockhouse stood always for some big, clumsy and rather incompetent animal, while the insurgents, scattered on two sides of it, were little enterprising creatures of another species, too wise to come too near, but joyously ragging at its easiest flanks and dirling the lead into its sides in a way to make it fume and spit and rave like the tomcat when the glad, free-band foxhound pups catch him in the lane.

The men, outlying in the grass, chuckled deliriously at the fury of the Spanish fire. They howled opprobrium to encourage the Spaniards to fire more ill-used, incapable bullets. Whenever an insurgent was about to fire he ordinarily prefixed the affair with a speech. "Do you want something to eat? Yes? All right." Bang! "Eat that." The more common expressions of the incredibly foul Spanish tongue were trifles light as the air in this badinage which was shrieked out from the grass during the spin of bullets and the dull rattle of the shooting.

But at some time there came a series of sounds from the east that began in a few disconnected pruts and ended as if an amateur was trying to play the long roll upon a muffled drum. Those of the insurgents in the blockhouse attacking party who had neighbors in the grass turned and looked at them seriously. They knew what the new sound meant. It meant that the twenty men who had gone to the eastward were now engaged. A column of some kind was approaching from that direction and they knew by the clatter that it was a solemn occasion.

In the first place, they were now on the wrong side of the road. They were obliged to cross it to rejoin the main body, provided, of course, that the main body succeeded itself in crossing it. To accomplish this the party at the blockhouse would have to move to the eastward until out of sight or good range of the maddened little fort. But judging from the heaviness of the firing the party of twenty who protected the east were almost sure to be driven immediately back. Hence travel in that direction would become exceedingly hazardous. Hence a man looked seriously at his neighbor. It might easily be that in a moment they were to become an isolated force and woefully on the wrong side of the road.

Any retreat to the westward was absurd, since primarily they would have to widely circle the blockhouse, and more than that they could hear even now in that direction Spanish bugle calling to Spanish bugle, far and near, until one would think that every man in Cuba was a trumpeter and had come forth to parade his talent.

VI

The insurgent General stood in the middle of the road gnawing his lips. Occasionally he stamped a foot and beat his hands passionately together. The carriers were streaming past him, patient, sweating fellows, bowed under their burdens, but they could not move fast enough for him when others of his men were engaged both to the east and to the west, and he, too, knew from the sound that those to the east were in a sore way. Moreover, he could hear that accursed bugling, bugling, bugling in the west.

He turned suddenly to the new lieutenant who stood behind him, pale and quiet. "Did you ever think a hundred men were so many?" he cried, incensed to the point of beating them. Then he said longingly: "Oh, for a half an hour! Or even twenty minutes!"

A practico racked violently up from the east. It is characteristic of these men that, although they take a certain roadster gait and hold it for ever, they cannot really run, sprint, race. "Captain Rodriguez is attacked by two hundred men, señor, and the cavalry is behind them. He wishes to know—"

The General was furious. He pointed. "Go! Tell Rodriguez to hold his place for twenty minutes, even if he leaves every man dead."

The practico shambled hastily off.

The last of the carriers were swarming across the road. The rifle-drumming in the east was swelling out and out, evidently coming slowly nearer. The General bit his nails. He wheeled suddenly upon the young lieutenant. "Go to Bas at the blockhouse. Tell him to hold the devil himself for ten minutes and then bring his men out of that place."

The long line of bearers was crawling like a dun worm toward the safety of the foot-hills. High bullets sang a faint song over the aide as he saluted. The bugles had in the west ceased, and that was more ominous than bugling. It meant that the Spanish troops were about to march, or perhaps that they had marched.

The young lieutenant ran along the road until he came to the bend which marked the range of sight from the blockhouse. He drew his machete, his stunning new machete, and hacked feverishly at the barbed wire fence which lined the north side of the road at that point. The first wire was obdurate, because it was too high for his stroke, but two more cut like candy, and he stepped over the remaining one, tearing his trousers in passing on the lively serpentine ends of the severed wires. Once out in the field the bullets seemed to know him and call for him and speak their wish to kill him. But he ran on because it was his duty, and because he would be shamed before men if he did not do his duty, and because he was desolate out there all alone in the fields with death.

A man running in this manner from the rear was in immensely greater danger than those who lay snug and closer. But he did not know it. He thought because he was five hundred—four hundred and fifty—four hundred yards away from the enemy and others were only three hundred yards away that they were in far more peril. He ran to join them because of his opinion. He did not care to do it, but he thought that was what men of his kind would do in such a case. There was a standard and he must follow it, obey it, because it was a monarch, the Prince of Conduct.

A bewildered and alarmed face raised itself from the grass and a voice cried to him: "Drop, Manolo! Drop! Drop!" He recognized Bas and flung himself to the earth beside him.

"Why," he said, panting, "what's the matter?"

"Matter?" said Bas. "You are one of the most desperate and careless officers I know. When I saw you coming I wouldn't have given a peseta for your life."

"Oh, no," said the young aide. Then he repeated his orders rapidly. But he was hugely delighted. He knew Bas well. Bas was a pupil of Maceo. Bas invariably led his men. He never was a mere spectator of their battle; he was known for it throughout the western end of the island. The new officer had early achieved a part of his ambition—to be called a brave man by established brave men.

"Well, if we get away from here quickly it will be better for us," said Bas bitterly. "I've lost six men killed and more wounded. Rodriguez can't hold his position there, and in a little time more than a thousand men will come from the other direction."

He hissed a low call, and later the young aide saw some of the men sneaking off with the wounded, lugging them on their backs as porters carry sacks. The fire from the blockhouse had become a-weary, and as the insurgent fire also slackened, Bas and the young lieutenant lay in the weeds listening to the approach of the eastern fight which was sliding toward them like a door to shut them off.

Bas groaned. "I leave my dead. Look there." He swung his hand in a gesture and the lieutenant looking saw a corpse. He was not stricken as he expected. There was very little blood; it was a mere thing.

"Time to travel," said Bas suddenly. His imperative hissing brought his men near him. There were a few hurried questions and answers; then, characteristically, the men turned in the grass, lifted their rifles, and fired a last volley into the blockhouse, accompanying it with their shrill cries. Scrambling low to the ground, they were off in a winding line for safety. Breathing hard, the lieutenant stumbled his way forward. Behind him he could hear the men calling each to each: "Segue! Segue! Segue! Go on! Get out! Git!" Everybody understood that the peril of crossing the road was compounding from minute to minute.

VII

When they reached the gap through which the expedition had passed, they fled out upon the road like scared wild-fowl tracking along a sea-beach. A cloud of blue figures far up this dignified shaded avenue fired at once. The men already had begun to laugh as they shied one by one across the road. "Segue! Segue!" The hard part for the nerves had been the lack of information of the amount of danger. Now that they could see it, they accounted it all the more lightly for their previous anxiety.

Over in the other field Bas and the young lieutenant found Rodriguez, his machete in one hand, his revolver in the other, smoky, dirty, sweating. He shrugged his shoulders when he saw them and pointed disconsolately to the brown thread of carriers moving toward the foot-hills. His own men were crouched in line just in front of him, blazing like a prairie fire.

Now began the fight of a scant rear-guard to hold back the pressing Spaniards until the carriers could reach the top of the ridge, a mile away. This ridge, by the way, was more steep than any roof; it conformed more to the sides of a French war-ship. Trees grew vertically from it, however, and a man burdened only with his rifle usually pulled himself wheezingly up in a sort of ladder-climbing process, grabbing the slim trunks above him. How the loaded carriers were to conquer it in a hurry, no one knew. Rodriguez shrugged his shoulders as one who would say with philosophy, smiles, tears, courage: "Isn't this a mess!"

At an order the men scattered back for four hundred yards with the rapidity and mystery of a handful of pebbles flung in the night. They left one behind, who cried out, but it was now a game in which some were sure to be left behind to cry out.

The Spaniards deployed on the road, and for twenty minutes remained there, pouring into the field such a fire from their magazines as was hardly heard at Gettysburg. As a matter of truth the insurgents were at this time doing very little shooting, being chary

of ammunition. But it is possible for the soldier to confuse himself with his own noise, and undoubtedly the Spanish troops
thought throughout their din that they were being fiercely
engaged. Moreover, a firing-line—particularly at night or when
opposed to a hidden foe—is nothing less than an emotional
chord, a chord of a harp that sings because a puff of air arrives or
when a bit of down touches it. This is always true of new troops
or stupid troops, and these troops were rather stupid troops. But
the way in which they mowed the verdure in the distance was a
sight for a farmer.

Presently the insurgents slunk back to another position, where
they fired enough shots to stir again the Spaniards into an opinion
that they were in a heavy fight. But such a misconception could
only endure for a number of minutes. Presently it was plain that
the Spaniards were about to advance, and, moreover, word was
brought to Rodriguez that a small band of guerillas were already
making an attempt to worm around the right flank. Rodriguez
cursed despairingly; he sent both Bas and the young lieutenant
to that end of the line to hold the men to their work as long as
possible.

In reality the men barely needed the presence of their officers.
The kind of fighting left practically everything to the discretion
of the individual, and they arrived at concert of action mainly
because of the equality of experience in the wisdoms of bush-
whacking.

The yells of the guerillas could plainly be heard, and the insurgents answered in kind. The young lieutenant found desperate
work on the right flank. The men were raving mad with it, bab-
bling, tearful, almost frothing at the mouth. Two terrible bloody
creatures passed him, creeping on all fours, and one in a whimper
was calling upon God, his mother, and a saint. The guerillas, as
effectually concealed as the insurgents, were driving their bullets
low through the smoke at sight of a flame, a movement of the
grass or sight of a patch of dirty brown coat. They were no

column-o'-four soldiers; they were as slinky and snaky and quick as so many Indians. They were, moreover, native Cubans, and because of their treachery to the one-star flag they never by any chance received quarter if they fell into the hands of the insurgents. Nor, if the case was reversed, did they ever give quarter. It was life and life, death and death; there was no middle ground, no compromise. If a man's crowd was rapidly retreating and he was tumbled over by a slight hit, he should curse the sacred graves that the wound was not through the precise centre of his heart. The machete is a fine broad blade, but it is not so nice as a drilled hole in the chest; no man wants his death-bed to be a shambles. The men fighting on the insurgent right knew that if they fell they were lost.

On the extreme right the young lieutenant found five men in a little saucer-like hollow. Two were dead, one was wounded and staring blankly at the sky, and two were emptying hot rifles furiously. Some of the guerillas had snaked into positions only a hundred yards away.

The young man rolled in among the men in the saucer. He could hear the barking of the guerillas and the screams of the two insurgents. The rifles were popping and spitting in his face, it seemed, while the whole land was alive with a noise of rolling and drumming. Men could have gone drunken in all this flashing and flying and snarling and din, but at this time he was very deliberate. He knew that he was thrusting himself into a trap whose door, once closed, opened only when the black hand knocked, and every part of him seemed to be in panic-stricken revolt. But something controlled him; something moved him inexorably in one direction; he perfectly understood, but he was only sad, sad with a serene dignity, with the countenance of a mournful young prince. He was of a kind—that seemed to be it—and the men of his kind, on peak or plain, from the dark northern ice-fields to the hot wet jungles, through all wine and want, through all lies and unfamiliar truth, dark or light, the men of his kind were governed by their gods, and each man knew the law and yet could not give tongue to it; but it was the law, and if the spirits of the men of his kind were all sitting in critical judgment upon him even then in the sky, he could not have bettered his conduct; he needs must obey the law, and always with the law there is only one way. But from peak and plain, from dark northern ice-fields and hot wet jungles, through wine and want, through all lies and unfamiliar truth, dark or light, he heard breathed to him the approval and the benediction of his brethren.

He stooped and gently took a dead man's rifle and some cartridges. The battle was hurrying, hurrying, hurrying, but he was in no haste. His glance caught the staring eye of the wounded soldier, and he smiled at him quietly. The man—simple doomed peasant—was not of his kind, but the law on fidelity was clear.

He thrust a cartridge into the Remington and crept up beside the two unhurt men. Even as he did so, three or four bullets cut so close to him that all his flesh tingled. He fired carefully into the smoke. The guerillas were certainly not now more than fifty yards away.

He raised him coolly for his second shot, and almost instantly it was as if some giant had struck him in the chest with a beam. It whirled him in a great spasm back into the saucer. As he put his two hands to his breast, he could hear the guerillas screeching exultantly, every throat vomiting forth all the infamy of a language prolific in the phrasing of infamy.

One of the other men came rolling slowly down the slope, while his rifle followed him, and striking another rifle, clanged out. Almost immediately the survivor howled and fled wildly. A whole volley missed him, and then one or more shots caught him as a bird is caught on the wing.

The young lieutenant's body seemed galvanized from head to foot. He concluded that he was not hurt very badly, but when he tried to move he found that he could not lift his hands from his breast. He had turned to lead. He had had a plan of taking a photograph from his pocket and looking at it.

There was a stir in the grass at the edge of the saucer, and a man appeared there looking where lay the four insurgents. His negro face was not an eminently ferocious one in its lines, but now it was lit with an illimitable blood-greed. He and the young lieutenant exchanged a singular glance; then he came stepping eagerly down. The young lieutenant closed his eyes, for he did not want to see the flash of the machete.

VIII

The Spanish Colonel was in a rage, and yet immensely proud—immensely proud, and yet in a rage of disappointment. There had been a fight, and the insurgents had retreated leaving their dead, but still a valuable expedition had broken through his lines and escaped to the mountains. As a matter of truth, he was not sure whether to be wholly delighted or wholly angry, for well he knew that the importance lay not so much in the truthful account of the action as it did in the heroic prose of the official report, and in the fight itself lay material for a purple splendid poem. The insurgents had run away—no one could deny it; it was plain even to whatever privates had fired with their eyes shut. This was worth a loud blow and splutter. However, when all was said and done, he could not help but reflect that if he had captured this expedition, he would have been a brigadier-general, if not more.

He was a short, heavy man with a beard, who walked in a manner common to all elderly Spanish officers and to many young ones. That is to say, he walked as if his spine was a stick and a little longer than his body; as if he suffered from some disease of the backbone which allowed him but scant use of his legs. He toddled along the road, gesticulating disdainfully and muttering, "Ca! Ca! Ca!"

He berated some soldiers for an immaterial thing, and as he approached the men stepped precipitately back as if he were a fire-engine. They were most of them young fellows, who displayed when under orders the manner of so many faithful dogs. At present they were black, tongue-hanging, thirsty boys, bathed in the nervous weariness of the after-battle time.

Whatever he may truly have been in character, the Colonel closely resembled a gluttonous and libidinous old pig, filled from head to foot with the pollution of a sinful life. "Ca!" he snarled as he toddled. "Ca! Ca!" The soldiers saluted as they backed to the side of the road. The air was full of the odor of burnt rags. Over on the prairie guerillas and regulars were rummaging the grass. A few unimportant shots sounded from near the base of the hills.

A guerilla, glad with plunder, came to a Spanish captain. He held in his hand a photograph. "Mira, señor. I took this from the body of an officer whom I killed machete to machete."

The captain shot from the corner of his eye a cynical glance at the guerilla, a glance which commented upon the last part of the statement. "M-m-m," he said. He took the photograph and gazed with a slow faint smile, the smile of a man who knows bloodshed and homes and love, at the face of a girl. He turned the photograph presently, and on the back of it was written: "One lesson in English I will give you—this: I love you, Margharita." The photograph had been taken in Tampa.

The officer was silent for a half-minute, while his face still wore the slow faint smile. "Pobrecito," he murmured finally with a philosophic sigh which was brother to a shrug. Without deigning a word to the guerilla he thrust the photograph in his pocket and walked away.

High over the green earth, in the dizzy blue heights, some great birds were slowly circling with down-turned beaks.

IX

Margharita was in the garden. The blue electric rays shone through the plumes of the palm and shivered in feathery images on the walk. In the little foolish fish-pond some stalwart fish was apparently bullying the others, for often there sounded a frantic splashing.

Her mother came to her rapidly. "Margharita, Mr. Smith is here! Come!"

"Oh, is he?" cried the girl. She followed her mother to the house. She swept into the little parlor with a grand air, the egotism of a savage. Smith had heard the whirl of her skirts in the hall, and his heart, as usual, thumped hard enough to make him gasp. Every time he called he would sit waiting, with the dull fear in his breast that her mother would enter and indifferently announce that she had gone up to heaven or off to New York with one of his dream-rivals, and he would never see her again in this wide world. And he would conjure up tricks to then escape from the house without any one observing his face break up into furrows. It was part of his love to believe in the absolute treachery of his adored one. So whenever he heard the whirl of her skirts in the hall he felt that he had again leased happiness from a dark fate.

She was rosily beaming and all in white. "Why, Mr. Smith!" she exclaimed, as if he was the last man in the world she expected to see.

"Good evenin'," he said, shaking hands nervously. He was always awkward and unlike himself at the beginning of one of these calls. It took him some time to get into form.

She posed her figure in operatic style on a chair before him and immediately galloped off a mile of questions, information of herself, gossip and general outcries, which left him no obligation but to look beamingly intelligent and from time to time say: "Yes?" His personal joy, however, was to stare at her beauty.

When she stopped and wandered as if uncertain which way to

talk, there was a minute of silence which each of them had been educated to feel was very incorrect—very incorrect indeed. Polite people always babbled at each other like two brooks.

He knew that the responsibility was upon him, and although his mind was mainly upon the form of the proposal of marriage which he intended to make later, it was necessary that he should maintain his reputation as a well-bred man by saying something at once. It flashed upon him to ask: "Won't you please play?" But the time for the piano ruse was not yet; it was too early. So he said the first thing that came into his head: "Too bad about young Manolo Prat being killed over there in Cuba, wasn't it?"

"Wasn't it a pity?" she answered.

"They say his mother is heartbroken," he continued. "They're afraid she's goin' to die."

"And wasn't it queer that we didn't hear about it for almost two months?"

"Well, it's no use tryin' to git quick news from there."

Presently they advanced to matters more personal, and she used upon him a series of star-like glances which rumpled him at once to squalid slavery. He gloated upon her, afraid, afraid, yet more avaricious than a thousand misers. She fully comprehended; she laughed and taunted him with her eyes. She impressed upon him that she was like a will-o'-the-wisp, beautiful beyond compare, but impossible, almost impossible, but at least very difficult; then again, suddenly, impossible—impossible—impossible. He was glum; he would never dare propose to this radiance; it was like asking to be Pope.

A moment later there chimed into the room something that he knew to be a more tender note. The girl became dreamy as she looked at him; her voice lowered to a delicious intimacy of tone. He leaned forward; he was about to outpour his bully-ragged soul in fine words, when—presto—she was the most casual person he had ever laid eyes upon, and was asking him about the route of the proposed trolley line.

But nothing short of a fire could stop him now. He grabbed her hand. "Margharita," he murmured gutturally, "I want you to marry me!"

She glared at him in the most perfect lie of astonishment. "What do you say?"

He arose, and she thereupon arose also and fled back a step. He could only stammer out her name. And thus they stood, defying the principles of the dramatic art.

"I love you," he said at last.

"How—how do I know you really, truly love me?" she said, raising her eyes timorously to his face, and this timorous glance, this one timorous glance, made him the superior person in an instant. He went forward as confident as a grenadier, and, taking both her hands, kissed her.

That night she took a stained photograph from her dressing-table, and, holding it over the candle, burned it to nothing, her red lips meanwhile parted with the intentness of her occupation. On the back of the photograph was written: "One lesson in English I will give you—this: I love you."

For the word is clear only to the kind who on peak or plain, from dark northern ice-fields to the hot wet jungles, through all wine and want, through lies and unfamiliar truth, dark or light, are governed by the unknown gods, and though each man knows the law no man may give tongue to it.

GRAHAM GREENE
(1 9 0 4 – 1 9 9 1)

Graham Greene's cinematic prose creates worlds of international intrigue that, no matter how complex, are always navigated by a moral compass. Born in 1904, Greene studied at Oxford and there he wrote for student magazines and was an editor of *The Oxford Outlook*. His first novel, *The Man Within,* came out in 1929, and was followed by a contract for his next three novels, enabling him to resign from newspaper work and devote more time to his fiction. At the outbreak of the Second World War, Greene, already a seasoned traveler, worked for the Ministry of Information, and in August 1941 he joined the Secret Service and was assigned to tracking German agents in Portugal. There he learned about a German agent charged with developing a spy ring in England for the Nazis. This man, "García," never left Lisbon but rather used a map, *A Blue Guide to England,* and fictional data to convey false information to the German government. "García" became the model for the character Wormold in Greene's novel *Our Man in Havana,* a dark comedy about a British vacuum cleaner salesman who unwittingly finds himself swept up into the revolution of 1959 in Cuba. Greene, seasoned at the absurdities of spying, and struck by the decadence in Cuba and the corruption of the Batista government, wrote, "I had visited Havana several times in the early fifties. . . . Suddenly it struck me that here in this extraordinary city, where every vice was permissible and every trade possible, lay the true background for my comedy."

from OUR MAN IN HAVANA

At every corner there were men who called "Taxi" at him as though he were a stranger, and all down the Paseo, at intervals of a few yards the pimps accosted him automatically without any real hope. "Can I be of service, sir?" "I know all the pretty girls." "You desire a beautiful woman." "Postcards?" "You want to see a dirty movie?" They had been mere children when he first came to Havana, they had watched his car for a nickel, and though they had aged alongside him they had never got used to him. In their eyes he never became a resident; he remained a permanent tourist, and so they went pegging along—sooner or later, like all the others, they were certain that he would want to see Superman performing at the San Francisco brothel. At least, like the clown, they had the comfort of not learning from experience.

By the corner of Virdudes Dr. Hasselbacher hailed him from the Wonder Bar. "Mr. Wormold, where are you off to in such a hurry?"

"An appointment."

"There is always time for a Scotch." It was obvious from the way he pronounced Scotch that Dr. Hasselbacher had already had time for a great many.

"I'm late as it is."

"There's no such thing as late in this city, Mr. Wormold. And I have a present for you."

Wormold turned in to the bar from the Paseo. He smiled unhappily at one of his own thoughts. "Are your sympathies with the East or the West, Hasselbacher?"

"East or West of what? Oh, you mean *that*. A plague on both."

"What present have you got for me?"

"I asked one of my patients to bring them from Miami," Hasselbacher said. He took from his pocket two miniature bottles of whiskey: one was Lord Calvert, the other Old Taylor. "Have you got them?" he asked with anxiety.

"I've got the Calvert, but not the Taylor. It was kind of you to remember my collection, Hasselbacher." It always seemed strange to Wormold that he continued to exist for others when he was not there.

"How many have you got now?"

"A hundred with the Bourbon and the Irish. Seventy-six Scotch."

"When are you going to drink them?"

"Perhaps when they reach two hundred."

"Do you know what I'd do with them if I were you?" Hasselbacher said. "Play checkers. When you take a piece you drink it."

"That's quite an idea."

"A natural handicap," Hasselbacher said. "That's the beauty of it. The better player has to drink more. Think of the finesse. Have another Scotch."

"Perhaps I will."

"I need your help. I was stung by a wasp this morning."

"You are the doctor, not me."

"That's not the point. One hour later, going out on a sick call beyond the airport, I ran over a chicken."

"I still don't understand."

"Mr. Wormold, Mr. Wormold, your thoughts are far away. Come back to earth. We have to find a lottery-ticket at once, before the draw. Twenty-seven means a wasp. Thirty-seven a chicken."

"But I have an appointment."

"Appointments can wait. Drink down that Scotch. We've got to hunt for the ticket in the market." Wormold followed him to his car. Like Milly, Dr. Hasselbacher had faith. He was controlled by numbers as she was by saints.

All round the market hung the important numbers in blue and red. What were called the ugly numbers lay under the counter; they were left for the small fry and the street sellers to dispose of. They were without importance, they contained no significant figure, no number that represented a nun or a cat, a wasp or a chicken. "Look. There's 2 7 4 8 3," Wormold pointed out.

"A wasp is no good without a chicken," said Dr. Hasselbacher. They parked the car and walked. There were no pimps around this market; the lottery was a serious trade uncorrupted by tourists. Once a week the numbers were distributed by a government department, and a politician would be allotted tickets according to the value of his support. He paid $18 a ticket to the department and he resold to the big merchants for $21. Even if his share were a mere twenty tickets he could depend on a profit of sixty dollars a week. A beautiful number containing omens of a popular kind could be sold by the merchants for anything up to thirty dollars. No such profits, of course, were possible for the little man in the street. With only ugly numbers, for which he had paid as much as twenty-three dollars, he really had to work for a living. He would divide a ticket up into a hundred parts at twenty-five cents a part; he would haunt car parks until he found a car with the same number as one of his tickets (no owner could resist a coincidence like that); he would even search for his numbers in the telephone-book and risk a nickel on a call. "Señora, I have a lottery-ticket for sale which is the same number as your telephone."

Wormold said, "Look, there's a 37 with a 72."

"Not good enough," Dr. Hasselbacher flatly replied.

Dr. Hasselbacher thumbed through the sheets of numbers which were not considered beautiful enough to be displayed. One never knew; beauty was not beauty to all men—there might be some to whom a wasp was insignificant. A police siren came shrieking through the dark round three sides of the market, a car rocked by. A man sat on the kerb with a single number displayed on his shirt like a convict. He said, "The Red Vulture."

"Who's the Red Vulture?"

"Captain Segura, of course," Dr. Hasselbacher said. "What a sheltered life you lead."

"Why do they call him that?"

"He specializes in torture and mutilation."

"Torture?"

"There's nothing here," Dr. Hasselbacher said. "We'd better try Obispo."

"Why not wait till the morning?"

"Last day before the draw. Besides, what kind of cold blood runs in your veins, Mr. Wormold? When fate gives you a lead like this one—a wasp and a chicken—you have to follow it without delay. One must deserve one's good fortune."

They climbed back into the car and made for Obispo. "This Captain Segura"—Wormold began.

"Yes?"

"Nothing."

It was eleven o'clock before they found a ticket that satisfied Dr. Hasselbacher's requirements, and then as the shop which displayed it was closed until the morning there was nothing to do but have another drink. "Where is your appointment?"

Wormold said, "The Seville-Biltmore."

"One place is as good as another," Dr. Hasselbacher said.

"Don't you think the Wonder Bar . . . ?"

"No, no. A change will be good. When you feel unable to change your bar you have become old."

They groped their way through the darkness of the Seville-Biltmore bar. They were only dimly aware of their fellow guests, who sat crouched in silence and shadow like parachutists gloomily waiting the signal to leap. Only the high proof of Dr. Hasselbacher's spirits could not be quenched.

"You haven't won yet," Wormold whispered, trying to check him, but even a whisper caused a reproachful head to turn towards them in the darkness.

"Tonight I have won," Dr. Hasselbacher said in a loud firm voice. "Tomorrow I may have lost, but nothing can rob me of my victory tonight. A hundred and forty thousand dollars, Mr. Wormold. It is a pity that I am too old for women—I could have made a beautiful woman very happy with a necklace of rubies. Now I am at a loss. How shall I spend my money, Mr. Wormold? Endow a hospital?"

"Pardon me," a voice whispered out of the shadows, "has this guy really won a hundred and forty thousand bucks?"

"Yes, sir, I have won them," Dr. Hasselbacher said firmly before Wormold could reply, "I have won them as certainly as you exist, my almost unseen friend. You would not exist if I didn't believe you existed, nor would those dollars. I believe, therefore you are."

"What do you mean I wouldn't exist?"

"You exist only in my thoughts, my friend. If I left this room . . ."

"You're nuts."

"Prove you exist, then."

"What do you mean, prove? Of course I exist. I've got a first-class business in real estate: a wife and a couple of kids in Miami: I flew here this morning by Delta: I'm drinking this Scotch, aren't I?" The voice contained a hint of tears.

"Poor fellow," Dr. Hasselbacher said, "you deserve a more imaginative creator than I have been. Why didn't I do better for you than Miami and real estate? Something of imagination. A name to be remembered."

"What's wrong with my name?"

The parachutists at both ends of the bar were tense with disapproval; one shouldn't show nerves before the jump.

"Nothing that I cannot remedy by taking a little thought."

"You ask anyone in Miami about Harry Morgan . . ."

"I really should have done better than that. But I'll tell you what I'll do," Dr. Hasselbacher said, "I'll go out of the bar for a minute and eliminate you. Then I'll come back with an improved version."

"What do you mean, an improved version?"

"Now if my friend, Mr. Wormold here, had invented you, you would have been a happier man. He would have given you an Oxford education, a name like Pennyfeather . . ."

"What do you mean, Pennyfeather? You've been drinking."

"Of course I've been drinking. Drink blurs the imagination. That's why I thought you up in so banal a way: Miami and real estate, flying Delta. Pennyfeather would have come from Europe by KLM, he would be drinking his national drink, a pink gin."

"I'm drinking Scotch and I like it."

"You think you're drinking Scotch. Or rather, to be accurate, I have imagined you drinking Scotch. But we're going to change all that," Dr. Hasselbacher said cheerily. "I'll just go out in the hall for a minute and think up some real improvements."

"You can't monkey around with me," the man said with anxiety.

Dr. Hasselbacher drained his drink, laid a dollar on the bar, and rose with uncertain dignity. "You'll thank me for this," he said. "What shall it be? Trust me and Mr. Wormold here. A painter, a poet—or would you prefer a life of adventure, a gunrunner, a Secret Service agent?"

He bowed from the doorway to the agitated shadow. "I apologize for the real estate."

The voice said nervously, seeking reassurance, "He's drunk or nuts," but the parachutists made no reply.

Wormold said, "Well, I'll be saying good night, Hasselbacher. I'm late."

"The least I can do, Mr. Wormold, is to accompany you and explain how I came to delay you. I'm sure when I tell your friend of my good fortune he will understand."

"It's not necessary. It's really not necessary," Wormold said. Hawthorne, he knew, would jump to conclusions. A reasonable Hawthorne, if such existed, was bad enough, but a suspicious Hawthorne . . . His mind boggled at the thought.

He made towards the lift with Dr. Hasselbacher trailing behind. Ignoring a red signal light and a warning Mind the Step, Dr. Hasselbacher stumbled. "Oh dear," he said, "my ankle."

"Go home, Hasselbacher," Wormold said with desperation. He stepped into the lift, but Dr. Hasselbacher, putting on a turn of speed, entered too. He said, "There's no pain that money won't cure. It's a long time since I've had such a good evening."

"Sixth floor," Wormold said. "I want to be alone, Hasselbacher."

"Why? Excuse me. I have the hiccups."

"This is a private meeting."

"A lovely woman, Mr. Wormold? You shall have some of my winnings to help you stoop to folly."

"Of course it isn't a woman. It's business, that's all."

"Private business?"

"I told you so."

"What can be so private about a vacuum cleaner, Mr. Wormold?"

"A new agency," Wormold said, and the liftman announced, "Sixth floor."

Wormold was a length ahead and his brain was clearer than Hasselbacher's. The rooms were built as prison-cells round a rectangular balcony; on the ground floor two bald heads gleamed upwards like traffic globes. He limped to the corner of the balcony where the stairs were, and Dr. Hasselbacher limped after him but Wormold was practised in limping. "Mr. Wormold," Dr. Hasselbacher called, "Mr. Wormold, I'd be happy to invest a hundred thousand of my dollars . . ."

Wormold got to the bottom of the stairs while Dr. Hasselbacher was still manoeuvring the first step; 501 was close by. He unlocked the door. A small table-lamp showed him an empty sitting-room. He closed the door very softly—Dr. Hasselbacher had not yet reached the bottom of the stairs. He stood listening and heard Dr. Hasselbacher's hop, skip and hiccup pass the door and recede. Wormold thought, I feel like a spy, I behave like a spy. This is absurd. What am I going to say to Hasselbacher in the morning?

The bedroom door was closed and he began to move towards it. Then he stopped. Let sleeping dogs lie. If Hawthorne wanted

him, let Hawthorne find him without his stir, but a curiosity about
Hawthorne induced him to make a parting examination of the
room.

On the writing desk were two books—identical copies of
Lamb's *Tales from Shakespeare*. A memo pad—on which perhaps
Hawthorne had made notes for their meeting—read, "1. Salary.
2. Expenses. 3. Transmission. 4. Charles Lamb. 5. Ink." He was
just about to open the Lamb when a voice said, "Put up your
hands. *Arriba los manos.*"

"*Las manos*," Wormold corrected him. He was relieved to see
that it was Hawthorne.

"Oh, it's only you," Hawthorne said.

"I'm a bit late. I'm sorry. I was out with Hasselbacher."

Hawthorne was wearing mauve silk pyjamas with a monogram
H.R.H. on the pocket. This gave him a royal air. He said, "I fell
asleep and then I heard you moving around." It was as though he
had been caught without his slang; he hadn't yet had time to put it
on with his clothes. He said, "You've moved the Lamb," accus-
ingly as though he were in charge of a Salvation Army chapel.

"I'm sorry. I was just looking round."

"Never mind. It shows you have the right instinct."

"You seem fond of that particular book."

"One copy is for you."

"But I've read it," Wormold said, "years ago, and I don't like
Lamb."

"It's not meant for reading. Have you never heard of a book-
code?"

"As a matter of fact—no."

"In a minute I'll show you how to work it. I keep one copy. All
you have to do when you communicate with me is to indicate the
page and line where you begin the coding. Of course it's not so
hard to break as a machine-code, but it's hard enough for the mere
Hasselbachers."

"I wish you'd get Dr. Hasselbacher out of your head."

"When we have your office here properly organized with sufficient security—a combination-safe, radio, trained staff, all the gimmicks, then of course we can abandon a primitive code like this, but except for an expert cryptologist it's damned hard to break without knowing the name and edition of the book."

"Why did you choose Lamb?"

"It was the only book I could find in duplicate except *Uncle Tom's Cabin.* I was in a hurry and had to get something at the C.T.S. bookshop in Kingston before I left. Oh, there was something too called *The Lit Lamp: A Manual of Evening Devotion,* but I thought somehow it might look conspicuous on your shelves if you weren't a religious man."

"I'm not."

"I brought you some ink as well. Have you got an electric kettle?"

"Yes. Why?"

"For opening letters. We like our men to be equipped against an emergency."

"What's the ink for? I've got plenty of ink at home."

"Secret ink of course. In case you have to send anything by the ordinary mail. Your daughter has a knitting needle, I suppose?"

"She doesn't knit."

"Then you'll have to buy one. Plastic is best. Steel sometimes leaves a mark."

"Mark where?"

"On the envelopes you open."

"Why on earth should I want to open envelopes?"

"It might be necessary for you to examine Dr. Hasselbacher's mail. Of course, you'll have to find a sub-agent in the post office."

"I absolutely refuse . . ."

"Don't be difficult. I'm having traces of him sent out from London. We'll decide about his mail after we've read them. A good tip—if you run short of ink use bird shit, or am I going too fast?"

"I haven't even said I was willing . . ."

"London agrees to $150 a month, with another hundred and fifty as expenses—you'll have to justify those, of course. Payment of sub-agents, etc. Anything above that will have to be specially authorized."

"You are going much too fast."

"Free of income-tax, you know," Hawthorne said and winked shyly. The wink somehow didn't go with the royal monogram.

"You must give me time . . ."

"Your code number is 59200 stroke 5." He added with pride, "Of course *I* am 59200. You'll number your sub-agents 59200 stroke 5 stroke 1 and so on. Got the idea?"

"I don't see how I can possibly be of use to you."

"You are English, aren't you?" Hawthorne said briskly.

"Of course I'm English."

"And you refuse to serve your country?"

"I didn't say that. But the vacuum cleaners take up a great deal of time."

"They are an excellent cover," Hawthorne said. "Very well thought out. Your profession has quite a natural air."

"But it *is* natural."

"Now if you don't mind," Hawthorne said firmly, "we must get down to our Lamb."

ERNEST HEMINGWAY
(1 8 8 9 – 1 9 6 1)

The Old Man and the Sea, the 1954 story of an old Cuban fisherman who goes out on one last run for a giant marlin, forever cemented Ernest Hemingway's legacy in Cuba. Inspired by his passion for sport fishing, Hemingway traveled from his home in Key West, Florida, to Cuba several times, staying for long stretches at the Ambos Mundos, a hotel not far from La Floridita, where he helped to invent the daiquiri. He eventually began living in the Ambos Mundos, where he began his novel about the Spanish civil war, *For Whom the Bell Tolls.* After he married Martha Gelhorn, she found them a country home just outside Havana called Finca Vigia. Hemingway spent the last twenty years of his life in Cuba, and these proved to be his most prolific as a writer. He completed *For Whom the Bell Tolls* and wrote *Across the River and into the Trees, A Moveable Feast, Islands in the Stream,* and *The Old Man and the Sea* at Finca Vigia. Currently, in a joint Cuban–North American effort, scholars are working to preserve the thousands of letters, photographs, and rough drafts left in Finca Vigia from Hemingway's final years in Cuba, recording both his most debilitating depressions and the highest summits in his career.

from THE GREAT BLUE RIVER

Holiday · July 1949

People ask you why you live in Cuba and you say it is because you like it. It is too complicated to explain about the early morning in the hills above Havana where every morning is cool and fresh on the hottest day in summer. There is no need to tell them that one reason you live there is because you can raise your own fighting cocks, train them on the place, and fight them anywhere that you can match them and that this is all legal.

Maybe they do not like cockfighting anyway.

You do not tell them about the strange and lovely birds that are on the farm the year around, nor about all the migratory birds that come through, nor that quail come in the early mornings to drink at the swimming pool, nor about the different types of lizards that live and hunt in the thatched arbor at the end of the pool, nor the eighteen different kinds of mangoes that grow on the long slope up to the house. You do not try to explain about our ball team— hardball, not softball—where, if you are over forty, you can have a boy run for you and still stay in the game, nor which are the boys in our town that are really the fastest on the base paths.

You do not tell them about the shooting club just down the road, where we used to shoot the big live-pigeon matches for the large money, with Winston Guest, Tommy Shevlin, Thorwald Sanchez and Pichon Aguilera, and where we used to shoot matches against the Brooklyn Dodgers when they had fine shots like Curt Davis, Billy Herman, Augie Galan and Hugh Casey. Maybe they think live-pigeon shooting is wrong. Queen Victoria did and barred it in England. Maybe they are right. Maybe it is wrong. It certainly is a miserable spectator sport. But with strong, really fast birds it is still the best participant sport for betting I know; and where we live it is legal.

You could tell them that you live in Cuba because you only have to put shoes on when you come into town, and that you can plug the bell in the party-line telephone with paper so that you won't have to answer, and that you work as well there in those cool early mornings as you ever have worked anywhere in the world. But those are professional secrets.

There are many other things you do not tell them. But when they talk to you about salmon fishing and what it costs them to fish the Restigouche, then, if they have not talked too much about how much it costs, and have talked well, or lovingly, about the salmon fishing, you tell them the biggest reason you live in Cuba is the great, deep blue river, three quarters of a mile to a mile deep and sixty to eighty miles across, that you can reach in thirty minutes from the door of your farmhouse, riding through beautiful country to get to it, that has, when the river is right, the finest fishing I have ever known.

When the Gulf Stream is running well, it is a dark blue and there are whirlpools along the edges. We fish in a forty-foot cabin cruiser with a flying bridge equipped with topside controls, oversize outriggers big enough to skip a ten-pound bait in summer, and we fish four rods.

Sometimes we keep Pilar, the fishing boat, in Havana harbor, sometimes in Cojimar, a fishing village seven miles east of Havana, with a harbor that is safe in summer and imminently unsafe in winter when there are northers or nor'westers. Pilar was built to be a fishing machine that would be a good sea boat in the heaviest kind of weather, have a minimum cruising range of five hundred miles, and sleep seven people. She carries three hundred gallons of gasoline in her tanks and one hundred and fifty gallons of water. On a long trip she can carry another hundred gallons of gas in small drums in her forward cockpit and the same extra amount of water in demijohns. She carries, when loaded full, 2,400 pounds of ice.

Wheeler Shipyard, of New York, built her hull and modified it to our specifications, and we have made various changes in her since. She is a really sturdy boat, sweet in any kind of sea, and she has a very low-cut stern with a large wooden roller to bring big fish over. The flying bridge is so sturdy and so reinforced below you can fight fish from the top of the house.

Ordinarily, fishing out of Havana, we get a line out with a Japanese feather squid and a strip of pork rind on the hook, while we are still running out of the harbor. This is for tarpon, which feed around the fishing smacks anchored along the Morro Castle-Cabañas side of the channel, and for kingfish, which are often in the mouth of the main ship channel and over the bar, where the bottom fishermen catch snappers just outside the Morro.

This bait is fished on a twelve-foot No. 10 piano-wire leader from a 6/0 reel, full of fifteen-thread line and from a nine-ounce Tycoon tip. The biggest tarpon I ever caught with this rig weighed 135 pounds. We have hooked some that were much bigger but lost them to outgoing or incoming ships, to port launches, to bumboats and to the anchor chains of the fishing smacks. You can plead with or threaten launches and bumboats when you have a big fish on and they are headed so that they will cut him off. But there is nothing you can do when a big tanker, or a cargo ship, or a liner is coming down the channel. So we usually put out this line when we can see the channel is clear and nothing is coming out; or after seven o'clock in the evening when ships will usually not be entering the harbor due to the extra port charges made after that hour.

Coming out of the harbor I will be on the flying bridge steering and watching the traffic and the line that is fishing the feather astern. As you go out, seeing friends along the water front— lottery-ticket sellers you have known for years, policemen you have given fish to and who have done favors in their turn, bum-boatmen who lose their earnings standing shoulder to shoulder with you in the betting pit at the jai-alai fronton, and friends passing in motorcars along the harbor and ocean boulevard who wave and you wave to but cannot recognize at that distance, although they can see the Pilar and you on her flying bridge quite clearly— your feather jig is fishing all the time.

Behind the boulevards are the parks and buildings of old Havana and on the other side you are passing the steep slopes and walls of the fortress of Cabañas, the stone weathered pink and yellow, where most of your friends have been political prisoners at one time or another; and then you pass the rocky headland of the Morro, with O'Donnell, 1844, on the tall white light tower and then, two hundred yards beyond the Morro, when the stream is running well, is the great river.

JIM SHEPARD

(1 9 5 6 –)

Jim Shepard teaches creative writing and film at Williams College. His novels and short stories are intense psychological profiles, frequently of historical people and the labyrinthine paths their ambitions take them down. His novels include *Flights* (1983), *Paper Doll* (1986), *Lights Out in the Reptile House* (1990), *Kiss the Wolf* (1994), *Nosferatu* (1998), and *Project X* (2004). His short story "Batting Against Castro" was originally published in *The Paris Review* and included in *The Best American Short Stories* in 1994. It is the title story in his 1996 collection of stories and is also included in his 2004 collection, *Love and Hydrogen: New and Selected Stories*. In this tale, Shepard brings his stylistic virtuosity together with his love of sports to provide a unique angle on history. From the perspective of a North American baseball player signed to a Cuban team during Batista's final years, the story explores political conflicts through the lens of a sport that is passionately loved both in Cuba and in the United States.

BATTING AGAINST CASTRO

In 1951 you couldn't get us to talk politics. Ballplayers then would just as soon talk bed-wetting as talk politics. Tweener Jordan brought up the H-bomb one seventh inning, sitting there tarring up his useless Louisville Slugger at the end of a Bataan Death March of a road trip when it was one hundred and four on the field and about nine of us in a row had just been tied in knots by Maglie and it looked like we weren't going to get anyone on base in the next five weeks except for those hit by pitches, at which some point someone down the end of the bench told Tweener to put a lid on it, and he did, and that was the end of the H-bomb as far as the Philadelphia Phillies were concerned.

I was one or two frosties shy of outweighing my bat and wasn't exactly known as Mr. Heavy Hitter, in fact, me and Charley Caddell, another Pinemaster from the Phabulous Phillies, were known far and wide as such banjo hitters that they called us—right to our faces, right during a game, like confidence or bucking up a teammate was for noolies and nosedroops—Flatt and Scruggs. Pick us a tune, boys, they'd say, our own teammates, when it came time for the eighth and ninth spots in the order to save the day. And Charley and I would grab our lumber and shoot each other looks like we were the Splinter himself, misunderstood by everybody, and up we'd go to the plate against your basic Newcombe or Erskine cannon volleys. Less knowledgeable fans would cheer. The organist would pump through the motions and the twenty-seven thousand who did show up (PHILS WHACKED IN TWI-NIGHTER; SLUMP CONTINUES; LOCALS SEEK TO SALVAGE LAST GAME OF HOME STAND) wouldn't say boo. Our runners aboard would stand there like they were watching furniture movers. One guy in our dugout would clap. A pigeon would set down in right field and gook around. Newcombe or Erskine would look in at us like litter was blowing across their line of sight. They'd paint the corners with a few unhittable ones just to let us know what a mismatch this was. Then Charley would dink one to second. It wouldn't make a sound in the glove. I'd strike out. And the fans would cuff their kids or scratch their rears and cheer. It was like they were celebrating just how bad we could be.

I'd always come off the field looking at my bat, trademark up, like I couldn't figure out what happened. You'd think by that point I would've. I tended to be hitting about .143.

Whenever we were way down, in the 12–2 range, Charley played them up, our sixth- or seventh- or, worse, ninth-inning Waterloos—tipped his cap and did some minor posing—and for his trouble got showered with whatever the box seats didn't feel like finishing: peanuts, beer, the occasional hot-dog bun. On what was the last straw before his whole Cuba thing, after we'd gone down one-two and killed a bases-loaded rally for the second time that day, the boxes around the dugout got so bad that Charley went back out and took a curtain call, like he'd clubbed a round-tripper. The fans howled for parts of his body. The Dodgers across the way laughed and pointed. In the time it took Charley to lift his cap and wave, someone caught him in the mouth with a metal whistle from a Cracker Jack box and chipped a tooth.

"You stay on the pine," Skip said to him while he sat there try-ing to wiggle the ivory in question. "I'm tired of your antics." Skip was our third-year manager who'd been through it all, seen it all, and lost most of the games along the way.

"What's the hoo-ha?" Charley wanted to know. "We're down eleven–nothing."

Skip said that Charley reminded him of Dummy Hoy, the deaf-mute who played for Cincinnati all those years ago. Skip was always saying things like that. The first time he saw me shagging flies he said I was the picture of Skeeter Scalzi.

"Dummy Hoy batted .287 lifetime," Charley said. "I'll take that anytime."

The thing was, we were both good glove men. And this was the Phillies. If you could do anything right, you were worth at least a spot on the pine. After Robin Roberts, our big gun on the mound, it was Katie bar the door.

"We're twenty-three games back," Skip said. "This isn't the time for bush-league stunts."

It was late in the season, and Charley was still holding that tooth and in no mood for a gospel from Skip. He let fly with something in the abusive range, and I'm ashamed to say that I became a disruptive influence on the bench and backed him up.

Quicker than you could say Wally Pipp, we were on our way to Allentown for some Double-A discipline.

Our ride out there was not what you'd call high-spirited. The Allentown bus ground gears and did ten, tops. It really worked over those switchbacks on the hills, to maximize the dust coming through the windows. Or you could shut the windows and bake muffins.

Charley was across the aisle, sorting through paper. He'd looked homicidal from the bus station on.

"We work on our hitting, he's got to bring us back," I said. "Who else has he got?" Philadelphia's major-league franchise was at that point in pretty bad shape, with a lot of kids filling gaps left by the hospital patients.

Charley mentioned an activity involving Skip's mother. It colored the ears of the woman sitting in front of us.

It was then I suggested the winter leagues, Mexico or Cuba.

"How about Guam?" Charley said. "How about the Yukon?" He hawked out the window.

Here was my thinking: The season was almost over in Allentown, which was also, by the way, in the cellar. We probably weren't going back up afterward. That meant that starting October, we either cooled our heels playing pepper in Pennsylvania, or we played winter ball. I was for Door Number Two.

Charley and me, we had to do something about our self-esteem. It got so I'd wince just to see my name in the sports pages— before I knew what it was about, just to see my name. Charley's full name was Charles Owen Caddell, and he carried a handsome suitcase around the National League that had his initials, C.O.C., in big letters near the handle. When asked what they stood for, he always said, "Can o' Corn."

Skip we didn't go to for fatherly support. Skip tended to be hard on the nonregulars, who he referred to as "you egg-sucking noodle-hanging gutter trash."

Older ballplayers talked about what it was like to lose it: the way your teammates would start giving you the look, the way you could see in their eyes, "Three years ago he'd make that play," or

"He's lost a step going to the hole; the quickness isn't there." The difference was, Charley and me, we'd seen that look since we were twelve.

So Cuba seemed like the savvy move: a little seasoning, a little time in the sun, some señoritas, drinks with hats, maybe a curveball Charley *could* hit, a heater I could do more than foul off.

Charley took some convincing. He'd sit there in the Allentown dugout, riding the pine even in Allentown, whistling air through his chipped tooth and making faces at me. This Cuba thing was stupid, he'd say. He knew a guy played for the Athletics went down to Mexico or someplace, drank a cup of water with bugs in it that would've turned Dr. Salk's face white, and went belly-up between games of a doubleheader. "Shipped home in a box they had to *seal*," Charley said. He'd tell that story, and his tooth would whistle for emphasis.

But really what other choice did we have? Between us we had the money to get down there, and I knew a guy on the Pirates who was able to swing the connections. I finished the year batting .143 in the bigs and .167 in Allentown. Charley hit his weight and pulled off three errors in an inning his last game. When we left, our Allentown manager said, "Boys, I hope you hit the bigs again. Because we sure can't use you around here."

So down we went on the train and then the slow boat, accompanied the whole way by a catcher from the Yankees' system, a big bird from Minnesota named Ericksson. Ericksson was out of Triple A and apparently had a fan club there because he was so fat. I guess it had gotten so he couldn't field bunts. He said the Yankee brass was paying for this. They thought of it as a fat farm.

"The thing is, I'm not fat," he said. We were pulling out of some skeeter-and-water stop in central Florida. One guy sat on the train platform with his chin on his chest, asleep or dead. "That's the thing. What I am is big boned." He held up an arm and squeezed it the way you'd test a melon.

"I like having you in the window seat," Charley said, his Allentown hat over his eyes. "Makes the whole trip shady."

Ericksson went on to talk about feet. This shortened the feel of the trip considerably. Ericksson speculated that the smallest feet in the history of the major leagues belonged to Art Herring, who wore a size three. Myril Hoag, apparently, wore one size four and one size four and a half.

We'd signed a deal with the Cienfuegos club: seven hundred a month and two-fifty for expenses. We also got a place on the beach, supposedly, and a woman to do the cleaning, though we had to pay her bus fare back and forth. It sounded a lot better than the Mexican League, which had teams with names like Coatzacoalcos. Forget the Mexican League, Charley'd said when I brought it up. Once I guess he'd heard some retreads from that circuit talking about the Scorpions, and he'd said, "They have a team with that name?" and they'd said no.

When Ericksson finished with feet he wanted to talk politics. Not only the whole Korean thing—truce negotiations, we're on a thirty-one-hour train ride with someone who wants to talk truce negotiations—but this whole thing with Cuba and other Latin American countries and Kremlin expansionism. Ericksson could get going on Kremlin expansionism.

"Charley's not much on politics," I said, trying to turn off the spigot.

"You can talk politics if you want," Charley said from under his hat. "Talk politics. I got a degree. I can keep up. I got a B.S. from Schenectady." The B.S. stood for "Boots and Shoes," meaning he worked in a factory.

So there we were in Cuba. Standing on the dock, peering into the sun, dragging our big duffel bags like dogs that wouldn't cooperate.

We're standing there sweating on our bags and wondering where the team rep who's supposed to meet us is, and a riot breaks out a block and a half away. We thought it was a block party at first. This skinny guy in a pleated white shirt and one of those cigar-ad pointed beards was racketing away at the crowd, which was yelling and carrying on. He was over six feet. He looked strong, wiry, but in terms of heft somewhere between flyweight and poster child. He was scoring big with some points he was making holding up a bolt of cloth. He said something that got them all going, and up he went onto their shoulders, and they paraded him around past the storefronts, everybody shouting, "Cas*tro*! Cas*tro*! Cas*tro*!" which Charley and me figured was the guy's name. We were still sitting there in the sun like idiots. They circled around past us and stopped. They got quiet, and we looked at each other. The man of the hour gave us his fearsome *bandido* look. He was tall. He was skinny. He was just a kid. He didn't look happy to see us.

He looked about ready to say something that was not a welcome when the *policia* waded in, swinging clubs like they were getting paid by the concussion. Which is when the riot started. The team rep showed up. We got hustled out of there.

We'd arrived, it turned out, a few weeks into the season. Cienfuegos was a game down in the loss column to its big rival, Marianao. Charley called it Marianne.

Cuba took more than a little getting used to. There was the heat: One team we played had a stadium that sat in a kind of natural bowl that held in the sun and dust. The dust floated around you like a golden fog. It glittered. Water streamed down your face and back. Your glove dripped. One of our guys had trouble finding the plate, and while I stood there creeping in on the infield dirt, sweat actually puddled around my feet.

There were the fans: One night they pelted each other and the field with live snakes. They sang, endlessly. Every team in the *Liga de Baseball Cubana* had its own slogan, to be chanted during rallies, during seventh-inning stretches, or just when the crowd felt bored. The Elefantes' was *"El paso del elefante es lento pero aplastante."*

Neither of us knew Spanish, and by game two we knew our slogan by heart.

"What *is* that? Charley finally asked Ericksson who *habla*'d okay. "What are they saying?"

"The Elephant passes slowly," Ericksson said, "but it squashes."

There were the pranks: As the outsiders, Charley and me expected the standards—the shaving-cream-in-the-shoe, the multiple hotfoot—but even so never got tired of the bird-spider-in-the-cap, or the crushed-chilies-in-the-water-fountain. Many's the time, after such good-natured ribbing from our Latino teammates, we'd still be holding our ribs, toying with our bats, and wishing we could identify the particular jokester in question.

There was the travel: The bus trips to the other side of the island that seemed to take short careers. I figured Cuba, when I figured it at all, to be about the size of Long Island, but I was not close. During one of those trips Ericksson, the only guy still in a good mood, leaned over his seat back and gave me the bad news: If you laid Cuba over the eastern United States, he said, it'd stretch from New York to Chicago. Or something like that.

And from New York to Chicago the neighborhood would go right down the toilet, Charley said, next to me.

Sometimes we'd leave right after a game, I mean without showering, and that meant no matter how many open windows you were able to manage you smelled bad feet and armpit all the way back. On the mountain roads and switchbacks we counted roadside crosses and smashed guardrails on the hairpin turns. One time Charley, his head out the window to get any kind of air, looked way down into an arroyo and kept looking. I asked him what he could see down there. He said a glove and some bats.

And finally there was what Ericksson called a Real Lack of Perspective. He was talking, of course, about that famous South of the Border hotheadedness we'd all seen even in the bigs. In our first series against Marianao after Charley and I joined the team (the two of us went two for twenty-six, and we got swept; so much for gringos to the rescue), an argument at home plate—not about whether the guy was out, but about whether the tag had been too hard—brought out both managers, both benches, a blind batboy who felt around everyone's legs for the discarded lumber, a drunk who'd been sleeping under the stands, reporters, a photographer, a would-be beauty queen, the radio announcers, and a large number of interested spectators. I forget how it came out.

After we dropped a doubleheader in Havana our manager had a pot broken over his head. The pot held a plant, which he kept and replanted. After a win at home our starting third baseman was shot in the foot. We asked our manager, mostly through sign language, why. He said he didn't know why they picked the foot.

But it was more than that, too: On days off we'd sit in our hammocks and look out our floor-to-ceiling windows and screened patios and smell our garden with its flowers with the colors from Mars and the breeze with the sea in it. We'd feel like DiMaggio in his penthouse, as big league as big league could get. We'd fish on the coral reefs for yellowtail and mackerel, for shrimp and rock lobster. We'd cook it ourselves. Ericksson started eating over, and he did great things with coconut and lime and beer.

And our hitting began to improve.

One for five, one for four, two for five, two for five with two doubles: The box scores were looking up and up, Spanish or not. One night we went to an American restaurant in Havana, and on the place on the check for comments I wrote, *I went 3 for 5 today.*

Cienfuegos went on a little streak: nine wins in a row, fourteen out of fifteen. We caught and passed Marianao. Even Ericksson was slimming down. He pounced on bunts and stomped around home plate like a man killing bees before gunning runners out. We were on a winner.

Which is why politics, like it always does, had to stick its nose in. The president of our tropical paradise, who reminded Charley more of Akim Tamiroff than Harry Truman, was a guy named

Batista who was not well liked. This we could tell because when we said his name our teammates would repeat it and then spit on the ground or our feet. We decided to go easy on the political side of things and keep mum on the subject of our opinions, which we mostly didn't have. Ericksson threatened periodically to get us all into trouble or, worse, a discussion, except his Spanish didn't always hold up, and the first time he tried to talk politics everyone agreed with what he was saying and then brought him a bedpan.

Neither of us, as I said before, was much for the front of the newspaper, but you didn't have to be Mr. News to see that Cuba was about as bad as it got in terms of who was running what: The payoffs got to the point where we figured that guys getting sworn in for public office put their hands out instead of up. We paid off local mailmen to get our mail. We paid off traffic cops to get through intersections. It didn't seem like the kind of thing that could go on forever, especially since most Cubans didn't get expense money.

So this Batista wasn't doing a good job, and it looked like your run-of-the-mill Cuban was hot about that. He kept most of the money for himself and his pals. If you were on the outs and needed food or medicine, it was your hard luck. And according to some of our teammates, when you went to jail—for whatever, for spitting on the sidewalk—bad things happened to you. Relatives wrote you off.

So there were a lot of *demonstraciones* that winter, and driving around town in cabs we always seemed to run into them, which meant trips out to eat or to pick up the paper might run half the day. It was the only nonfinable excuse for showing up late to the ballpark.

But then the demonstrations started at the games, in the stands. And guess who'd usually be leading them, in his little pleated shirt and orange-and-black Marianao cap? We'd be two or three innings in, and the crowd out along the third-base line would get up like the chorus in a Busby Berkeley musical and start singing and swaying back and forth, their arms in the air. They were not singing the team slogan. The first time it happened Batista himself was in the stands, surrounded by like forty bodyguards. He had his arms crossed and was staring over at Castro, who had *his* arms crossed and was staring back. Charley was at the plate, and I was on deck.

Charley walked over to me, bat still on his shoulder. I'm not sure anybody had called time. The pitcher was watching the crowd, too. "Now what is this?" Charley wanted to know.

I told him it could have been a religious thing, or somebody's birthday. He looked at me. "I mean like a national hero's, or something," I said.

He was still peering over at Castro's side of the crowd, swinging his bat to keep limber, experimenting with that chipped-tooth whistle. "What're they saying?" he asked.

"It's in Spanish," I said.

Charley shook his head and then shot a look over to Batista on the first-base side. "Akim's gonna love this," he said. But Batista sat there like this happened all the time. The umpire straightened every inch of clothing behind his chest protector and then had enough and signaled play to resume, so Charley got back into the batter's box, dug in, set himself, and unloaded big-time on the next pitch and put it on a line without meaning to into the crowd on the third-base side. A whole side of the stands ducked, and a couple of people flailed and went down like they were shot. You could see people standing over them.

Castro, in the meantime, stood in the middle of this with his arms still folded, like Peary at the Pole, or Admiral Whoever taking grapeshot across the bow. You had to give him credit.

Charley stepped out of the box and surveyed the damage, cringing a little. Behind him I could see Batista, his hands together over his head, shaking them in congratulation.

"Wouldn't you know it," Charley said, a little rueful. "I finally get a hold of one and zing it foul."

"I hope nobody's dead over there," I said. I could see somebody holding up a hat and looking down, like that was all that was left. Castro was still staring out over the field.

"Wouldn't that be our luck," Charley said, but he did look worried.

Charley ended up doubling, which the third-base side booed, and then stealing third, which they booed more. While he stood on the bag brushing himself off and feeling quite the pepperpot, Castro stood up and caught him flush on the back of the head with what looked like a burrito of some sort. Mashed beans flew.

The crowd loved it. Castro sat back down, accepting congratulations all around. Charley, when he recovered, made a move like he was going into the stands, but no one in the stadium went for the bluff. So he just stood there with his hands on his hips, the splattered third baseman pointing him out to the crowd and laughing. He stood there on third and waited for me to bring him home so he could spike the catcher to death. He had onions and ground meat on his cap.

That particular Cold War crisis ended with my lining out, a rocket, to short.

In the dugout afterward I told Charley it had been that same guy, Castro, from our first day on the dock. He said that that figured and that he wanted to work on his bat control so he could kill the guy with a line drive if he ever saw him in the stands again.

This Castro came up a lot. There was a guy on the team, a light-hitting left fielder named Rafa, who used to lecture us in Spanish, very worked up. Big supporter of Castro. You could see he was upset about something. Ericksson and I would nod, like we'd given what he was on about some serious thought, and were just about to weigh in on that very subject. I'd usually end the meetings by giving him a thumbs-up and heading out onto the field. Ericksson knew it was about politics, so he was interested. Charley had no patience for it on good days and hearing this guy bring up Castro didn't help. Every so often he'd call across our lockers, "He wants to know if you want to meet his sister."

Finally Rafa took to bringing an interpreter, and he'd find us at dinners, waiting for buses, taking warm-ups, and up would come the two of them, Rafa and his interpreter, like this was sports day at the UN. Rafa would rattle on while we went about our business, and then his interpreter would take over. His interpreter said things like, "This is not your tropical playground." He said things like, "The government of the United States will come to under-stand the Cuban people's right to self-determination." He said things like, "The people will rise up and crush the octopus of the north."

"He means the Yankees, Ericksson," Charley said.

Ericksson meanwhile had that big Nordic brow all furrowed, ready to talk politics.

You could see Rafa thought he was getting through. He went off on a real rip, and when he finished the interpreter said only, "The poverty of the people in our Cuba is very bad."

Ericksson hunkered down and said, "And the people think Batista's the problem?"

"Lack of money's the problem," Charley said. The interpreter gave him the kind of look the hotel porter gives you when you show up with seventeen bags. Charley made a face back at him as if to say, Am I right or wrong?

"The poverty is very bad," the interpreter said again. He was stubborn. He didn't have to tell us: On one road trip we saw a town, like a used-car lot, of whole families, big families, living in abandoned cars. Somebody had a cradle thing worked out for a baby in an overturned fender.

"What do you want from us?" Charley asked.

"You are supporting the corrupt system," the interpreter said. Rafa hadn't spoken and started talking excitedly, probably asking what'd just been said.

Charley took some cuts and snorted. "Guy's probably been changing everything Rafa wanted to say," he said.

We started joking that poor Rafa'd only been trying to talk

about how to hit a curve. They both gave up on us, and walked off. Ericksson followed them.

"Dag Hammarskjöld," Charley said, watching him go. When he saw my face he said, "I read the papers."

But this Castro guy set the tone for the other ballparks. The demonstrations continued more or less the same way (without the burrito) for the last two weeks of the season, and with three games left we found ourselves with a two-game lead on Marianao, and we finished the season guess where against guess who.

This was a big deal to the fans because Marianao had no imports, no Americans, on their team. Even though they had about seven guys with big-league talent, to the Cubans this was David and Goliath stuff. Big America vs. Little Cuba, and our poor Rafa found himself playing for Big America.

So we lost the first two games, by ridiculous scores, scores like 18–5 and 16–1. The kind of scores where you're playing out the string after the third inning. Marianao was charged up and we weren't. Most of the Cuban guys on our team, as you'd figure, were a little confused. They were all trying—money was involved here—but the focus wasn't exactly there. In the first game we came unraveled after Rafa dropped a pop-up and in the second we were just wiped out by a fat forty-five-year-old pitcher that people said, when he had his control and some sleep the night before, was unbeatable.

Castro and Batista were at both games. During the seventh-inning stretch of the second game, with Marianao now tied for first place, Castro led the third-base side in a Spanish version of "Take Me Out to the Ball Game."

They jeered us—Ericksson, Charley, and me—every time we came up. And the more we let it get to us, the worse we did. Ericksson was pressing, I was pressing, Charley was pressing. So we let each other down. But what made it worse was with every roar after one of our strikeouts, with every stadium-shaking cele-bration after a ball went through our legs, we felt like we were letting America down, like the poor guy on the infantry charge who can't even hold up the flag, dragging it along the ground. It got to us.

When Charley was up, I could hear him talking to himself: "The kid can still hit. Ball was in on him, but he got that bat head out in front."

When I was up, I could hear the chatter from Charley: "Gotta have this one. This is where we need you, big guy."

On Friday Charley made the last out. On Saturday I did. On Saturday night we went to the local bar that seemed the safest and got paralyzed. Ericksson stayed home, resting up for the rubber match.

Our Cuban skipper had a clubhouse meeting before the last game. It was hard to have a clear-the-air meeting when some of the teammates didn't understand the language and were half paralyzed with hangovers besides, but they went on with it anyway, pointing at us every so often. I got the feeling the suggestion was that the Americans be benched for the sake of morale.

To our Cuban skipper's credit, and because he was more contrary than anything else, he penciled us in.

Just to stick it in Marianao's ear, he penciled us into the 1-2-3 spots in the order.

The game started around three in the afternoon. It was one of the worst hangovers I'd ever had. I walked out into the Cuban sun, the first to carry the hopes of Cienfuegos and America to the plate, and decided that as punishment I'd been struck blind. The crowd chanted, "The Elephant passes slowly, but it squashes." I struck out, though I have only the umpire's say-so on that.

Charley struck out too. Back on the bench he squinted like someone looking into car headlights. "It was a good pitch," he said. "I mean it sounded like a good pitch. I didn't see it."

But Ericksson, champion of clean living, stroked one out. It put the lid on some of the celebrating in the stands. We were a little too hungover to go real crazy when he got back to the dugout, but I think he understood.

Everybody, in fact, was hitting but us. A couple guys behind Ericksson, including Rafa, put together some doubles, and we had a 3–0 lead which stood up all the way to the bottom of the inning, when Marianao batted around and through its lineup and our starter and went into the top of the second leading 6–3.

Our guys kept hitting, and so did their guys. At the end of seven we'd gone through four pitchers and Marianao five, Charley and I were regaining use of our limbs, and the score was Cuba 11, Land of the Free 9. We got another run on a passed ball. In the ninth we came up one run down with the sun setting in our eyes over the center-field fence and yours truly leading off. The crowd was howling like something I'd never heard before. Castro had everybody up on the third-base side and pointing at me. Their arms moved together like they were working some kind of hex. Marianao's pitcher—by now the sixth—was the forty-five-year-old fat guy who'd worked the day before. The bags under his eyes were bigger than mine. He snapped off three nasty curves, and I beat one into the ground and ran down the first-base line with the jeering following me the whole way.

He broke one off on Charley, too, and Charley grounded to first. The noise was solid, a wall. Everyone was waving Cuban flags.

I leaned close to Charley's ear in the dugout. "You gotta lay off those," I said.

"I never noticed anything wrong with my ability to pull the ball on an outside pitch," he said.

"Then you're the only one in Cuba who hasn't," I said.

But in the middle of this local party with two strikes on him Ericksson hit his second dinger, probably the first time he'd had two in a game since Pony League. He took his time on his home-run trot, all slimmed-down two-hundred-sixty pounds of him, and at the end he did a somersault and landed on home plate with both feet.

For the Marianao crowd it was like the Marines had landed. When the ball left his bat the crowd noise got higher and higher pitched and then just stopped and strangled. You could hear Ericksson breathing hard as he came back to the bench. You could hear the pop of the umpire's new ball in the pitcher's glove.

"The Elephant passes slowly, but it squashes," Charley sang, from his end of the bench.

That sent us into extra innings, a lot of extra innings. It got dark. Nobody scored. Charley struck out with the bases loaded in the sixteenth, and when he came back to the bench someone had poured beer on the dugout roof and it was dripping through onto his head. He sat there under it. He said, "I deserve it," and I said, "Yes, you do."

The Marianao skipper overmanaged and ran out of pitchers. He had an outfielder come in and fling a few, and the poor guy walked our eighth and ninth hitters with pitches in the dirt, off the backstop, into the seats. I was up. There was a conference on the mound that included some fans and a vendor. Then there was a roar, and I followed everyone's eyes and saw Castro up and moving through the seats to the field. Someone threw him a glove.

He crossed to the mound, and the Marianao skipper watched him come and then handed him the ball when he got there like his relief ace had just come in from the pen. Castro took the outfielder's hat for himself, but that was about it for a uniform. The tails of his pleated shirt hung out. His pants looked like Rudolph Valentino's. He was wearing dress shoes.

I turned to the ump. "Is this an exhibition at this point?" I said. He said something in Spanish that I assumed was "You're in a world of trouble now."

The crowd, which had screamed itself out hours ago, got its second wind. Hurricanes, dust devils, sandstorms in the Sahara—

I don't know what the sound was like. When you opened your mouth it came and took your words away.

I looked over at Batista, who was sitting on his hands. How long was this guy going to last if he couldn't even police the national pastime?

Castro toed the rubber, worked the ball in his hand, and stared at me like he hated everyone I'd ever been associated with.

He was right-handed. He fussed with his cap. He had a windmill delivery. I figured, Let him have his fun, and he wound up and cut loose with a fastball behind my head.

The crowd reacted like he'd struck me out. I got out of the dirt and did the pro brush-off, taking time with all parts of my uniform. Then I stood in again, and he broke a pretty fair curve in by my knees, and down I went again.

What was I supposed to do? Take one for the team? Take one for the country? Get a hit, and never leave the stadium alive? He came back with his fastball high, and I thought, Enough of this, and tomahawked it foul. We glared at each other. He came back with a change-up—had this guy pitched somewhere, for somebody?—again way inside, and I thought, Forget it, and took it on the hip. The umpire waved me to first, and the crowd screamed about it like we were cheating.

I stood on first. The bases were now loaded for Charley. You could see the Marianao skipper wanted Castro off the mound, but what could he do?

Charley steps to the plate, and it's like the fans had been holding back on the real noisemaking up to this point. There are trumpets, cowbells, police whistles, sirens, and the godawful noise of someone by the foul pole banging two frying pans together. The attention seems to unnerve Charley. I'm trying to give him the old thumbs-up from first, but he's locked in on Castro, frozen in his stance. The end of his bat's making little circles in the air. Castro gave it the old windmill and whipped a curve past his chin.

Charley bailed out and stood in again. The next pitch was a curve, too, which fooled him completely. He'd been waiting on the fastball. He started to swing, realized it was a curve breaking in on him, and ducked away to save his life. The ball hit his bat anyway. It dribbled out toward Castro. Charley gaped at it and then took off for first. I took off for second. The crowd shrieked. Ten thousand people, one shriek. All Castro had to do was gun it to first and they were out of the inning. He threw it into right field.

Pandemonium. Our eighth and ninth hitters scored. The ball skipped away from the right fielder. I kept running. The catcher'd gone down to first to back up the throw. I rounded third like Man o' War, Charley not far behind me, the fans spilling out onto the field and coming at us like a wave we were beating to shore. One kid's face was a flash of spite under a Yankee hat. A woman with long scars on her neck was grabbing for my arm. And there was Castro blocking the plate, dress shoes wide apart, Valentino pants crouched and ready, his face scared and full of hate like I was the entire North American continent bearing down on him.

ISADORA TATTLIN

With two small children in tow Isdora Tattlin followed her husband, an energy consultant, to his post in Havana in the 1990s, just after the fall of the Socialist bloc. This time was known in Cuba as *El Período Especial en Tiempo de Paz,* or "The Special Period in Peacetime," an innocuous-sounding term for a four-year crisis during which raw material imports to Cuba dropped nearly 90 percent. Tattlin records her life in a country suffering shortages of fuel, food, and almost all amenities. Although the Tattlins had a big house in Havana staffed by servants, her diaries chronicle the struggles of trying to provide her children with a "normal" life, including clandestine swimming lessons, ballet classes on cement floors, and family excursions where no amount of money could purchase food in a country of bare shelves. In addition to her struggle to run a household, Tattlin also views these troubled times in Cuba through the lens of parties she threw, plays and concerts she attended, and relationships with artists and scholars she befriended. Her tongue-in-cheek diary entries chronicle the everyday chores of a housewife: ironing, planning dinner, and finding a pediatrician, in a place and time that is anything but "everyday."

from CUBA DIARIES: AN AMERICAN HOUSEWIFE IN HAVANA

IV.1

Back from vacation with four hundred pounds of luggage, the usual haul. Twelve hours and three different airplanes, it takes us, to get from Newark to Havana.

Tums, we bring back for the help, Pepto-Bismol, Advil, Tagamet, foot powder, corn pads, false-teeth adhesive, hemorrhoidal suppositories, antibacterial soap, vitamins E and C, multivitamins, calcium pills, cod-liver oil pills, support stockings, underpants, bras, socks, raincoats, and sneakers. For ourselves, we bring tennis balls, books, a dish rack, ten pounds of kids' snack food, and sneakers, sandals, and dress shoes one and two sizes bigger so the kids won't run out, as well as every size of Ziploc bag and photo sleeve so we won't have to depend on visitors.

I am wondering if this is the last time I will have to make such a haul.

I hold out my hand to shake hands with the baby-faced guard who was there before we left, and before I know it, he kisses me on both cheeks.

There were four bombs in one day while we were gone—three fifteen minutes apart at the Triton, Chateau Miramar, and Copacabana and one later in the day at the Bodeguita del Medio. An Italian was killed at the Copacabana while sitting in the bar with his father. He was hit in the jugular vein by a shard from a glass ashtray and bled to death. An El Salvadoran was caught, a mercenary trained in Georgia, the TV says, and paid by the Cuban-American National Foundation.

I find a satin bow among my stash of present-wrapping supplies and carry it to the veranda along with a small aluminum suitcase I have brought from the United States. It's the kind of suitcase used for carrying camera equipment, lined with foam rubber. I tie the bow on the handle and put it on Nick's chair before he comes down for breakfast.

"Surprise!" I say as Nick unlocks the suitcase with a tiny key. Nick has already been back in Cuba for two weeks.

Inside are two dozen half-ripe beefsteak tomatoes.

*   *   *

A smirking Cuban newscaster reports that the Cuban government finds it incredible that security forces as efficient as those in the United States were not able to know about attempts beforehand.

No sugar or flour at the Diplo, Lorena reports.

The pope is coming. It is confirmed now. He will come in January.

IV. 2

Jaime, a gay Cuban man in his fifties, comes for dinner. Jaime tells us he was out for dinner with a friend at a *paladar* when they got the idea to go to the nightclub Perikiton because his friend had never been. The Perikiton, basically a large fenced-in open-air space, started as a place for gays, but now more than half the people who go there are straight. There were between three and four thousand people there the night Jaime and his friend went. The Spanish director Almodóvar was there, as well as the actress Bibi Andersson and the French fashion designer Jean-Paul Gaultier. Jaime and his friend were standing there, remarking how whenever they were in a place like that, they always felt that they had to be on their guard, because of what used to happen in the old days. They were just saying that, when suddenly there were screams and they felt themselves being shoved by a wave of people. Plainclothes policemen scattered throughout the crowd pulled out guns. They herded everyone outside—foreigners on one side, and Cubans on the other. They had waited for Almodóvar and Bibi Andersson to leave before they busted the club, but they didn't know about Gaultier. All the Cubans were photographed, then loaded into one set of buses, and all foreigners were loaded into another. Cubans had to pay fines of thirty pesos each, but the foreigners were set free. We ask Jaime what the charges were, but Jaime says he doesn't know. Jaime says that he and his friend, for some reason, were allowed to leave. "*Pasa, pasa,*" a guard said to them. They got in their car and started to drive away, when another guard stood in front of their car and said, "Who do you think you are? Diplomats?" They had to get out of their car and be checked all over again.

I say that I thought it was no big deal anymore in Cuba when someone was gay.

Jaime says the roundup was designed to humiliate.

I say you can humiliate large numbers of people up to a certain point, but humiliating *four thousand* people on an island of eleven million seems kind of counterproductive.

Jaime says they don't see it that way.

IV. 3

Mrs. Fleites *se quedó* ("stayed," which in Cuba means "went for a visit to another country and stayed"), another teacher tells me. She will not be coming back. She is making a living for the time being giving private English lessons in Miami.

"But what about her husband?"

"It's *divorcio a lo cubano.* He will get to Miami someday, or maybe not."

Mrs. Fleites is gone, the first-grade teacher is gone, too, and the school's Spanish teacher and Gonzalo and Raulito, a man who sold us fruit out of the back of his 1959 Nash Rambler. Now they live in Miami, in Venezuela, in Michigan, in Canada. Most slip away, but the fruit man announced, "I'm going. Maybe I will stay." One friend's brother left in a boat. He now has a job in a bakery, and a house and car. A film critic, too, has gone. He went to teach a course at a U.S. university and stayed. His wife and children are trying to join him and have been given refugee status so that they can now travel to the United States, but they still have not been allowed to leave Cuba. The film critic's wife lived all right for a year after her husband left, but now that she has been given refugee status, her son and daughter have been kicked out of school and she has lost her job. Still the family has not been given an exit permit.

A teacher at the school gives me a slip of paper. "This is Mrs. Fleites's telephone number in Miami. She wants you to call her the next time you are there."

I spend the next few minutes thinking about how much I will not call Mrs. Fleites.

IV. 4

I go to Lola's. A friend of a friend has gotten in touch with me over the summer. She is a Cuban American who left Cuba in the early sixties, along with her whole family. She married an American American and has one son. She meant never to return to Cuba, but now she is feeling more like visiting if only to show Cuba to her son. I tell Lola that she doesn't want to visit like a regular tourist. She wants a car, a driver. She wants to stay in people's houses.

Lola moves her abundant body to the edge of her chair. She asks me where the woman is from. I say her family is from Camagüey. They had a ranch there, but she grew up in Havana. Lola says she can find her and her husband and son a car, a driver, and places to stay in Havana, in Camagüey, and in places along the way to Camagüey if they are interested in stopping. Lola then says she also knows someone in the archives department and that if my friend needs any deeds or any other kind of documentation, her friend could get them for her.

I ask Lola if her friend could get into trouble for that.

Lola explains patiently to me that the deeds in the archives are the deeds of *private* properties that were taken over, just taken over by the government . . .

I ask Lola if she could get into trouble for that, and Lola explains patiently that people have to make a living.

IV. 5

A party in yet another spacious but dilapidated mansion in Cubanacán. The host is yet another European man of about fifty-five with adolescent Cuban girlfriend, this time a six-footer in a backless polyester evening dress and sixties updo. Her long face is sullen, as if she doesn't know who to blame for being in that dress with that hair in that place. A Middle Eastern ambassador, about fifty, is also there with his adolescent girlfriend. Both the host and the ambassador look utterly unembarrassed. The Middle Eastern ambassador tells us he knew the Italian who was blown up in the blast.

There is a buffet of rice casserole colored bright green with food dye and pasta salad heavy on the mayo. The host says he hasn't been back to Europe in a long time. Nick whispers in my ear that this is obvious. The host, squeezing the waist of his slouching girlfriend, says he doesn't know why anyone would want to go. The host wears a white linen suit over a black T-shirt. He is in the import-export business. Medicines, he says.

Nick says he has to get his secretary to explain better to him, when an invitation comes, who exactly is inviting us.

AFICIONADOS

"The drumming never stops in Cuba—congas, mostly, skin on skin beating out eerie rhythms soft as Cuba itself. . . . Drumming in Cuba seems always to touch on desire."

—*Elizabeth Hanly*

LANGSTON HUGHES

(1 9 0 2 – 1 9 6 7)

A central voice in the Harlem Renaissance, Langston Hughes forever changed American literature, making the blues and jazz central to the rhythm and language of his poetry. Cuba, struggling with its own issues of racial identity, had early on been receptive to Hughes's work, and many of his poems had been translated into Spanish and published there. While visiting Cuba as a young poet in 1930, Hughes encouraged the poet Nicolás Guillén to use the music of Cuban *son* to capture the struggles and longing of black people in Cuba. This music Hughes described as the "heartbeat and songbeat of Africa." Guillén went on to become one of the most famous poets in Cuban history and one of the first writers to celebrate Cuba's rich African heritage. While Hughes left an indelible footprint on Cuban culture, we see in his essay "Havana Nights" that Cuban music cast quite a spell on Hughes as well. The popular song lyrics he heard there, celebrating "mulatto beauties" and "chocolate sweeties," would be echoed in Hughes's later poem "Harlem Sweeties," where he describes the walnut-tinted, cocoa brown, pomegranate-lipped women on Sugar Hill in Harlem.

HAVANA NIGHTS

In Miami, Zell and I put the Ford in the garage. We went by rail to Key West, thence by boat to Cuba. It was suppertime when we got to El Moro with Havana rising white and Moorish-like out of the sea in the twilight. The evening was warm and the avenues were alive with people, among them many jet-black Negroes in white attire. Traffic filled the narrow streets, auto horns blew, cars' bells clanged, and from the wineshops and fruit-juice stands radios throbbed with drumbeats and the wavelike sounds of maracas rustling endless rumbas. Life seemed fluid, intense, and warm in the busy streets of Havana.

Our hotel was patronized mostly by Cubans from the provinces, with huge families. Its inner balconies around an open courtyard were loud with the staccato chatter of stout mamas and vivacious children. Its restaurant on the first floor—with the entire front wall open to the street—was as noisy as only a Cuban restaurant can be, for, added to all the street noises, were the cries of waiters and the laughter of guests, the clatter of knives and forks, and the clinking of glasses at the bar.

I liked this hotel because, since tourists never came there, the prices were on the Cuban scale and low. None of the rooms had any windows, but they had enormous double doors opening onto the tiled balconies above the courtyard. Nobody troubled to give anyone a key. The management simply took for granted all the guests were honest.

I went the next day to look up José Antonio Fernandez de Castro to whom, on a previous trip to Cuba, I had been given a letter of introduction by Miguel Covarrubias. José Antonio was a human dynamo who at once set things in motion. A friend of many American artists and writers, he drank with, wined and dined them all; fished with Hemingway; and loved to go to Marianao— the then nontourist amusement center. He knew all the taxicab drivers in town—with whom he had accounts—and was, in general, about the best person in Cuba to know, if you'd never been there before.

José Antonio was a newspaperman on the *Diario De La Marina.* He later became an editor of *Orbe,* Cuba's weekly pictorial magazine. Then he went into the diplomatic service to become the first secretary of the Cuban Embassy in Mexico City, and from there to Europe. Painters, writers, newsboys, poets, fighters, politicians and rumba dancers were all José's friends. And, best of all for me, he knew the Negro musicians at Marianao, those fabulous drum beaters who use their bare hands to beat out rhythm, those clave knockers and maraca shakers who somehow have saved—out of all the centuries of slavery and all the miles and miles from Guinea—the heartbeat and songbeat of Africa. This ancient heartbeat they pour out into the Cuban night from a little row of café hovels at Marianao. Or else they flood with song those smoky low-roofed dance halls where the poor of Havana go for entertainment after dark.

Most Cubans who lived in Vedado, Havana's fashionable section, had no idea where these dance halls were. That is why I liked José Antonio. He lived in Vedado, but he knew *all* Havana. Although he was a white Cuban of aristocratic background, he knew and loved Negro Cuba. That first night in town we went straight to Marianao.

This was my third trip to Cuba. Once I had been there as a sailor, and I had known the life of the water front and San Isidro Street. The winter preceding my present trip, I had come in search of a Negro composer to do an opera with me at the behest of my New York patron. So I had by now many friends in Havana, including the then unknown Nicolás Guillén, who later became a famous poet. My own poems had been published in Spanish in a number of Cuban magazines and papers, and I had given readings of them previously for Havana cultural organizations. The Club Atenas, leading club of color, had entertained me.

The Club Atenas occupied a large building with a staircase of marble, beautiful reception rooms, a ballroom, a comfortable library, a fencing room and a buffet. I had been astonished and delighted with its taste and luxury, for colored people in the United States had no such club. Diplomats, politicians, professional men and their families made up its membership—and a cultured and charming group they were. Then no rumbas were danced within the walls of the Atenas, for in Cuba in 1930 the rumba was not a respectable dance among persons of good breeding. Only the poor and declassé, the sporting elements, and gentlemen on a spree danced the rumba.

Rumbas and *sones* are essentially hip-shaking music—of Afro-Cuban folk derivation, which means a bit of Spain, therefore Arab-Moorish, mixed in. The tap of claves, the rattle of gourds, the dong of iron bells, the deep steady roll of drums speak of the earth, life bursting warm from the earth, and earth and sun moving in the steady rhythms of procreation and joy.

A group of young business and professional men of Havana once gave a rumba party in my honor. It was not unlike an American fraternity or lodge smoker—except that women were present. The women were not, however, wives or sweethearts of the gentlemen giving the rumba. Far from it. They were, on the whole, so a companion whispered to me, younger and prettier than most of their wives. They were ladies of the demimonde, playgirls, friends and mistresses of the hosts, their most choice females invited especially for zest and decorativeness.

The party was held in a large old Spanish colonial house, presided over by a stout woman with bold ways. It began about four in the afternoon. At dusk dinner was served; then the fiesta went on far into the night. It was what the Cubans call a *cumbancha*. Spree, I suppose, would be our best word.

When I arrived a Negro rumba band was playing in the courtyard, beating it out gaily, with maracas beneath the melody like the soft undertow of sea waves. Several kegs of wine sat on stools in the open air, and a big keg of beer decorated one end of the patio. Hidden in a rear court was a bar from which waiters emerged with Bacardi or whatever else one wished to drink that was not already in sight.

A few lovely mulatto girls sat fanning in wicker chairs. One or two couples were dancing as I came in, but the sun still shone in the courtyard and it was not yet cool enough for much action. Gradually more and more people began to arrive, girls in groups, men in ones or twos, but no men and women together. These were the women men kept, but did not take out. I had become acquainted with this custom of the mistress in Mexico and other Latin lands, where every man who was anybody at all had both a wife and a pretty mistress.

As the sun went down beyond the skyline, life began to throb in the cool enclosure. The taps on the wine kegs flowed freely. Lights were lighted on the patio, more chairs brought, and I was given a seat of honor near the orchestra. Most of the dancing pairs sat down, or disappeared inside the house. But the music seemed to take a new lease on life. Now various couples, one or two at a time, essayed the rumba in the center of the court as the rest of the party gathered to watch. I could not make out whether it was a dance contest or not, and my hosts were slightly tipsy by then so not very coherent in their explanations. But when the dancing couples seemed to tire, others took the floor. Sometimes a short burst of applause would greet an especially adept pair as the man swept around the woman like a cock about a hen, or the woman without losing a beat of the rhythm, went very slowly down to the floor on firm feet and undulated up again. Tirelessly the little Negro band played. Like a mighty dynamo deep in the bowels of the earth, the drums throbbed, beat, sobbed, grumbled, cried, and then laughed a staccato laugh. The dancing kept up until it was quite dark and the first stars came out.

Glass after glass was thrust into my hands as I sat looking and listening with various friends about me. Then after a while, a little tired of sitting still so long, I got up and moved to the other end of the courtyard. As soon as I rose, the music stopped. People began to drink and chatter, but there was no more exhibition dancing. Later I learned that I, as the guest of honor, controlled that part of the entertainment. By rising, I had indicated a lack of further interest, so the rumba stopped. Had I known, I might have not risen so soon.

After supper—delicious sea food served with boiled bananas

and Spanish rice—the general dancing began again. Several pretty girls did their best to teach me to rumba. Cuban dancing is not as easy as it looks, but I had a good time trying to learn, and I was interested in trying to understand the verses the musicians sang as they played. Some of the men who spoke English translated for me. Most of the songs were risqué in an ingenious folk way. One thing that struck me was that almost all the love lyrics were about the charms of *mi negra,* my black girl, *mi morena,* my dark girl, my chocolate sweetie or my mulatto beauty, plainly described as such in racial terms. These dusky nuances, I notice, are quite lost in the translations that Broadway makes of Cuban songs for American consumption.

As the night laughed on and big stars sparkled lazily over the festive courtyard, some of the men of the party explained to me that within the house there were rooms with big old-fashioned beds to which one might retire. "And here are girls," they said. "You are the guest of honor. Take your choice from any. Our women are your women, tonight."

So it goes at a rumba party in Havana to which one does not invite one's wife, one's mother, or one's sweetheart.

JAYNE CORTEZ

(1 9 3 6 –   )

Music and poetry are fused in the work of Jayne Cortez, author of ten books of poetry and nine recordings of music and spoken word. A jazz fan and word maven, Cortez echoes the percussions of American jazz and funk in her work while embracing a global concern for women and people of color, whether in the United States, Cuba, Africa, or Brazil. From marching as part of the civil rights movements in Mississippi in the sixties, to teaching writing workshops in Watts, the troubled neighborhood of L.A., Cortez is unflinching in her beliefs and celebratory of the hope that arises in even the most difficult circumstances. Her poems "Visita" and "In 1985 I Met Nicolás Guillén" celebrate Cuba, capturing the country's fiery splendor, its elusive rhythms, and the indomitable spirit of African culture thriving in this Caribbean island. Cortez has received many awards, including the Langston Hughes Award for excellence in the arts and letters, the American Book Award, and the International African Festival Award. She is cofounder and president of the Organization of Women Writers of Africa.

VISITA

1981
in Cuba
looking for
the great poet
Nicolás Guillén
in La Habana
in El Vedado
& on street corners

with 'Johnny Ordinary'
in bars with
'Johnny Nobody' &
between receptions and presentations
at Union of Artists & Writers
in office of Vice Minister of Culture
in the forest of ruffled tail feathers
at Tropicana night club
& in Santiago
Santiago de Cuba
Where José Martí is buried like
           a perfect poem
where spirit of Antonio Maceo sits like
           a bronze sunrise
where beauty of Mariana Grajales who
saw her fifteen sons fall into
claws of fifteen buzzards
           circulates
where blood of heroes illuminate in
deepness of Moncada barracks
where old trova come leaping from new trova
& we are the trovas on the road to Bayamo
the road where I swear I hear
bass droning voice of Jesús Menéndez
I swear I see those black facial gestures
meeting my facial gestures
in brightness of the cane field that
spins before me like a dream of
the sun dressed in fuchsia and
melting into folk lyrics of Camaquey
& merging with lime colored palm leaves
& blowing with tobacco smoke through
X cross section of
everything cross & criss-crossing like bulls

flywings   goats   dry grass   horses   gauchos
& this bus this guagua pulling
into city of huge clay pots
city of clear water
city of charcoal reddish mud
city of caramel sand
city with Indian name Camaquey
Camaquey City
birthplace of Nicolás Guillén
special like the clay pots
caramel like the sand &
in advance of walking on
       Trinidad cobblestones
& before passing Sancti Spíritus
       Sierra del Escambray
then returning to
       La Habana
for homage
to Wilfredo Lam
it would be so nice
to meet Nicolás Guillén
here at the friendship house
or in a study circle
or with the Federation of Women
it would be so nice
to meet the poet who
gave us the Riddles
the Tropics
the Great Zoo
& Che Comandante
I would like to meet Nicolás Guillén
before leaving the
1952 turquoise Studebaker
the 1948 red painted Dynaflow Buick

the 1955 lemon yellow Chevy
& the steamrolling
diesel truck in the sky
honk   honk   honk
I would like to meet Nicolás Guillén while
I'm dazzling in the pure energy of Cuba
& getting the same serene feeling I get
after arriving in West Africa
no heavy load of racism on my shoulders
& while I feel happy
about nothing in particular
just happy
like a baby in the baby brigade
like children in child care centers
not fearful of knowing each other
just free & jaunty
you know jauntiness
not in the dumps of
constant depression
not hanging on edge
of an epidemic of stress
but cheerful & sunny
like sun bursting through pollution
on late stormy afternoons understand
not soft not hard core not threatened
but protected
& I would like to
meet Nicolás Guillén
in this mood
in this place
at this time

IN 1985 I MET NICOLÁS GUILLÉN

In 1985 I met Nicolás Guillén while
he sat with admirers in Havana
I met Nicolás Guillén
as he listened to
school children sing his poems
I met Nicolás Guillén
introduced by Nancy Morejón
to the delegation of
African American women writers
I met Nicolás Guillén
while he joked & flirted
& made poetry out of
simple human kinds of things
I met Nicolás Guillén
with his wit
with his smile
with his social criticism
& Spanish all fast
& dished up spicy

ALLEN GINSBERG
(1 9 2 6 – 1 9 9 7)

Journalist Allen Young traveled to Cuba during its infamous Gray Period, not too long after the revolution of 1959. In the sixties a disturbing Stalinist atmosphere held sway in Cuba, when artists, writers, and homosexuals were harshly persecuted. In 1965 the government created forced-labor camps in rural provinces, dubbed Military Units to Aid Production. Homosexuals were forced into brutal labor there for the purpose of changing them into "real" men. Young visited Cuba during this dark time to report on the situation in his book, *Gays Under the Cuban Revolution.* In an interview with Allen Ginsberg, Young records Ginsberg's experience in Cuba when the poet publicly spoke out against the repression of gays in Cuba.

Poet Allen Ginsberg was no stranger to controversy before his visit to Cuba. During the turbulent sixties in the United States, he was arrested at antiwar rallies, teargassed at the Democratic National Convention, and jailed for demonstrating against President Nixon at the Republican National Convention. His first book of poetry, *Howl,* prompted the San Francisco Police Department to arrest the publisher, Lawrence Ferlinghetti. Although Ginsberg's fame is due to his poetry, his interviews are also considered works of art in their own right. Ginsberg stated, "A long time ago I figured out that the interview and media was a way to teaching. If you talk to people as if they were future Buddhas, or present Buddhas, then any bad karma coming out of it will be their problem rather than yours, so you can say anything you want, and you can talk on about the highest level possible." In 1965, while speaking at the Casa de las Américas in Havana, Ginsberg offended authorities and was promptly escorted from the country. In this interview, Ginsberg philosophizes on homosexuality, drug use, and the Cuban revolution.

from AN INTERVIEW WITH ALLEN YOUNG IN *GAY SUNSHINE*

AY: There were some vague stories going around about your visit to Cuba in 1965 and departure. I'd like to know more about what you did in Cuba and what you said that eventually got you deported.

AG: Well, the worst thing I said was that I'd heard, by rumor, that Raul Castro was gay. And the second worst thing I said was that Che Guevara was cute. The most substantial thing was that I went around wondering why their marijuana policy, as of 1965, was so down and unscientific. I didn't accept the answer I got which was that the Batista soldiers used to get high and shoot at them, because I didn't think that was true. By hindsight, it doesn't seem really relevant to their needs, but at the same time, the denial of marijuana doesn't seem relevant to their needs, either.

There was persecution of homosexuals in the primarily gay-oriented theater group at the time. Instead of finding a place for that, they tried to break it up and sent everybody out to the sugar-cane fields to work. This was an attempt to humiliate them, to use sugarcane for humiliation rather than community. And it wasn't in the newspapers. It was a secret campaign, with all the Young Communist League party-hack, flag-waving kids, like the Nixonettes, so to speak, accusing everybody they didn't like of being faggots.

It was considered bad form to wear beards and long hair, even though that was the characteristic style of Castro and the liberators up on the main drag, La Rampa. People were being stopped by the police and busted for having long hair, accused of being existentialists and degenerates. A bunch of young kids belonging to a poetry group I knew, El Puente (The Bridge), were being bugged by the police, not allowed to publish, and were called fairies. One evening the whole group of Escritores del Encuentro

Inter-Americana, sponsored by Casa de las Américas, went to the theater to hear a concert of "feeling" music. We were joined there by a whole bunch of young poet kids. When we left the theater, they were all stopped by the police, arrested and told to stop hanging around with foreigners. Some of the young poet kids were translating my work.

So there was this police bureaucracy in Cuba that was very heavy and was coming down heavy on culture, in terms of beards, sexual-revolution tendencies, sociability, and homosexuality. In other words, there was no real cultural revolution; it was still basically a Catholic mentality. As in many Communist countries, the police bureaucrat party hacks were like Mayor Daley ward-healers: flag-waving, fat-assed square types. Self-seeking squares, not at all spiritually Communist, were getting control of the police and emigration bureaucracies and setting themselves at odds against the people who screw with their eyes open, listen to the Beatles and read interesting books like Genet, and *fought* at the Bay of Pigs against the Americans. Even people who had been up in the mountains with Castro were very secretive about smoking grass. The press was monolithically controlled and boring, and the newspaper reporters for the press reminded me very much of the self-righteous newspaper reporters from the *Daily News* as far as their opinionation and argumentativeness.

I just continued talking there as I would talk here in terms of being antiauthoritarian. But my basic feeling there was sympathetic to the revolution. I had friends living there, was invited there as a guest, and I took part as a judge in a literary contest, and I just shot my mouth off! The worst thing was the talk about homosexuality and the challenge to the official position about it. Castro had taken an official position in a speech at the university in which he had attacked homosexuality. He called it degenerate or abnormal, saw it as a cabal, perhaps, a conspiracy. I think he praised the Young Communist League for turning in fairies.

I suggested to Haydee Santamaria that they invite the Beatles and got the answer: "They have no ideology; we are trying to build a revolution with an ideology." Well, that's true, but what was the ideology they were proposing? A police bureaucracy that persecutes fairies? I mean, they're wasting enormous energy on that. Some of those "fairies" were the best revolutionaries—people that fought at the Bay of Pigs, Playa Girón.

I slept with one young poet, secretively. I took one stick of grass one day, walking along a shady street with a bearded fellow who said he'd been up in the mountains with Castro and that they had smoked up there. But that was the extent of my "criminal behavior."

I was in my hotel room one morning toward the end of my stay in Cuba when three uniformed, olive-clothed, mute soldiers came in with an officer. He said he was head of immigration, that I had to pack my bags, and that I was being deported on the next plane out, to Prague. I asked if they had informed the Casa de las Américas, and the answer was, no; there will be time enough later. They wouldn't let me make a phone call to the Casa, which was my host, and they took me downstairs. I shouted in the lobby to Nicanor Parra that I was being deported and they should get in touch with the Casa de las Américas and warn them. I was driven out to the airport. On the way I asked why I was being deported. The officer said, "For breaking the laws of Cuba." And I said, "What laws?" He responded, "You'll have to ask yourself that." And that answer, I thought, was like the answer I got from Dean McKnight at Columbia University when I got kicked out for staying overnight in my room with Jack Kerouac. And we hadn't made love at all. We just slept there because Kerouac had no place to sleep that night.

I didn't go round screaming to *Time* magazine that I'd been unjustly kicked out of Cuba. I just gave them the benefit of the doubt, understanding that I was like a pawn. It was a fight between the liberal groups and the military bureaucracy groups. I realized also that the more the United States put pressure on Cuba, the more power the right-wing military, police bureaucracy and party hacks would get. The real problem was to relieve the pressure in America, to end the blockade rather than to "blame" the Cuban Revolution, Castro, or Marxism—although I don't think Castro was very tactful on the question of homosexuality. There was an excessively macho thoughtlessness on his part, and insensitivity.

I thought one of the most brilliant and interesting results of gay liberation was the confrontation with the repressive, conservative police bureaucracy in Cuba. I think the confrontation between the Venceremos Brigade* and gay lib showing the Cuban mental block on the subject of homosexuality was one of the most useful things that gay lib did on an international scale. At least it brought the question to front-brain consciousness. Gay lib people went there to offer themselves and, I think, less to confront the Cubans than to find out what the scene was. They were, obviously, faithful in terms of change and sympathy with the revolution. Since it was a gay lib group, the right-wing, capitalist press couldn't take advantage of the confrontation to put shame on Cuba, because otherwise they'd have to defend gay lib! So, it was gay lib taking the bull by the horns, within the context of brotherhood, challenging the Cuban macho, repressive mentality in a constructive way. I don't think the Communist Party there reacted very well. What was the result?

AY: In the interim period the brigade has adopted a policy of excluding gay liberation people. There was a fifth brigade that did not have gay liberation people on it. The Cubans have since come up with a detailed, rather specific policy statement on homosexuality, declaring it to be a "social pathology." The pro-Cuban

---

*The Venceremos Brigades were groups of young Americans sympathetic to the Cuban revolution who went by ship to help the Cubans harvest the sugar crop in 1969 and 1970. Allen Young had helped set up the initial Venceremos Brigades. See Toby Marotta, *The Politics of Homosexuality* (Boston, Houghton Mifflin, 1981), and Young's own *Gays Under the Cuban Revolution* (Grey Fox, 1981).

Venceremos Brigade people have related with hostility to the radical gay lib movement. Large numbers of New Left people who formerly were very sympathetic to Cuba have reduced their expression of sympathy for Cuba because of the gay question The Cubans, basically, have forced a lot of people to choose between the Cuban revolution and gay liberation, and they're quite surprised to find people choosing the gays.

AG: When Castro originally had his revolution, he said it's a Marxist revolution but it's still a humanist revolution. If it's a humanist revolution, they cannot put down gays. Otherwise, it's doubletalk. I think it's important to support any separation out from American imperialism and conspicuous consumption, and any sort of independence from American psychological domination. But, on the other hand, the reason for doing so is to become human again and independent.

If the definition of human and independent means sustaining an old, authoritarian viewpoint toward sexuality—the monotheistic, Catholic viewpoint—then it would be better that American radicals at least realized that they're dealing with human beings in the Cuban situation rather than with divine authorities. I am willing to accept the fact that the Cuban revolution is a genuine relief from Mafia capitalist domination, the previously corrupt society of Cuba, and a release from America.

In other words, I feel the Cuban revolution is important and should be supported. They'll learn, soon enough. They're gonna see the end of the world anyway and end up with long hair and pansexualities. They're going to have to take it as state policy before they're over, just to relieve their population problem. I think the gays are dealing in the long run from a position of great strength, because their position is founded in ancient rules of mammal behavior and ecological necessity as far as the future and the recognition of common humanity. So I think gays can afford to say, "Ahhh."

ELIZABETH HANLY
(1 9 5 1 –   )

Elizabeth Hanly has been traveling back and forth to Cuba for nearly two decades, writing articles about the island for a wide variety of magazines and newspapers, ranging from *Allure* to *The Literary Supplement* of the *Guardian* of London. As she has pointed out, the term "magic realism" was coined by a Cuban; this is fitting from an island fueled by a Creole religiosity. The predominant religion on the island, Santería, is a combination of African nature gods and Catholic saints, with a dose of Chinese plant lore mixed in. Its system of beliefs is both sublime and superstitious; it relies on magic, and its mysteries are communicated through the body. Ballet diva Alicia Alonso once said, "Our genius as Cubans is our ability to communicate with our bodies." In Santería, worship is expressed through drumming and dance, and the nature gods possess the bodies of the initiated, creating an ecstatic experience where the divine walk among their followers. This is one of the mysteries—startling, fascinating, and slightly unreal to the outsider—that pulls Hanly back to Cuba again and again. She is currently working on a novel titled *Undress Me Slowly* that delves further into the sensual and sacred in Cuban culture.

SANTERÍA:
AN ALTERNATIVE PULSE

The drumming never stops in Cuba—congas, mostly, skin on skin beating out eerie rhythms soft as Cuba itself. Drumming can be heard from jails and from cemeteries and on some nights even from the middle of the woods as old men teach their great-grandchildren as they were taught, at the roots of what Afro-Cubans have always regarded as the sacred ceiba tree. Similar drumming underpins the parade of showgirls, dressed often as chandeliers, in Cuba's grand old cabaret, the Tropicana, where the songs are all about sex and longing and growing old. During worker-day celebrations, that drumming undercuts the militancy of revolutionary anthems: something languid is added to the mix. Drumming in Cuba seems always to touch on desire. And every bit of the drumming, like the island's soul itself, is seeped in the sacred rhythms of Santería.

Today Cuba is desperate, with its economy in free fall and many people hungry. And still the island remains feisty. "Cuba must be made of cork," one joke goes, "otherwise the island would have sunk long ago." Its religion deserves at least some of the credit.

The Catholic Church never had the hold in Cuba that it did in most other Latin countries. Perhaps the influence of Africa was just too strong. (As a sugar producer, Cuba was a major center for slave traffic in the nineteenth and early twentieth centuries.) Perhaps an island "born out of whoring, smuggling, and drinking," as Cuban art critic Gerardo Mosquera put it, needed a faith as worldly as the Creole amalgam which became known as Santería.

Some ethnographers have described Santería as cultural masquerade. Yoruba slaves "converted" by their masters simply figured out which saint seemed closest to which god and dressed one in the other's clothing. This is certainly true, but things were more complex than that. Even before the Yoruba religion reached the New World it was a mix of Egypt, Greece, Jerusalem, and Africa. Once in Cuba not only did Spain's Catholicism enter in, but that country's tradition of spiritism and gypsy magic as well.

Santería became a wellspring of Cuba's baroque imagination and a reminder of magic and earthly delights during those years when the island was most driven by collective, even ascetic values. "'The Religion,' as Santería is called on the island, was always there, always palpable, an alternative pulse," says Cuba's National Institute of Science psychologist Elena Suarez. Monsignor Carlos Manuel de Cespedes, Vicar of the Catholic Church in Havana,

goes further. "One simply can't understand Cuba without understanding Santería," he says.

I was returning to Cuba for the fourth time in five years and
trying to decide which of two friends to visit first: Elena Suarez, a
psychologist who had spent the better part of a lifetime trying to
come to terms with the religion, or Juan BenComo, who not only
practiced it but made the sacred drums said to call down the gods.

I ended up not even stopping at the hotel before going to Ben-
Como's home. Within the hour, as usual, he was walking me
through Havana. I was seeing it again after a year: the maze of
columned walkways, the bodegas strewn with Florentine tile,
valentines, and little else, the lovers pushed against wrought-iron
fences, the laundry and the filigree.

By noon, we'd reached the *toque*. I knew on my first day back
BenComo would bring me where I could greet the gods. A central
sacrament in Santería, a *toque* is more like a party than a mass.
Hundreds, perhaps thousands of them take place in private
homes in Havana every weekend. Teams of musicians beat out
complex polyrhythms. Those gathered together dance to the
rhythms. Sacred stories—gospels—are being relived in that dancing and in the polyrhythms themselves. Sooner or later somebody
falls into a trance, "mounted" by a god come to hang out with his
community for a while.

We'd been there two hours and still no *orisha,* as the African
gods were called. But the energy was rising. The air seemed to
thicken. As usual it was all becoming hypnotic, claustrophobic.
The drums wouldn't stop. I couldn't tell anymore where they
ended and my body began. The place was at a slow boil.

Then a husky young fellow was in convulsions on the ground.
Still convulsing, he charged toward the edge of the roof. Six or
seven men held him back. I've been watching such events for
years, but still I find them unnerving. When the young man re-
appeared about a half an hour later, he'd been dressed by the elders
in the *orisha* Changó's red-and-white vestments, his face was

ashen, his eyes dilated, the possession complete. For eight hours in the tropical sun, the god and his people danced together.

But today the casual ecstasy I was used to seeing was missing. Today the god wasn't giving his usual advice: where to find an apartment or gasoline, or how to deal with a reluctant lover or a recurrent illness. Again and again Changó called to his community. At one point he fell to his knees pleading for the prayers and sacrifices which would perhaps fortify the pantheon sufficiently to enable them to save Cuba from the civil war they feared was ahead.

I had first come to Cuba as a cultural rather than a political reporter. I was to write on some of the island's popular bands. That was my pretext. Actually, I'd come on a treasure hunt. My dad had visited the island in 1929. Even forty years after his trip I had watched a rather fearsome man grow soft talking about the light in Cuba, or a musician or feathers and some outrageous flirt. My father had been one of the literally millions of Americans who found their way to Cuba. What was it about the island that captured so many imaginations? Had the revolution, for better or for worse, altered that Cuba beyond recognition? In finding the answers to my questions, like so many before me, I've become haunted by Cuba. I've returned again and again trying to make sense of what I've felt there, most especially of Santería and BenComo.

I first met BenComo at a rumba party. Back in 1988, Cuba's Union of Writers and Artists could still afford to have them every Wednesday night at its center. That night everybody was getting drunk. Not BenComo, fiftyish and slight, who sat as ever watchful with his periscope eyes. By the time we met, I had come to understand that most of the popular music of Cuba had its roots in the sacred rhythms of Santería and its sister faith Palo, or Kongo. (Ever wondered about the title of that Gloria Estefan song, "Rhythm Is Gonna Get You"?) Doing some research into the visual arts on the island, I had seen how much of the work of Cuba's young painters grew out of Santería's imagery.

I couldn't have realized then just how dry BenComo's response was when I told him I wanted to know more about "the religion." "Ah, you must be a Marxist then," he smiled, and proceeded to ask me a series of hard questions about my purpose. The following morning he arrived unannounced at the old Hilton, the Havana Libre, where I was staying, skirted the security police who until recently have tried to keep Cubans and foreigners apart, and with his trademark old-world manners slipped my arm through his. And so began the first of what would be our myriad long walks. Like many Cubans, BenComo doesn't sit still easily. He walked me all over Havana, teaching Santería all the while.

According to BenComo, Santería is all about balance in the face of life's constant change. The gods are basic energy patterns. They're force fields, some wildly erotic, some Christlike, some sullen, all of which must be respected and reconciled. Santería is as much a psychology as a theology. Its ideal: being able to ride the mean in the face of all this energy. (An ideal which, according to Yale Africanist Robert Farris Thompson, created "the aesthetics of cool.") The gods are quintessentially immanent in Santería. Everything in the world, from stars to stones, is a manifestation of a particular *orisha*—everything, even color, belongs to one god or another. There simply are no secular objects. Likewise each activity, each profession, each time of day has its guiding *orisha*. Neither then are there secular moments. Santería teaches that by using sacred recipes—a few herbs belonging to one god, a bit of food belonging to another—by properly administering the energies of life's various force fields, it is possible to bring about concrete changes in individual lives—magic. (According to Ben-Como, the sacred ceiba tree cries when asked to lend its root to black magic, but the supreme creator, Olofi, gave permission for everything. The ceiba must do as it's bid, i.e., magic works even if those working it don't have the ethics to handle it wisely.)

As BenComo and I walked, we didn't go a block without somebody stopping to greet us. Often we'd be brought home by a friend for coffee. I sat among life-size statues of the *orishas*—a.k.a. various Catholic saints—in modest living rooms and wealthy ones all over Havana. Over the coffee often there was talk of Santería's miracles. An economist spoke of his daughter, diagnosed as schizophrenic. The family consulted the gods via Santería's elaborate divination system. She was to be initiated, not institutionalized, the gods advised. That was ten years ago, and according to her father, the girl has had no psychotic episodes since. I heard similar stories of cancers and remissions. There was talk of more modest miracles as well. Havana today is in such disrepair that buildings quite literally are falling down. One Santería priest, a primary-school teacher, told us his *orishas* whisper about where to turn to avoid falling bricks.

On one of our walks BenComo and I ran into Sara Vasquez. She's an old woman now, but still quite stunning. Ever since she was a girl she's worked as a model for Cuba's painters. "The Black Pearl," she was called in her heyday. When I admired the blue scarf she wore, she winked. The blue belongs to Yemayá, goddess of deep waters, who manages to be extraordinarily seductive without necessarily letting herself be touched. "Nobody can be lost," Sara told me once. "The gods are so close, you just have to know how to reach them."

One afternoon, BenComo brought me to a ritual party given for the dead, as well as for the *orishas,* where Richard Edgues, cocreator of the chachacha, played his famous flute for the spirits. After a few hours of sacred rhythms, of trances where sweet old women turned into seers after crawling around the floors in trance, gobbling up the sacred herbs scattered about in the corners, the musicians and the hundred or so attending broke into chachacha. I left wondering if it were possible in Cuba even to separate the secular from the sacred.

Cuban ethnographer Natalia Bolivar estimates that 90 percent of all Cubans practice Santería. That figure may well be high. I did meet intellectuals and bureaucrats who said that they believed in none of this, although almost always they'd add, "but that which can fly, flies." "Santería has created such a thick atmosphere in Cuba," added a churchman who prefers to remain anonymous, "that even those of us outside the faith float about in it."

One day Pedro Vasquez, the brother of my friend Elena, came to tell me about a dream. Pedro was an architect, a man who had believed all his adult life only in Fidel's New Man. Yet his dream counseled that insulin treatments alone wouldn't control his daughter's diabetes. The girl must also scatter the white blossoms and jars of honey sacred to Ochún (the *orisha* of love and sweetness) around her room. "Is there no escape from this shit?" he asked.

Both Elena and her brother had been forbidden to talk about Santería as they grew up in their prerevolutionary upper-middle-class home. But unlike her brother, Elena has spent her entire adult life colliding with "the religion." In the 1960s, during the revolution's early days, while leading literacy programs that reached deep into the Cuban countryside, she heard every day of Santería's wonders. "Then one afternoon in the mountains, I saw a procession pass. I swear it was raining only on the hands of those carrying gifts for the gods. Since then I've become ever more confounded by Santería." After Suarez's work with the literacy campaigns, she was part of the effort to set up cultural networks in tiny towns all over the island. Today she is part of a research unit in Cuba's National Academy of Sciences that studies the efficacy of Santería's "green medicine." "I'm never really comfortable with Santería," she says. "It seems we Cubans have some kind of tiger by the tail."

Seven years ago, on my first trip to Cuba, a singer in a band had introduced us. For all her perfect Spanish manners, Elena can boogie. Fifty-something, too skinny by Cuban standards, with a crazy mane of curls, it was Elena who brought me together with everybody in Havana who in her estimation had thought seriously about "the religion." We'd talk together long into the night about our lives. My measured friend restored my equilibrium in Cuba far more often than she knew. Still, for reasons I don't completely understand, I never introduced her to BenComo. Neither did I tell her what went on between us. I'm not talking romance. There was none. Neither did any money change hands. To this day I don't understand why BenComo ever adopted me or why from the first I was willing to accompany him not only on walks but on buses— for buses were still running seven years ago—over much of the island.

Still, it took BenComo most of that first trip to convince me to go ahead with the sacrifice. Every priest with whom we had talked apparently had seen the crisis in my immediate family. In such circumstances a sacrifice—returning to life some of the energy living a life has taken away—is often said to be appropriate, even necessary. I wouldn't consider it. But finally, after a few weeks with BenComo, fascination won out.

Using a journalist's justification, I stood with BenComo and two more Santería priests, waiting for a bus, live chicken in hand. Nobody looked at us twice. It was a hot, clear day. We were down on the rocks by the bay in no time. Fishermen were casual with their greetings. We searched together for an appropriate "sacred" stone. Changó's lightning began at the same time as the priests' prayers. A wind came up as I joined in. The sky got darker and darker. The water began pulsing, pulsing like the innards of something, pulsing like a drum, a convulsion, an orgasm. All of us were kneeling now. In one quick stroke, one of the priests had cut the animal's throat. As blood washed over the stone, the sky and water turned silver. Only when the chicken was out to sea did Changó's rains come. Back in the hotel, I downed more than one tranquilizer.

Suffice it to say, during those early weeks with BenComo I was nervous. A Cuban, a devoted Marxist, once asked me if I ever prayed. God knows, I've wanted to, but the symbols of my own tradition have seemed bone dry. The poetry of William Blake seemed like prayer to me. And BenComo's world at times seemed close to Blake. Yet during much of that first trip, I don't know who I was more suspicious of: myself or BenComo. Was I after exotica? And who exactly was this fellow at my side? Occasionally as we walked he'd hum a line from an old chachacha. *"¿Qué quiere el negro, Mami?"*—What does the black man want, Mommy?

Elena Suarez was full of stories of how deeply Santería and its sister faiths have penetrated the island's history—at least according to popular imagination. Cuba's strong man of the 1930s, dictator Geraldo Machado, allegedly buried a *prenda*—a sort of magic stick—beneath a ceiba tree in Havana's Central Park to avenge himself on his people. According to ethnographer Natalia Bolivar, such stories are far from rumor. She points to the multi-million-dollar collection of gold and silver sacred objects still in the hands of the widow of Rogelio, one of prerevolutionary Cuba's most important Santería priests. Bolivar claims these were the gifts of Carlos Prío, Cuba's last democratically elected president, and General Fulgencio Batista, whose coup toppled Prío as Fidel's revolution would topple Batista. "Yet before the revolution," she says, "Santería was kept in the shadows—at least among the oligarchy [which included Bolivar's family]." Many of Cuba's rich and powerful may have had their Santería priests, a whole island may have been dancing to Santería's rhythms, yet according to Bolivar prerevolutionary Cuba insisted on seeing itself as white, Catholic, and Spanish.

And after the revolution? There were Santería initiates in Fidel's inner circle. That much is certain. Longtime confidant Celia Sanchez was one. (Curiously many Cubans feel it was when Celia died in the early 1980s that Fidel began to lose touch with Cuba.) But what about the myriad rumors that Fidel himself is an initiate? Many of his friends and foes alike agree upon the name he received at that alleged initiation: "He who survives, king for all his days."

"Communist Cuba's relationship with Santería was convoluted

at best," says a Havana University historian. "Fidel couldn't resist playing with it even as he tried (at least initially) to break it. State attacks were subtle. Santería itself was never banned, but especially early on permissions for *toques* were so regularly denied that it became difficult at best to practice the religion—at least openly. Those who did receive permission were often those working for state security as informers. Meanwhile, 1960s media campaigns were insinuating that members of these religions were criminals or social deviants." According to many of those I met at *toques,* at various times in revolutionary Cuba, if parents were found to have initiated a child that parent would be jailed for weeks or months. One old woman took me aside. "I was his legs," she said, referring to her husband, a Santería priest. "During the hardest times when it was too dangerous for Maximo, I would go out into the night. Sometimes I'd be out many hours but I always came home with the herbs Maximo needed. Or the animals. It was me who said the prayers to the ceiba. I was his legs." Until relatively recently, the party line on Santería went something about it being born out of the desperation of the poor, and that as a religion it would simply "fade away, outgrown once the revolution's social-service networks had done their work." Often a Party member would wink then and add: "One or the other has to go—it's us or them."

All the while postrevolutionary Cuba tried to use Santería to forge a politically correct national identity, one which would turn away from the legacy of white "imperialist" Spain and the developed world, one which would not incidentally further confirm Fidel as the leader of the third world. In the early 1960s, three Santería museums were opened in the Havana vicinity alone. Children were taken to them on school trips. The Ministry of Culture let it be known that Afro-Cuban themes in the arts would be appreciated. And the island's most popular dance band, Los Van Van, began working lyrics into their songs that married Afro-Cuban religions and revolutionary consciousness. (In one song, all of Central America's guerrilla wars are described as unstoppable, as close to nature's secrets as is Santería's sister faith, Palo.) Meanwhile, something unexpected was happening. The revolution's cultural and educative networks were so good and so extensive that a whole new class of artists was being produced. Many of these artists were poor or from rural areas. Their themes brought an explosion of Santería into Cuban high culture. (Leaving aside Santería's profound influence on Cuban music and dance, few prerevolutionary artists would touch its themes. Novelist Alejo Carpentier and painter Wifredo Lam are the two most notable exceptions.)

Today Cuba is "a country very nearly obsessed with its magical side," says José Bedia, one of the island's premier young painters. According to a librarian at the University of Havana, no matter the quality of book the revolution prints on Santería, it's sold out in less than a week. Nearly every volume on Santería that any library has had in its collection has been stolen.

All week BenComo had been reminding me that we were expected in Guanabacoa, a small town across the bay from Havana, early on Sunday afternoon. This was to be a double *toque,* with six drums instead of the usual three. He thought it was something I should see. There were already five Ochúns present when BenComo and I arrived. One of them would nuzzle a devotee and it would all begin again: another possession/trance, another Ochún incarnated. There was no end in sight. Each *orisha* has dozens of *caminos* (roads), variations on a single theme. A handful of them danced together here. They seemed to have a strange pull on one another, these pieces of the goddess. A move from one necessitated a move from another. And for the initiated, each move told a story. I would have expected something more lyrical from the goddess of beauty. These dances were desperate: the hunted keeping a watch. Still, the possessed, tall, thin men mostly (the gods/goddesses aren't particular about possessing those of the corresponding sex) shimmered in Ochún's gold cloth. I kept trying to shake off energy. Too much had seeped inside. Perhaps with enough dancing, a climax, a release would come. But I stood there frozen, caught between worlds.

"Stay away from all this," a correspondent covering Cuba for one of the States' prestigious newspapers warned me. "If I really gave in to those drums," he says, "my life would change in ways I can't begin to know. Better to leave it all alone." "Stay away from all this," echoed my friend Elena Suarez. "I've seen what happens to my friends. Santería becomes an addiction."

Still I couldn't seem to take anybody's advice. Granted there was plenty to disturb me in Santería. Blood sacrifices were the least of it. As Elena suggested, this is a world so full of meaning, with so many signs and messages, that finally one can become paralyzed, unable even to cross a street without incantations. There's so much paranoia in Santería, especially in today's Cuba. A run of bad luck is almost always considered active intervention—the magic of one's enemies. (Perhaps this is the underside of a culture so given to intimacy.) Besides, I grew tired of priests whose religiosity was often all about how much the gods could do for them and how quickly. "In many ways Santería is the perfect paradigm for Cuba's notorious practicality," anthropologist Virgilio Moreno told me. "Santería isn't so simple," countered devil's advocate Monsignor Carlos Manuel de Cespedes. More than once he reminded me, "Within the religion you can find every kind of faith." Psychologist Isabel Sanchez put it another way. "Cuba's soul," she said, "is always caught between poles. You'll never find one tendency here without its opposite. Santería is at least as much a paradigm for Cuba's idealism as its practicality." (I thought of those huge revolutionary posters displayed everywhere in Havana. All of them are wordplays on "faithfulness.")

Elena Suarez may have warned me away from Santería— "Frankly, I'm afraid of it," she's said. Yet paradoxically my friend

describes the religion as "underpinning the deepest stratum of
Cuban culture, marking even the way we think. Santería," she says,
"has created a whole island fascinated by magical transformation.
You can hear it in our music." "Even the youngest children here
have a need to transform themselves," Sanchez notes. "It's part of
a whole cluster of spiritual concerns that penetrate everything
from the political to the cultural life of Cuba." "We Cubans," adds
poet Omar Perez, "have a need not so much to be different from
one another but to be able to move easily in and out of ordinary
reality." "Just look at Cuban women's obsession to reverse their
hair color," says Minerva Lopez, a hairdresser and painter whose
work focuses on Afro-Cuban gremlins. Perhaps Politboro Chief
Jose Carniedad put it most succinctly. A few months before his
death he rather grudgingly told me, "To be human, at least in
Cuba, seems to indicate a magical sensibility."

BenComo has little patience with such theorizing. Instead he
teaches me the sacred dances said to call down Santería's gods.
There's Ogún, lord of iron, lord of Thanatos—his movements
are more frenzy than dance. And Yemayá, goddess of deep
waters—during her dances one's back seems somehow open to
the ocean. And Changó, lord of lightning and just cause—during
these sequences, one hand indicates the testicles, the other throws
the lightning bolts which are said to originate from his testicles.
Dance these dances and any theory about the religion pales. Perhaps more than anything else, Santería is about imprints on the
body. I spoke once with Alicia Alonso, a former Balanchine
soloist who heads Cuba's National Ballet. "Our genius as Cubans,"
she told me, "is our ability to communicate with our bodies."

For over half a century, psychologists such as Carl Jung have
been writing about our culture's need to reconnect the primal with
the divine. Humanist Joseph Campbell describes the symbols of
the Afro-Caribbean faiths which do just that as "luminous." Here
in the States, our answer has been Robert Bly's weekend adven-
tures and New Age retreats. Obviously in Cuba something far

more organic is going on. I've wondered if it isn't the underworld of Santería that makes Cuba as haunting as it is. I've wondered if a glimmer of all this—best described perhaps as body as soul—doesn't explain why my dad and so many other U.S. tourists found their way here.

"We Cubans do indeed believe too easily in too much," says Monsignor Carlos Manuel de Cespedes. "It may be heresy to say so, but I wouldn't have it any other way. At least my people are able to feel excitement. At least my people are able to feel." I thought of all the couples I'd seen at dance halls—a good number of them octogenarians—dancing to rhythms so close to those sacred to Santería, couples who couldn't seem to get out of each other's arms.

PICO IYER

(1 9 5 7 –)

Pico Iyer, a prolific and restless travel writer, brings both a fresh sensitivity and a cynical irony to his reporting on such places as Ethiopia, Llasa, and Tibet. His travel books include *The Lady and the Monk, Four Seasons in Kyoto, The Global Soul: Jet Lag, Shopping Malls, and the Search for Home, Video Night in Kathmandu: And Other Reports from the Not-So-Far-East,* and a collection of essays, *Tropical Classical: Essays from Several Directions.* In the words of Iyer, "We travel, in essence, to become young fools again—to slow time down and get taken in, and fall in love once more." His evocations of Cuba have enticed readers for years. In his novel *Cuba and the Night,* Iyer delves deeply into the yearnings Cuba inspires through his portrayal of a relationship between a young Cuban woman and a man visiting from South Africa. In their story, travel and love, romance and politics, are entwined in a doomed affair under the starry Cuban skies.

from CUBA AND THE NIGHT

We went all together, the two of us and Nelida, after the rain had subsided, to Artemisa, the old car jouncing along the open sea, the driver singing *canciones de amor,* my arm around her shoulder, she leaning against me and whispering a line I couldn't follow: *"'Luego, Después del rayo, y del fuego, Tendré tiempo de sufrir.'"* We drove past processions of small towns, and it felt as if we were going to a wedding: every province had dressed itself up in its prettiest skirts, with new pictures of Che, and SOCIALISM OR DEATH posted up on every pillar and restaurant and doorway, and little red-and-black flags with "26" on them pasted on every inch of space. WE

FOLLOW YOU, said the signs on every wall, on every house. WE WILL NOT FAIL. Take note of our Revolutionary fervor, they were saying; pass by us, Angel of Death.

It reminded me of what José had said once, about Pascal's wager: the Revolution was the same, he'd said. No one knew what it was going to do next, whether it was benign, whether it was god or devil; but the safest thing was always to say that it was good. Believe in it, and at least you had a chance of coming out on the winning side; doubt it, and you were doomed from the beginning.

When we got to Artemisa, the streets were strung with party lights, and on every door, on every wall, there was a slogan. SIEMPRE ES 26. ESTAMOS CONTIGO. VIVA FIDEL! There was a fiesta feeling everywhere, and the bars were open round the clock: like a permanent Saturday night when school is let out, a white night of the soul. Every night was prom night in Cuba in those days, but this was something special.

"You know the Moncada?" she asked, as we wended our way through the crowds, toward the main plaza and its stores. "You know every fighter in the Moncada was an *artimiseño*? Ramiro Valdés, Julio Díaz, Ismael Ricondo? *Todo, todo,* from Artemisa!"

I'd never heard her so caught up in the Revolutionary spirit, and I couldn't tell whether it was the day or the place that had brought it out in her, but I decided to can my Moncada spiel, and not ask her what it said about the Revolution that its great heroic moment was a fiasco in which the rebels were slaughtered, and their leader himself, Fidel, had left his glasses at home. This was not the moment for that: every year, the anniversary of the Revolution was celebrated in some "model town," and this year Artemisa was the chosen one, the place where the old man would shout hoarse promises to his bride.

Everywhere around us, people were moving. Little girls dressed up as for church, and electric bulbs running on wires above the parks, and somewhere there was a rumor that Los Van Van was going to be playing in the park. We went to Lourdes's aunt's house, and when she saw us, she kissed us all, and took us in, and there were shouts and cries and kisses. A few minutes later, we were out again—some ancient family feud, and some cousin asking Lourdes why she'd been to jail.

"Okay, Richard, tonight we sleep in the street," she said. "You learn the Cuban way."

We made our way back to the plaza then, and it was more packed than ever, and I didn't know if it was a rock-concert gig or a town-hall meeting. In a bare patch of grass next to a school, someone had set up speakers, and the word was that Grupo Sierra Maestra was going to be here any minute. For now, there was some local group, pounding out salsa dance tunes, and one whole field of young Cubans wriggling in place with the moves their mothers had taught them.

I bought a couple of beers for the girls, and we found some seats, and they began dancing. Nelida wiggling with a cabaret dancer's frenzy, Lula moving more slowly in place, like a rich girl in a Kuwaiti disco.

"*Hey, compañero, qué pasa?*" said the black man who suddenly appeared beside us, a trim, muscular guy with a close-fitting shirt: he could have passed for Pelé.

"*Hola!*"

Lula pinched my palm, and I knew what that meant: stay quiet, say nothing, this guy was trouble.

"My name is Fredo," he was saying, in English, and I pretended I didn't hear him, and jived closer over to Lula. If he wanted to hit on Nelida, this was his cue.

But he didn't take the hint, and came moving over to us, dancing all the while, arms moving back and forth, in a leisurely, controlled way that had more power to it than sex. "Is good, no?" he said, not leaving the English. "You like this country?"

"I dislike this guy," Lula whispered, with her back turned. "He's making my skin move."

"Hey, *compañero?*" he said again, smiling to the beat. "What part of Havana do you live in?"

I kept on dancing.

"Ah, maybe you are an *extranjero*. You come from Canada, maybe? *Estados Unidos?*"

"South Africa," I finally answered.

"South Africa? What part?"

We were dancing all the while, Lourdes in a kind of distracted way, her mind not moving with her body, Nelida in some drum-beating trance of her own, the guy in short, compact motions, like a piston.

"You will hear Fidel tomorrow?"

"Come on," said Lourdes. "Let's move." We tried to sidle away then, and he kept following us: to run was like setting off a burglar alarm, to stay was like admitting our guilt. "Come on," she said more urgently, and then we were snaking through the dancers, and he was beginning to follow us, and then at last Nelida came out of her spell, and grabbed his arm, and said, *"Baila conmigo, niño,"* and she was rubbing herself against him and puckering her lips, and we figured that that was the last we'd see of her tonight.

That left the rest of the night before us, and nowhere to go. We couldn't stay at her aunt's house, and we'd let the taxi go, so there was nothing for it but waiting at the bus station for a bus to Havana they said might never come. Outside the bars and restaurants, people were sitting on steps or standing against walls, looking into the distance: the usual three-hour *cola*. Every house looked like a party or a Christmas cake, but there was a man watching in every entrance, and when you turned off the main drag, you stumbled into dirty puddles.

For a while, we made a kind of makeshift home in front of a closed door, and I bought us some beers, and we cuddled and got close. But then things started getting heavy, and she got nervous, and every time I kissed her, she looked around for the security man. So we headed back to the bus station and got into the line. There was nothing to do there, as usual, but hold one another, and gossip, and wait.

"You know, Richard, once there was a long *cola,* a *super cola,* a *tremendo cola,* the longest *cola* in the history of Cuba. And a guy came up, with a beard, wearing army clothes, and said, *'El último?'* and they led him to the back of the line. And as soon as everyone else saw him there, they all found ways to leave the line or go back home, until the guy was alone at the front. 'Hey,' he said to the last guy to leave, 'what is this line for?' 'Oh, it's for leaving the island,' the man told him."

I wondered why she was telling me this kind of story in a crowded place like this—on the eve of Fidel's visit, no less—but I figured she knew what she was doing, and decided to go with it.

"Here," she said, as we were pushed closer together by the line. "Let me show you this." She pulled out from her pocket her pink wallet, and, searching through it, drew out an old sad black-and-white mug shot, not much bigger than her nail.

"Your *esposo?*"

"No. My father. I never told you his story?" She stopped for a moment. "He was a *Fidelista* before; he loved Fidel. He used to say that Cuba was the only country that was free. That had no bosses. He went to Russia to study for him, he gave everything to the Party. And then he fell in love with a woman, and her husband found out, and this husband was in the police, and my father was sent to jail, and that was it. The one true friend of Fidel, and they let him die.

"I believed in Fidel too, before. He had so many dreams; he was so strong; he gave himself only to his country. I was a good *Pionera* in school; I wrote essays about Che. But then they killed my father. And after, I told you, there was one time I was engaged. He was a good boy. Very good. Kind. Patient. Not like the others. It was my first love. And then, one day, it was like this: there was a fiesta, and there was a *cola,* and I was young, and I could not control myself, and the police were trying to command us, and telling women they could go first if they would go behind the wall with them for five minutes, and I got mad, and I kicked a policeman there, and they took me to prison. My *esposo,* he was there, and he shouted at them, and told them to go to hell, and they called him a traitor, an imperialist, and he was in jail for six months. When he came out—it was different. It was never the same again."

I looked at her then, and saw that it was about something more than bread and plane tickets, and as tangled as any family history. "That is why I learned English," she went on. "That is why I love Martí. Because he wanted to so something with his life. Not only to wait, to sit, to visit a foreign country and hope that things will change. He tried to change things himself, to make things better." She smiled up at me then, and said, "Better we kiss. You must enjoy this Cuban evening," and she relaxed her body into mine.

The minutes passed, the hours passed, it seemed, and the line got longer, and there was never a bus in sight. At one point—it must have been three A.M. or later—someone got out a guitar, and a few drunken boys began beating out a rhythm on the walls, and a girl started singing, and Lula joined in from where she was standing, and, in a faint, high voice, she sang boleros and then Cuban songs, and then Yoruba songs and Beatles songs and even Russian songs. The time moved more quickly then, and the *cola* itself became a party, with frantic strumming and the beating of walls, and voices, two or three, taking melodies for a walk. Then the bus came, and suddenly the line, so patient, broke into ranks, and there was a scuffle, and someone shouted *Hijo é puta,* and a big white guy took a swing at a black, and someone kicked at Lourdes, and hit her in the leg, and we climbed up amid the mob, and grabbed some seats, and she fell asleep in my lap as we lurched back toward Havana. It must have been five-thirty then, and the

sun was just beginning to rise, but I was too wired to crash out—
I had too much to think about—so I just sat there, with her head
resting in my lap, stroking her hair and watching her face, and seeing the sun come up over the sugarcane, another morning-after in
the glorious Revolution.

TOM MILLER

(1 9 4 7 -   )

When Tom Miller embarked on an eight-month sojourn through Cuba during
the Special Period, he set out "not to write about sugarcane quotas or Marxist health care, but rather people who wake up in the morning, go to school,
go to work, come home, make dinner, make love, go dancing, go crazy." The
book that resulted from this journey, *Trading with the Enemy: A Yankee Travels Through Castro's Cuba,* is more than a travelogue, as it also provides an
excellent portrait of Cuban culture: the tensions between individuals and
communities, the love of country, and the conflicted views of the United
States as either the enemy or the promised land.

The excerpted section here is a description of his interview with Nitza Villapol, a television personality who used a philosophical approach to cooking
that would forever change Cubans' diets. She was embraced and rejected by
Cubans both in the country and by those who left. Although Villapol was never
credited as the author outside of Cuba, her first cookbook, *Cocina al minuto*
(*The Cuban Flavor*), is considered a classic for Cuban cuisine worldwide. During
the Special Period, when food was scarce, she continued cooking onscreen
with whatever was available to the people, encouraging simple recipes such
as cucumber lemonade. Rumor in Cuba has it that when she presented a
black bean dessert, cynicism ran too high, and her program was canceled.

from TRADING WITH THE ENEMY:
A YANKEE TRAVELS THROUGH
CASTRO'S CUBA

Despite my protestations, La Plume insisted on escorting me to
my afternoon appointment with Nitza Villapol, the television

cook. She had arranged it and, by God, she was going to see it through. When Nitza finally answered the doorbell she looked as if we had awakened her. She wore a sack dress, slippers, and no jewelry or makeup. Her neck-length light-colored hair was slightly tousled. Now in her midsixties, she was somewhat heavy, not quite dowdy. La Plume formally introduced herself and me.

Nitza Villapol, the friend in every Cuban's kitchen, was no friend in her own living room. She sat erect and glowered at us. I made small talk. She spoke curtly. I talked smaller. She was more brusque. I tried every conceit in the journalist's bag to get a conversation going—flattery, provocation, the weather, good cop–bad cop, subtlety, bluntness, flippancy, profundity. She was as likely to converse with me as José Martí was to cut a deal with the Spanish. The windchill factor on that eighty-nine-degree day was below zero. I thanked La Plume for arranging the interview and suggested that she leave. Inefficient yes, dumb no. She left.

Nitza began slower than my train to Cienfuegos. The question that finally pulled the queen of Cuban kitchens out of the station was about the typical Cuban kitchen. "It has a two-burner stove, up high, not on the floor. Some of them are charcoal, but most cook with gas or electricity. Most households now have refrigerators."

She glared, daring another question, then suddenly softened. "Do you know what I had for lunch today?" asked the country's most prominent expert on food. "Canned clam chowder." Her voice startled me with its sudden mix of exasperation, vengefulness, pity, and sorrow. "Cubans ruin their eating. I don't give a damn. All they want is pork, fried bananas, and rice. You don't need meat to be well fed. What the hell do I care about rice. Wheat is as good for you as rice. I won't stand in line for any food."

She spoke with fury: anger at Cubans, anger at their habits, resentment at everything. "People won't change their food habits. They eat what they like, not for their health. It's very frustrating. I used to think I could change their eating habits. Now I give them information, and if they don't change it's their tough luck. They're too finicky about what they eat."

A curious thing happened. A couple of words in English slipped out of her mouth. I responded in English and she continued in kind. She said she hadn't carried on a conversation in English with a native speaker in years. She spent most of her youth in the States, and she speaks fluent, accentless English, with a rich vocabulary acquired from movies, radio, and books. Personal emotions rushed to the fore. "I'm a sourpuss. That's what I am, a sourpuss. My life is like a jar of cookies—everyone wants to take something but no one wants to put something in. I'm old. I don't get out much. I don't go to the beach like I used to. My mother is old." Her mother, then ninety, was propped up in the next room, unable to walk or talk. "I have no family or friends." She scowled at me.

"She took care of me when I was young and now I'm taking care of her when she is old. It is my only priority. I don't invite people to come and visit. I don't cook for anyone. I don't care what they think. I used to think it was very important to be popular. Now I don't give a damn. Ask any man what he wants. He wants to be fed and he wants sex. I used to have friends. It's very sad. My mom is in the house. I have to feed her or she dies."

Silent tears suddenly gushed down Nitza Villapol's cheeks. We sat across a low table from each other; I reached out, not knowing what to do or say. "You look like you need a hug," I stammered. She grabbed my hands and squeezed.

"Ten million people think they know me. But in my private life I'm not very happy. I'm so alone. I do housework. I clean the goddamn place and I wash the dishes. That's what I do. I *hate* to wash dishes. I don't like housework." She mimicked a happy persona: "I ought to be glad to cook for anyone who comes by. Well," she continued, sternly, "I don't even bring a glass of water to anyone." In fact, I had been there almost an hour and she hadn't even carried out this most rudimentary etiquette offered in the most humble homes. "I don't give a good goddamn." She walked over to the window. She had the only venetian blinds I saw in a Cuban home.

She switched to Spanish. "I've been to England, Scotland, Italy, France, and Mexico. San Francisco, Boston, New York, Miami, and Africa. People have different objectives, but they're the same everywhere. José Martí said that you should love and construct rather than hate and destroy." Tears returned. "I try to belong with the first of those. I try to help because it's human. Usually people don't appreciate what doesn't cost them a centavo. Man is not very far from the ape."

Back to English. "It's not easy to grow old. Young people think we're dead but still breathing. They think we have no right to have things. I like things around me. Hell, I'm old. Fortunately I live in a country where old people have a lot more than in other countries. We have food, clothing, housing, and most important, work. In Cuba when you're old you may be lonely but you're not hungry."

Tears came once more. "I can't even talk to my mother anymore. All I have is this island that I love so much." She blubbered uncontrollably. "I wouldn't change my nationality for any place in the world. I'm so proud to be Cuban. The only misgiving I have is that my work has helped people who left Cuba to survive. People have stolen my works. I haven't received a penny for my books. Fortunately, I don't have to steal to live. I don't like people who leave Cuba. With a few exceptions here and there they are *mezquinos*," stingy people. "The petite bourgeoisie in the Miami community—they have my books and they follow my recipes. I resent that. I *hate* them."

Her cookbook, *Cocina al minuto,* originally published in the 1950s, has been reprinted a few times in Cuba. Abroad, it has been appropriated as if it were public domain, most insidiously in the States, where not only has no contract been signed nor royalties paid but even her name has been removed. Even more insulting, *Cocina al minuto* has been translated into English as *The Cuban Fla-*

vor, also published in Miami, again with no credit. It duplicates most of the recipes in Nitza's original book word for word: same contents in the same order, same number of servings, same measurements, ingredient by ingredient, right down to the *boniato.* Her bitterness is well founded.

Yet no one is fooled. In conversations with innumerable Cubans who have left their homeland, I have been told time after time that *Cocina al minuto* was among the most treasured possessions they packed in the one suitcase they were allowed to take. It is the Cuban *Joy of Cooking.* In households in Cuba and throughout the Diaspora, Nitza Villapol's *Cocina al minuto* has become the First Testament.

Nitza collected herself and spoke of the national diet. She bristles at the notion that she is a cook; she is a nutritionist first, she will tell you, and she teaches dietary basics through cooking. "I've tried for thirty years to change the Cuban diet. Cuba has a sweet tooth. Every country does, I suppose. Sugar is a baby taste, and people who have babies can help them by not feeding them sweets all the time. Sugar has a place in the human diet, of course. But people use it to replace other nutrients.

"I'm a diabetic. I use a little sugar, but not every day. The harm isn't in sugar but in the way people use it. In underdeveloped countries people are starving. With sugar they're still undernourished but they're not starving. Photographers in the fashion industry here and all over the world insist that the style is to be slim. Rubens's models wouldn't earn a centavo in Cuba. I would like to lose weight. I can do it if I exercise. I used to swim at a pool at one of the big hotels. They gave me permission to swim there because most foreigners don't recognize me." She got me that glass of water.

"Obesity is a problem in Cuba. We are trying to keep children from getting fat. Fat cells developed in childhood are like sponges—they may not hold anything for a long time, but they can still absorb later in life. If a child is obese, it's a lifelong prob-

lem fighting obesity. That's the most important thing happening
in Cuba right now, as far as nutrition goes. Now the adolescents
try all those freak diets."

Nitza Villapol's career goes back to 1951 when Cuba, one of
the first countries to have television, first went on the air with a
regular schedule. Nitza was in the first year's lineup and has
brought her studio kitchen into living rooms ever since. By all
accounts she has the longest-running television program in the
world. Her college background was in home economics and education, with courses in dietetics thrown in. "I felt the responsibility to learn more. I was already working in television. They used to
call me Cuba's Betty Furness. I sold Leonard's products, RCA Victor products, Stokley's food. I sold Osterizer blenders and Sun-
beam frying pans." Nitza smiled for the first time since I walked in.

Her program, *Cocina al minuto,* was broadcast daily in 1958. "I
didn't have the slightest idea what the Revolution was. I had no
personal connection to it except that three friends had signed
some document calling for change. It was common to see grown
men and women going through trash cans foraging for something
to eat. When many people were hungry, the rich in Cienfuegos
used to have lobster and jumbo shrimp and rich coffee. Now all
that good stuff is exported. I would *love* to sit down to a steak dinner with potatoes and tomato salad, and cheesecake for dessert. If
it's a porterhouse steak, so much the better. But instead of that we
have schools and hospitals.

"Anyway, my friends all left Cuba when they realized it was
Communist. I had a domestic worker, and she said, 'We'll see if
you'll be so happy when they take away what you have!' I said,
'Lolita, they can't. I work with my head and my hands. I'm not
exploiting anybody.'" Nitza got herself a glass of water.

"I like TV. I truly do. I like to communicate with the public. I'm
a teacher. I like to teach. The ways to good nutrition are difficult.
Many people think the Occidental way is the only way to eat. Ani-

mal protein and the like. I could eat rice every day of my life because I'm a Cuban, but I don't think a tourist could." She leaned back and spoke with animation for the first time since we began. "I enjoy precooked rice, but most Cubans don't. It's a little yellowish and nutty. I don't have as much trouble as most Cubans because my food habits are more international. I like fish, vegetables, and meat. I like food very simply prepared."

Gabriel García Márquez called her once. "I couldn't figure out why, but he wanted to interview me." She whispered conspiratorially: "I don't like his books. I couldn't even finish *One Hundred Years of Solitude*. I like to breathe while I read a book. I did like his book about Bolívar, but I don't like fiction very much. Well, it turned out he was doing some research about food and needed some advice."

Her office had a comfortable clutter to it. Bookshelves were full of cookbooks, books on nutrition, fine literature. She pointed out *Elena's Secrets of Mexican Cooking,* by Elena Zelayeta, as a favorite cookbook. Also, *Love and Knishes,* by Sara Kasdan. A Remington portable sat on her desk.

With the writers union next door, I said this block had some of the finest books to be found in the country. "UNEAC is shit," she retorted. She walked over to the window and looked down on it with contempt. "I have to look at that building every day of my life. For forty years I've been in radio, television, and film. I've written more than one book and countless articles. And when I applied for membership, they wouldn't admit me." She put on her cheerful, sarcastic voice: "They said, you're an entertainer, not a writer." Had the window been open, she would have spit on the UNEAC grounds.

In 1965 Nitza went to London and Africa as part of a United Nations survey team. "I lived in Queens Way in London for almost four months. The British Museum was near where I worked. English food—it's bad and tasteless. I usually ate lunch at an Italian restaurant." Low moans came from the next room, and Nitza excused herself to tend to her mother.

Her radio sits in the bedroom. "I listen to the BBC and short-wave from Canada and the English Caribbean so I can hear some English. The BBC is a good station."

Nitza's father, a Cuban, lived in New York in the 1920s, where he met her mother, an orphaned Cuban raised by Dominican nuns in Texas. He worked for Macy's in Latin American exports. "He lost his job after the stock market crash. Two of his brothers were closely linked to the dictator Machado. One was his private secretary, and the other was the majordomo of the *palacio.* My father had political inclinations to the left. That's why my name is Nitza—it's a Russian name. At least my dad thought it was. It was in honor of the October Revolution. After the Macy's job, my parents had to sell all they had to support the family, and my father sold Eskimo Pies on the streets. He would buy them in the morning, and if he didn't sell them we'd eat them at home that night. Many times that's all we had. This was during the Depression. I was very fat as a child." She smiled broadly.

"My father spoke English well but he had a foreign accent. In school they used to call me a Spanish onion. Once he came to school to pick me up and I ran up to him crying, 'Don't speak Spanish, Daddy, don't speak Spanish!' On weekends he'd take me to the Palisades or the Bronx Zoo. He used to think about Cuba so much. When he realized what society was doing to me, he'd take me to the Museum of Spanish Art near Riverside Drive every Sunday. I remember him saying, 'This is your culture. Never be ashamed of your heritage.'

"My father didn't want to come back to Cuba when Machado was president, but my mother said, 'If you want to stay you can, but I'm going back. No more New York winters for me.' So we sold all of our winter clothes and booked third-class passage. This was in July 1933. The women and the children were in one part,

and the men in another. We were *aplastados*," squished. Nitza
sobbed gently at the memory.

The Villapols sailed for three days on the *Orizaba,* the same
boat from which thirty-two-year old writer Hart Crane had
jumped to his death a year earlier. "My father cried as we entered
the Harbor. We could see the little Negroes dive into the filthy bay
for a penny from the tourists. The poor little children were almost
naked, underfed, and without any shoes. We arrived in Cuba just a
few days before the fall of Machado. I was nine."

Señor Villapol sold insurance and managed a press, where he
printed a Communist Party newspaper. Among his customers was
Carlos Rafael Rodríguez, now the country's vice president.

"He never asked me to give up my American citizenship or to
be a Cuban, but when I became of age I did anyway. He was so
happy.

"He wasn't fit for underground work, but if the Party needed
someone as a front to rent a house for a resting place, or an office
to work out of, he would do it. After Batista had staged his coup
and then Fidel attacked the Moncada, I said, what are you going to
do about it, join that crazy man? I meant Fidel, of course. Batista's
coup pushed Cuba back many years."

She stood up abruptly. "Let me get you something. Come with
me." She led me around the corner to the kitchen. "I'm a friendly
person, but I know I can be crazy. Here." She pulled a grapefruit
out of a bag. "We have the best grapefruit in the world. Our only
competitor is Israel." She squeezed two glasses of grapefruit juice.
Her sink overflowed with a week's dirty dishes. Every counter was
crowded with unwashed pots and pans, opened containers, spilled
food, unidentifiable leftovers, and drying liquid. The most envied
kitchen in the Pearl of the Antilles was a godawful mess. "On
weekends I clean up. I may have to hire someone. It's getting too
much to handle the house and my mother. I used to clean my
bathroom and kitchen with a toothpick. Now I've been told that

after the first of the year we won't have detergent because so much of it is imported."

"What will you clean with?"

"Soap! I remember the days before detergent when everything was washed with soap." She reached into a bag and pulled out some crackers. "And without detergent, we'll wash our things with *hoja de maguey*. Its juice is like soapwater, and the fiber is like an *estropajo*," a luffa. "The only hardship I won't be able to endure is if we have to stop the elevators. Those four floors will be a burden. I had polio when I was twenty-two. It's hard for me to walk. It's hard to take care of my mother and the apartment. But the Cuban people are not going to surrender. We're not going to go back! We're going to survive. It may be hard, but it's possible."

She opened her Coldspot. "Sometimes we have a power outage for two or three days and everything in the refrigerator spoils." She pulled out a cake and sliced two pieces. She loaded the cake, some crackers, and the fresh grapefruit juice on a small tray and we went back into the living room.

"I've been back to New York once since we left. I was at the Cloisters, and took a cab downtown. I told the driver, when you pass 137th Street, please go slowly. He asked me why, and I told him that I used to live there. He said, 'Lady, you wouldn't want to walk the streets there in the daytime now.'"

A soft dusk poured through the windows giving the apartment a nice muted glow. Or, put another way, it was almost dark and Nitza hadn't turned on a light.

"I think if I went back now I'd spend all my time at theaters and museums, and window shopping on Fifth Avenue. There's not much else worth doing there, is there? If I didn't live in Cuba I'd want to live in San Francisco or Rome."

The fresh-squeezed grapefruit was delicious.

"Last week's show was about grapefruit. I never work from a script. I just go to the studio and talk. I may repeat a recipe but what I say is different. I read. I read a lot. That's all my preparation. I love reading."

Nitza has earned the praise of three generations of Cubans for adapting to market conditions. When a shortage of tomatoes or an abundance of mangoes hits the produce bins, she knows, and adjusts her show accordingly. Her household food comes from the neighborhood market and bakery rather than the well-stocked Diplomercado, where, if she sought the privilege, she could surely buy groceries. *Cocina al minuto,* then weekly on Sunday mornings, could be like *Granma,* pretending that disaster hadn't struck, but her audience knows she uses only ingredients available to all. When she demonstrated bread making once, she mentioned that Cuba must import its wheat, while an unnamed country to the north actually pays its farmers *not* to grow wheat.

We finished our snack. "Whenever I make soup I put rum in it. Don't people put sherry in soup? Why not rum? One rainy night recently I put some rum into canned clam chowder. It was three-year-old rum. If it had been seven-year-old rum it would have been better. You can use seven-year-old rum in all recipes that call for sherry or brandy."

She finally turned a light on.

"You *must* see the prehistoric murals in Viñales." I had told Nitza that I was going to the province of Pinar del Río soon. "Before the Revolution, Pinar del Río was called La Cenicienta," Cinderella, "because it was so very poor. I was there once and I remember seeing a boy peeling sugarcane with his knife and a girl on a swing. An accident happened and she lost an eye. Her mother said, 'One eye is enough.' This was a very poor country. Before, the only hope was a lottery ticket. There was such a difference between the poor and the middle class. At the time of the Revolution you had to decide whether you were with the people or with those people who exploit the people. It's relatively easy to overthrow a dictatorship, but it's hard to build a society. It's very unfortunate that the so-called American way of life has blinded so many people. Most of my friends left the country. I couldn't because of the way I was brought up. I remember the day that Fidel said that this was to be a socialist society. I said, ah! This is what my father was talking about. He died two years before the Revolution."

The telephone rang, but the caller hung up before Nitza could reach the kitchen phone.

"We still have a hard time in front of us. We've done a lot, but we could've done more. What we have gained is not reversible. The only mistake Allende made in Chile was leaving the army with its old generals and its old people. I remember Fidel wouldn't come into Havana until the old guard had left. Stubborn men! *No se puede dejar la iglesia en manos de Lutero.*" You can't leave the church in Luther's hands.

"Fidel had an army of peasants. The people were illiterate, but they had fought the Revolution to be free. Lenin once said that no one escapes his time. I think that if you truly love something, you hang on. That's why a revolution has to be based on the people. I was a charter member of the Federación de Mujeres Cubanas," the Federation of Cuban Women, "and the Comités de Defensa de la Revolución. The first years of the Revolution were much harder than this. But with the help of the USSR we have survived. I'm not a member of the Communist Party but my feelings are Communist Party.

"I can understand that someone would not like it here if you didn't see this country before 1959. People used to dig in garbage cans for food. Whole families used to live on the streets. I had a teaching degree, and for five years I couldn't get a job because there simply weren't enough schools. And with so much illiteracy! To understand, you have to have lived it. It's not easy here. Between now and the end of the year we don't even know what will happen. It is a special period. Fidel has said it." She laughed.

"Lots of people think that this government will be overthrown.

But a true revolution brings so much to so many people, people who never had schools or hospitals, or who were discriminated against because of the color of their skin."

Nitza had talked with me for five hours. "I wonder if you see me as a fanatic. Because I'm sure, in spite of its problems, that what this country is doing is right. I'm sure we're on the right track."

HOLLY MORRIS

(1 9 6 5 –   )

As the editorial director of the publishing company Seal Press, Holly Morris edited books ranging in topic from domestic violence to international fiction to women's travel and adventure literature. Inspired by the stories but frustrated by being chained to a desk, Morris left her job and began a PBS television series, *Adventure Divas,* in which she searched the world for her own personal icons. The results are lively journeys through India, New Zealand, Iran, and Cuba, where she scouted out some of these nations' most intriguing women.

   This essay is based on Morris's pilot series, *Cuba: Paradox Found,* which began airing nationally in April 2000. In it, she describes encounters with an erotic poet in her eighties and the girls in a hip-hop group. Morris has published in two anthologies, *A Different Angle* and *Uncommon Waters,* about her long-standing passion, fishing. She is currently completing a book about women, globalization, and revolution, *Divadom,* that is forthcoming in 2005 and from which this is adapted.

ADVENTURE DIVAS

FIRST STOP: CUBA
Can the Revolution Really Be Televised?

Throughout the decades of Fidel Castro's revolution, Cuba had been just an enigmatic pinko blip on my radar and Fidel was an aging revolutionary stuck in a fatigued fashion rut. But then Cuba began to pulse in my consciousness. Friends who visited the country spoke of a place very different from the dour lockstep reality that one would expect from one of the last communist out-posts. The economic embargo had become a de facto information embargo, and we—a fledgling American documentary produc-tion company—were curious about what lay behind one of the last tinfoil curtains.

Whether you agree with the Cuban revolution's tenets or not, the revolution is still, in theory, going on. Witnessing the revolu-tion in action appealed to our underdog complex. Plus, a major thrust of Castro's socialist revolution was to liberate the poor and uneducated from the dire conditions created by a U.S.-backed dic-tator, Batista, who did not operate in the best interests of his people. To liberate the poor and uneducated, of course, is to transform women's lives. We wanted to know how the revolution was going, and what was up with our sisters ninety miles south. We wanted to explore Cuba through the lens of some of its divas.

The word "diva" articulated a zeitgeist I felt in the air—and the word's meaning had been morphing as it bubbled up through the cultural morass. No longer was "diva" weighed down by snotty prima donna opera singer baggage. I had started to see in diva-vision: to connect the dots, the acts, the ethos, the scrappy charge toward ideals that characterized the people I admired. The goal of finding these women around the world fueled our documentary series, *Adventure Divas*. In Cuba, a hip-hop group and an erotic poet were among our first subjects.

TRADING WITH THE ENEMY

We had not anticipated the antipathy (or in some cases, simple apathy) we received from the U.S. government and the Cuban Interests Section. For months we begged, we pleaded, we touted our professional stripes, we wore suits, for chrissakes, but no brass would okay our trip and grant us official credentials. We were a crew non grata. The ramifications of going on the sly for the shoot could be serious. Yet after four months of bureaucratic pandering we decided that toeing the line was overrated and that we would indeed go guerrilla, via Mexico. One by one, the crew was informed that we were going without permission (which, in government circles, could be construed as "trading with the enemy" should we have spent money there.) Were they still on board? "Not a problem," Cheryl, our cheerful New York–based reportage cinematographer responded. "Anything to stick it to Jesse Helms."

We made the clandestine trip through Cancún and eventually arrived in Havana, armed with our cameras and notebooks and a mad determination to capture a Cuba that is more complex than the three-bean "Fidel-Cigar-Salsa" salad that is a staple of the U.S. media diet.

The dashing Argentine revolutionary Che Guevara gazes intently over public squares and is lionized on every peso. He was intelligent, sensitive, literary—or so the legend goes. Cheryl dubs him El Hombre Guapo (The Handsome Man). Ironically, the living Fidel Castro's image is not prominently displayed, yet "El Lider" is omnipresent, like oxygen: all around, influencing everything, but invisible. Cheryl and I are laboriously translating a Marxist slogan, *Hasta La Victoria, Siempre!* (Until the Victory, Always!), which is splashed across the side of a building, when a young man walks up. *"¿De dónde eres? ¿Canadá? ¿Inglaterra?"* he says. *"Los Estados Unidos,"* Cheryl responds cautiously. He is surprised, but friendly. "The bar where Hemingway drank mojitos every afternoon is right around the corner." Hemingway. Thus the Fidel-Che-Ernest trifecta of Cuba's male cultural icons is complete. We cheerfully explain that we're more interested in finding our own brand of icon: "We want to interview women who are visionary and accomplished—you know—divas." The man backs away slowly, smiling kindly, and walks off.

INSTINTO: RAPPERS
"We are like a vitamin for other young women."

Filming guerrilla style, and doing so in Cuba, means that this is a far from seamless venture. We blame the economic embargo—which does in fact also behave like an information embargo—for our lack of research about divas. But, as with those Cubans who blame the embargo entirely for the failed economy, our explanation for our unpreparedness is only partly true.

By necessity, we are now committed to serendipity—and in fact banking on it—and we decide that it is time to get streetwise. Cheryl and I wander toward the local stickball game, which is taking place in a mostly vacant lot. Remnants of a building from an era past provide the bases in the Cuban version of America's favorite pastime. Baseball is probably our respective countries' most profound common love. Half a roll of film in, we talk to twelve-year-old Oscar. After Cheryl goes to bat (a double), we ask him what's happening around Havana, and Oscar says his cousin said he knows someone who knows someone who said that there's a girl rap group called Instinto performing in a basement near Revolution Square in "a little while."

We had heard about Instinto through some local contacts, but now we are hot on their trail. We grab our gear, pile into a '57 Bel Air hardtop, and ten minutes later are unloaded near a massive statue of José Martí. Revolution Square is home to a slew of ministry buildings (in all shades of gray), the requisite Che mural, the "Comité" of the Communist Party, and all the offices where Fidel and the council of ministers do politics. In short, we are inside the beltway, madly running toward a basement full of rappers.

The basement is pulsing with teenagers and twenty-somethings, all of whom are showing considerable skin. The place is absolutely in blossom—pheromones zinging between people and off walls with an abandon that only takes place below the Tropic of Cancer. The fourteen-year-old girl in her first tube top, working the brand-new goods, epitomizes the high-pitched atmosphere. It is dark, which creates difficulties for filming purposes. Yet, when Instinto takes the stage, it's like good art—you know it when you see it: divas. Suddenly, light is shed all over the dingy basement. Talent. Voice. Belly. Booty. Confidence. Instinto has a visceral liberation all of us gringas covet.

> *come on get closer*
> *i don't want to shock you*
> *i want to rap you close*
> *there is no wizard here*
> *what i do is art*

When Instinto climbs offstage I talk to their lead singer, Iramis.

"Would you mind doing an ad hoc show for us tomorrow, and perhaps an interview?" I ask after introducing myself.

"*Sin problema,*" (no problem), responds Janet.

The next day Janet, Iramis, and Dori show up in a cobblestone square at the appointed time and with three claps of their hands begin an a cappella street performance that would have MTV execs drooling. Born to perform—no choreographer, no microphones or advance preparation, Instinto commands the square.

Midperformance, a grammar school lets out, and little girls and boys in black and red school outfits organically merge into the performance. We keep shooting. Instinto's "mmmph" washes over the kids, who start doing their best to emulate them. Instinto performs three flawless takes for us, and in between each we talk about what fuels their music and the effect they have. With my limited Spanish, and instantly dashing to smithereens any chance of ever getting a gig with *Rolling Stone,* I ask the obvious, "*¿Hay instinto en su música?*" (Is there instinct in your music?)

"There is sooo much. Too much. Everything we do, we do with instinct. We are like a vitamin for other young women," says Janet (pronounced yan-nay).

Instinto's confidence is infectious and their style comes from deep within. The sensual is a food group here— and that isn't only evident where dark basements and pheromones intersect. Cuba is intrinsically sexy—in the best sense of the word. What seems to epitomize this high order of evolution is the way in which women totally "own" their butts. The ladies ownin' it is just representative of the sexy continuum, *sexus inherentus,* if you will, which seems to show itself in everything from a glance during a salsa move to the deliberate stir of a mojito.

I ask Instinto how they think they are perceived.

"We are seen as a symbol of courage, because rap is a genre that is almost always about protest. So we are different from other women's groups in Cuba, which are mostly salsa, and they don't have the flexibility to say what we say in our music. We are proud of that."

Wobbly antennas atop Soviet-designed high-rises may have yielded the first sounds of hijacked rap straight from the shores of Miami, but Afro-Cuban rhythms, identity politics, and local realities were quickly infused into Cuban rap to create a distinctive art form. Rap became a vehicle to express frustration about poverty, racism, and the daily challenges of living in contemporary Cuba— and successfully wedged a crack for freedom of expression in a state big on censorship. Unlike the United States, where racism is evident on all levels, it seems as if racism exists primarily on political and economic levels in Cuba, but less so in terms of daily interactions and petty discriminations. Clearly, Instinto would rather show than tell, and they hit the cobblestones again to do some more rhyming.

> *word is we're smooth as wine.*
> *we are instinct personified.*
> *rap is my addiction, to deny the affliction of prejudice.*
> *yes, this music has more americana flavor, but it's made by my people*
> *and me.*
> *we mix and we conquer. we do it for you.*

CARILDA OLIVER LABRA: POET
". . . it has lost the scent of Cuba"

Poets, of course, are the natural peddlers of love. They are the ones who torch up an eight-ball of life's giant je ne sais quoi and distill it down to a pot of sweet nectar. So, it is a poet we are going to see in Matanzas. We have noticed her volumes of award-winning poetry in the country's ubiquitous bookstalls. Her first collection, *Lyric Prelude,* established her as an important voice. In 1950, she won the National Prize for her book *At the South of My Throat.* She took considerable heat in the forties and fifties for the steamy content of some of her work, and her collection *Feverish Memory* sealed her reputation as an erotic writer. Now, with age and increased government tolerance, she has transformed from scandalous hellion into Cuban national treasure.

The little cobblestoned town of Matanzas is a port city of fabled austerity. In the early 1800s, booming with wealth from the slave and sugar trades, the town became a cultural mecca of sorts, and it remains so today as a home to many artists, poets, and writers. Labra's house, small and elegant, oozes with intellectual richness and sturdy supple-leather good taste. We walk in and the living room is abuzz with a small group of women who seem like handlers. They are fawning and doting and, well, handling. (I later find out they are representatives of the Cuban Women's Federation.)

Carilda is wearing a white linen blazer, and her big red hair frames a warm smile. She is as creased and sparkly and attractive as her home, but the most striking thing about her is that she is in a hurry. She is the first person I've met in Cuba who is actually in a hurry.

Carilda is on her way to give a reading in a nearby town but still has us in for a quick visit. Her forty-something-looking husband breezes through, and it occurs to me that she must still have that erotic spark that created so many poems. Carilda is eighty-one.

Despite her standing in Cuba, Carilda is little known in the

United States, and only one of her volumes of poetry has been translated into English. Most of the books by Cuban writers available in the United States are by Cubans who left with the revolution, or their offspring: first-generation Cuban Americans. When it comes to music—rap, say—illegal satellite dishes and bootleg tapes spread that Americana quickly through Cuba. Black market poetry has yet to become en vogue, though many organizations, such as Global Exchange, work hard to encourage a steady trickle of cultural to-and-fro. There is also the challenge of being published in her own country—not for lack of popularity but rather for lack of paper on which to print the books.

The Cuban Missile Crisis of 1962 inspired Carilda to write "Declaration of Love," which is a sheer tribute to eros and politics.

> *I ask if I'm wise*
> *when I awaken*
> *the danger between his thighs.*
> *or if I'm wrong*
> *when my kisses prepare only a trench*
> *in his throat.*
>
> *I know that war is probable*
> *especially today*
> *because a red geranium has blossomed open.*
>
> *Please don't point your weapons*
> *at the sky:*
> *the sparrows are terrorized,*
> *and it's springtime,*
> *it's raining,*
> *the meadows are ruminating.*
> *Please, you'll melt the moon, only night light of the poor.*
>
> *It's not that I'm afraid,*
> *or a coward,*

I'd do everything for my homeland;
but don't argue so much over your nuclear missiles,
because something horrible is happening
and I haven't had time enough to love.

Carilda offers to read us one poem before she leaves. I am secretly hoping for an erotic one, since I loathe how older women are regarded as asexual the world over.

"What are you going to read us?" I ask.

"When my grandmother came from Spain, married with her three little kids, one of which was my mother, she brought a little bit of Spanish soil in a bag. Once in a while, I would see my grandmother taking the little bag that contained the soil and smelling it, thinking 'Ay, my Spanish land, I will never go back to Spain,' with such nostalgia and sadness. Then, when my mother went into exile, I remember that she searched for a little bag and filled it with Cuban soil. When I visited her for the first time in the United States, she said to me: 'Didn't you bring a little bit of soil?' I said, 'But you already have a little bit of soil.' She said, 'Yes, but it has lost the scent of Cuba.'

"My mother never could come back to Cuba, and that is why this poem was born," she tells me as she settles back into a rocking chair and opens a volume to read.

When my grandmother came she brought a bit of Spanish soil
When my mother left, she took a bit of Cuban soil
I will carry no bit of homeland
I want it all above my grave.

THOMAS BARBOUR
(1 8 8 4 – 1 9 4 6)

Thomas Barbour coauthored *The Herpetology of Cuba* with Charles T. Ramsden in 1919, and it was hailed as the first English-language catalog of the frogs, toads, lizards, snakes, and turtles of Cuba. This was followed by his breakthrough book, *The Birds of Cuba,* in 1923, in which he chronicles the marvelous avian life on this lush, tropical island, including the three new species of birds Barbour himself identified. Both books are still considered seminal works and invaluable references for scientists, naturalists, and nature lovers interested in Cuba. While passionately exploring the caves, mountainsides, and mangrove forests of Cuba, Barbour befriended Cuban scientists, farmers, guides, and North American expatriates along the way. He recorded his experiences of the people and places of the largest of all islands in the West Indies in his marvelous book *A Naturalist in Cuba* (1945). In this book readers learn about American sugar planter Edwin Atkins, who lived most of his life in Cuba and whose land became known as the Soledad Gardens. This became the Atkins Institution, where Harvard students and professors joined Cuban scientists for tropical research on plants and trees that impacted botany in all tropical climates. After the revolution of 1959, Harvard terminated its support, and the area became the Cienfuegos Botanical Garden, and remains a very popular tourist destination. Since 1995, cultural and academic travel has sometimes been permitted to Cuba from the United States, and scientists from both countries are beginning to work together again to understand the natural wonders of Cuba. Although Barbour's aims were scientific, his musings and reports, his cataloging and collecting take on the feel of poetry, and readers experience Barbour's melancholy upon leaving this magical place he grew to know so intimately.

from A NATURALIST IN CUBA

My memories of Harvard House and the garden at Soledad stand among those at the very top on the list of all those which I hold treasured most affectionately. On that morning of which I am thinking I opened my eyes and then closed them again, to see in memory once more the opalescent light which suffuses the cane fields at dawn—that extraordinary lighting up in the early morning, whose beauty is matched in the tropics by the equally short period of waning light at evening. I saw the mist lying over the valley and then the waxing power of the sun; the glitter and the shimmer which is in the air at midday, and the hushing of the birds.

I said to myself, "It's rather a pity that we don't have at Soledad that strange rising and falling chorus of insects' voices which one may hear at noontide made by the cicadas as they sing in the highlands of Costa Rica"—their voices roaring out and then growing stilled again as clouds pass and repass the face of the sun at midday. Then I saw, in my half-closed eyes, that peculiar velvety texture of the sky by night and the preternaturally vivid stars. Such are the memories which haunt me now with an all-pervading aura more keenly since it has become clear that I shall never be well enough to go to the tropics again.

It is unfortunate that it is not within my powers to set forth the happy way in which the presence of different personalities has always impinged on my consciousness to produce within me a veritable kaleidoscope of impressions. I walk about the Garden with David Fairchild and his reactions produce one set of concomitant reflections on my part, and so on with all the great number of friends, some botanical, some zoological, and others both Cuban and American, simply those who never before have seen the innumerable wonders which this Garden offers. To me no two visits have ever produced sensations which were alike; even, for that matter, when I have been walking about alone.

Two shelters, where I often took refuge against a sudden shower, I always associated with birds. One little kiosk is nestled at the foot of a giant ceiba tree in a leafy copse which is always cool and tranquil. I don't think I ever rested there during the happy days when I smoked those most excellent cigars (procurable at the *tienda* down by the mill near Harvard House) without soon seeing a tody. I seldom if ever sat puffing away at my *breva,* my head buzzing with plans for new plantings, without hearing in a few moments that sudden snapping sound which often is so suddenly evident in the air but a few paces away. The todies are tiny verdigris busybodies far smaller than an English sparrow and they fly from perch to perch much like one of our flycatchers, except that they do not pounce on a moth miller or a droning beetle and then return to the same stance. They keep circulating about from pillar to post, so to speak, and as they make each foray their wings snap like those of a giant grasshopper at each take-off. They are tame as can be and I have often stared at one but a few feet from my very face and eyes as it perched with its flattened beak tipped up, the better to show its lovely rose-colored gorget. They look so incredibly like the miniature kingfisher, which, with due allowance for evolutionary modification for a forest habitat, they are. To be sure, they invade open fields at times and then how the beekeepers hate them!

My other favorite resting place where birds are always very much in evidence is on the hill in "Arizona," that little eminence in the midst of the collection of succulents where one may rest to gaze at the Trinidad Mountains, sitting down in a little tile-roofed mirador of *mampostería,* or stucco if you prefer. Here there is always a Cuban sparrow hawk to be seen balanced on the tip of some one of the many century-plant flower spikes which tower to fifteen or more feet in the air on either hand. Doves and meadow larks are always scuttling about on the ground and I promise you that you won't wait five minutes before one male Ricord's hummer arrives to chase another away from the rose-pink cluster of

blossoms of the Kalanchoe plants which are planted about the
walls of our sightly little hut. For years it has been a pleasure to
walk about with new-come bird lovers and to promise them these
joys morning and evening. I was almost going to say morning,
noon, or eve, but I might be drawing the long bow just a bit.

I appreciate the utter inadequacy of the pictures which I have
tried to draw. But who can hope to describe in words one's instant
impression as one suddenly comes face to face with a tree trunk
with gorgeous orchids nestled upon its drab bark? Clusters of any
of the myriad species which, here in the North, we cannot visual-
ize as they appear when they are growing at home. Many emerge
into their glory during the height of the dry season; on the other
hand, many of the flowering trees are brought into their first flush
of splendor by the rains of springtime.

It has been my good fortune to see the Garden during every
month of the year and I would not be able to say surely whether,
if I were to revisit it but once again, I should pray that the visit
might be during the dry time of our winter or during the rains of
Cuban summer.

I am not thinking of creature comforts either. I admit that,
considering these, the dry season wins. We can then keep the grass
and the myriad pricking burrs and the spiny seeds more easily in
control, and, in summer, Cuban soil makes the stickiest of gumbo
mud. Most visitors are a good deal more comfortable walking in
the dry season when the heat is somewhat less than it is in summer.

We are fortunate to have at the Garden not only those shelters
against sudden showers which I have described, but that other
excellent and spacious resting place built by one of my warm
friends who would scalp me did I but mention his name. Here
groups of students may sit comfortably protected from rain or
sun and listen to such informal instruction as we may offer from
time to time. The Soledad Garden was my first love in Cuba and
as I look back at it after thirty years' affiliation, I believe that the

Atkins Institution of the Arnold Arboretum, which is now the official and, I must confess, rather clumsy title, is destined to a great future. It will increase and grow as one of the brightest stars in Harvard's crown and grow also in beneficent activities to the end that Cuba may be ever more conscious of her own potentialities and our own country be more alive to those of its lovely neighbor.

So ends my little story; a curious hodgepodge, if you will, of sociology, natural history, geology, paleontology; mostly however my own observations and for that reason alone perhaps worthwhile. One final question, however, comes to the fore as I sit here in my garden in Beverly Farms. Why do I care, why do I have a strange feeling of sadness which is very difficult to shake off and which is simply because the realization is just a bit overwhelming that I shall probably never see Cuba again? I wonder what there is about the place that makes me feel this way.

I write in my garden at Beverly Farms. The surroundings are superlatively lovely. My wife is a born gardener and we live surrounded by a riot of color, infinitely more varied and more ebullient than anything which the tropics ever produce, and yet there is something, much as I love our country and our landscape, that is eternally missing. I think one absorbs through the nose more impressions than one suspects. Of course, here everything smells different. I miss the smell of smoke at dawn, of coffee roasting for the fresh day's supply. In the country in Cuba, too, so many flowers give off their fragrance with the coming on of dark, which is not so often the case with our garden plants.

Then what has been most impressive to me ever since I first went to the tropics was the recurring thrill of dawn and nightfall. The coming of our dawn is a dawdling affair, especially as the days shorten and winter comes on. In Cuba I step out in the morning and the great stars which seem so much larger than ours look like illuminated holes punched in black velvet. Then all of a sudden light appears in the east and in less time than it takes to talk about it the sun has appeared and it is broad daylight. So also in the evening. I remember years ago in Havana I often took a drive around the Malecón to wind up the day. All of a sudden the light on Morro Castle flashed, the policemen blew their whistles, and every cabby stepped down, scratched his little wax match, and lit the lamp. It was night, with that lovely soft cool freshness that comes in all but the very hottest weather.

I guess perhaps I have found the answer. I believe what I miss is daylight and the sudden gloaming, and then, of course, the beloved friends that I inevitably associate with my Cuban visits, and I might as well be quite earthy and admit it, I miss imaginative food—not the sort of material that Anglo-Saxons prepare for their meals. I think that completes the answer.

EXILES, IMMIGRANTS, AND THEIR OFFSPRING

///.

"My head buzzed with the sudden recognition of a place that held something for me beyond memory."

—*Rosa Lowinger*

OSCAR HIJUELOS

(1 9 5 1 –   )

The characters in the many novels of Oscar Hijuelos live and die by music, whether mournful boleros about broken hearts, memory-laden cha-cha-chas, or soulful mambo jazz rifts. Hijuelos was the first Hispanic American novelist to win the Pulitzer Prize for fiction, for his 1989 novel *The Mambo Kings Play Songs of Love*. For the characters in this book, music ties the past to the present, connecting a distant island receding into myth to the ambitions and dreams of immigrants living in Spanish Harlem. Born in the United States to parents from Cuba, Hijuelos provides an insightful look into the lives of musicians whose art is to shape desire into notes and stanzas, and who embody the evolution of salsa from the African rhythms of Cuba to the jazz big bands of New York City in the 1950s.

from THE MAMBO KINGS PLAY SONGS OF LOVE

Pending late nights out, they'd find themselves climbing the stairs to their cousin Pablo's fourth-floor apartment on La Salle Street at five in the morning. Rooftops burning red, and black birds circling the water towers. Cesar was thirty-one years old then and out to have a good time, preferring to look forward and never back into his past: he'd left a kid, a daughter, behind in Cuba. Sometimes he had pangs for his daughter, sometimes felt bad that things didn't work out with his former wife, but he remained determined to have a good time, chase women, drink, eat, and make friends. He wasn't coldhearted: he had moments of tenderness that surprised him toward the women he went out with, as if he wanted truly to fall in love, and even tender thoughts about his former wife. He had other moments when he didn't care. Marriage? Never again, he'd tell himself, even though he'd lie through his teeth about wanting to get married to women he was trying to seduce. Marriage? What for?

He heard a lot about "a family and love" from Pablo's plump little wife. "That's what makes a man happy, not just playing the mambo," she'd say.

He had moments when he thought about his wife, a hole of sadness through his heart, but it was nothing that a drink, a woman, a cha-cha-cha wouldn't fix. He had hooked up with her a long time ago because of Julián García, a well-known bandleader in Oriente Province. He was just a young upstart from Las Piñas then, a singer and trumpet player with a wandering troupe of *guajiro* musicians who would play in the small-town plazas and dance halls of Camagüey and Oriente Provinces. Sixteen years old, he fled to the dance halls, had a good time meeting and entertaining the people of small towns and bedding down poor country girls where he could find them. He was a handsome and exuberant singer, with an unpolished style and a tendency toward operatic flourishes that would take him off-key.

These musicians never made any money, but one day when they were playing at a dance in a small town called Jiguaní, his youthful exuberance and looks had impressed someone in the crowd who passed his name to Julián García. At the time he was looking for a new crooner and wrote a letter simply addressed "Cesar Castillo, Las Piñas, Oriente." Cesar was nineteen then, and not yet jaded. He took the invitation to heart and made the journey down to Santiago the week after he'd received it.

He'd always remember the steep hills of Santiago de Cuba, a city reminiscent in its hilliness, he would think years later, of San Francisco, California. Julián lived in an apartment over a dance hall which he owned. The sun radiating against the cobblestone streets and cool doorways from which one could smell the afternoon lunches and hear the comforting sounds of families dining at their tables. Brooms sweeping out a hallway, salamanders skulking along the arabesque tiles. García's dance hall was a refuge of shady arcades and a long, cool inner hallway. The place was deserted except for García, who sat in the middle of a colonnaded dance floor tinkling at the piano, stout, sweaty, and with a head damp with running hair dye.

"I'm Cesar Castillo, and you told me to come and sing for you one day."

"Yes, yes."

For his audition he opened with Ernesto Lecuona's "*María la O.*"

Nervous about performing for Julián García, Cesar sang his heart out in a flamboyant style, using extended high notes and long, slow phrasing, arms flailing dramatically. When he'd finished, Julián nodded encouragingly and kept him there, singing, until ten o'clock that night.

"You come back here tomorrow. The other musicians will be here, okay?"

And in a friendly, paternal manner, his hand on Cesar's shoulder, Julián led him out of the hall.

Cesar had a few dollars in his pocket. He was planning to wander around the harbor and have some fun, fall asleep on one of the piers by the ocean, as he had so many times before, arms thrown over his face, in fields in the countryside, in the plazas, on church steps. He was so used to looking out for himself that it surprised him to hear García ask, "And do you have a place to sleep tonight?"

"No." And he shrugged.

"*Bueno,* you can stay with me upstairs. Huh? I should have told you that in the letter."

Remaining that night, the future Mambo King basked in Julián's kindness. High on that hill and overlooking the harbor, that apartment was a pleasant change for him. He had his own room, which opened up to a balcony, and all the food he could eat. That was the order of the household: all of García's family, his wife and four sons, lived for their evening meals. His sons, who performed with him, were immense, overfed, with cheerful angelic dispositions. That was because Julián was so loving, an affectionate man who even challenged Cesar's macho resolve to need or want no one.

He began to sing with Julián's outfit, a twenty-piece orchestra, in 1937. They had a pleasant "tropical" sound, depending heavily on violins and sonorous flutes, and their rhythm section dragged as in the style of fox-trotters of the twenties, and Julián, who conducted and played the piano, had a penchant for dreamlike orchestrations, clouds of music that seemed to float upward on waves of tremolo-choked piano. The Mambo King would have one photograph of that orchestra—and this sat in that envelope in the Hotel Splendour—of himself in a formal black suit, wearing white gloves, sitting in a row with the others. Behind them, a backdrop of Havana Harbor and El Morro Castle, flanked by pedestals on which Julián had placed small statues of antique themes—a wingèd victory and a bust of Julius Caesar, and large ostrich-plume-filled vases. What was that look on Cesar's face? With his black hair combed back and parted in the middle, he was pleasantly smiling, in commemoration of that happy time in his life.

Julián's orchestra packed dance halls all over Oriente and Camagüey. He had conservative tastes, never playing original compositions but relying on the songs of the popular Cuban composers of the day: Eduardo Sánchez de Fuentes, Manuel Luna, Moisés Simón, Miguel Matamoros, Eliseo Grenet, Lecuona. He was the warmest human being Cesar Castillo would ever meet in his life. That portly orchestra leader exuded pure love for his fellowman—"A family and love, that's what makes a man happy"—and showed this affection to his musicians. That was a time when the Mambo King was close to becoming a different kind of human being.

Cesar never let go of his liking for women. He maintained his king-cock strut and manly arrogance, but around Julián and his family, he felt so peaceful that he calmed down. And it showed in his singing. He gained more control, became more lilting, and developed an affectionate tone in his songs, which people liked and responded to. He had not yet found a way of transforming that into the world-weariness of his records in the midfifties. (And if you heard the wrecked voice of Cesar in 1978 and compared it to the golden-toned voice of the 1930s and 1940s, you would have a hard time believing they came from the same singer.) They played all over the provinces in towns with names like Bayamo, Jobabo, Minas, Morón, Miranda, Yara, El Cobre, and in the larger cities of Camagüey, Holguín, and Santiago. They traveled in three trucks and they would make their way down dirt roads, struggling through the brush and forests of the countryside, and into the mountains. They played for *campesinos,* soldiers, bureaucrats, businessmen. They played for people who lived in houses with palm-thatch roofs, for those who lived in grand-style Spanish villas, and in the plantations and sugar mills, and in beautiful citrus groves, for the Americans who had constructed New England frame clapboard houses, with little back gardens and front porches. They played in towns without modern plumbing or electricity where people hardly knew the name of Hitler, in countryside so dark that the stars were a veil of light and where the thready luminescence of spirits moved through the streets and over the walls at night and where the arrival of Julián's orchestra was greeted like the Second Coming of Christ, with children and dogs and crowds of teenagers following behind it, clapping and whistling wherever they went. They played weddings, baptisms, and confirmation parties, *fiestas de quince,* and *fiestas blancas,* where the participants dressed in white from head to toe. They'd perform waltzes and *danzones* for the old people, and floor-sliding tangos and steamy rumbas for the young.

Julián was a good orchestra leader and a good man. Cesar would have thought of Julián as a "second father" if the word "father" did not make him want to punch a wall. In that time, he learned much about putting together an orchestra and singing from Julián, and enjoyed the glory of performance. He used to throw himself completely into his songs and lived for the moment when the entire ballroom would be on its feet either dancing or applauding.

"Just make them feel that you care for them. You don't have to overdo it, because they know that, but let them know all the same."

While singing with Julián's orchestra the Mambo King became well known. He could walk down the street of many a small town and there would always be someone to come up to him and say, "Aren't you Cesar Castillo the singer?" He started to acquire a lordly bearing, though one that fell apart when it came to chasing women. Returning to the farm in Las Piñas for his monthly visits, he would feel as if he had come home to a haunted house, the site of many of his fights with his father and the sadness of his mother's weeping that filled the halls. He would return with presents and advice and with a desire for peace that always erupted, after a day or so, into another fight with his father, Don Pedro, who considered musicians effeminate, doomed men. He'd return and give Nestor music lessons, take Nestor to town. Always impressed with his brother's musicianship, he had plans to take Nestor into Julián's orchestra when he was of age and the family would let him leave the house.

Now he remembers and sighs: the long approach to the farm along the riverbank and forest, the dirt road past the houses and over the water, the sun bursting through the treetops. The Mambo King riding on a borrowed mule, a guitar slung over his shoulders . . .

He had been in the orchestra for four years when he attended a weekend party at Julián's apartment in Santiago and there made the acquaintance of his niece, Luisa García. He was the handsome young crooner at the end of the table, reveling in the friendship of this older man, guzzling Spanish brandy all night and feeling light-headed enough to easily fall in love. And there she was, Luisa. Sitting across from her during the meal, he smiled and kept staring into her eyes, but she would turn away. Shy and thin, with a plain face, Luisa had a large beaked nose, pretty eyes, and a kindly expression. She liked to wear simple dresses. Although her body was not spectacular, her skin gave off a nice scent of oils and perfume, and when he stood beside her, filling a glass from a punch bowl, he knew she would turn out to be a passionate lover.

She was a schoolteacher and, at twenty-six, three years older than the Mambo King. No one in her family held out much hope that she would get married, but that night the way Cesar kept looking at her became a subject of family gossip. Julián could not have been more delighted. He would call them together and speak to them jointly. "I wanted to show you both the view from this window. Isn't that something there, the sun's rays spreading everywhere. *¿Qué bueno, eh?*"

RUTH BEHAR

(1 9 5 6 –   )

Ruth Behar's work as a writer and anthropologist has always been intimately
intertwined with the Spanish-speaking world. Professor of Anthropology at
the University of Michigan, she explores the themes of home, identity, and
loss from the perspective of both an immigrant and that of a Jewish woman
from Latin America. Behar was born in Havana and moved with her family to
New York in 1962. She has worked to create a dialogue between the splin-
tered camps of Cuban exiles and the denizens of Cuba with an anthology she
edited, *Bridges to Cuba,* that presents essays by Cuban American writers trying to reconcile their own lives within the context of bitter political conflict.
Ruth Behar's first book, *The Presence of the Past in a Spanish Village: Santa
María del Monte,* documents the social transformations of a village in Spain
during the late Franco years. Her second book, *Translated Woman: Crossing
the Border with Esperanza's Story,* an account of her friendship with a Mexican street peddler, gained her national prominence. The short story reprinted
here, "In the Absence of Love," was initially published in *The House of Memory,* a collection of stories by Jewish women from Latin America.

IN THE ABSENCE OF LOVE

"When I say that I no longer loved him, I mean
to say that you have no idea to what lengths one
can go in the absence of love."

"Give me some idea."

"I can't."

—Marguerite Duras,
The Ravishing of Lol Stein

In the absence of love, I am going to Cuba again. It's my seventh
trip. I no longer have a reason to return. There is nothing left to
find, nothing left to bring back. I have taken pictures of the forlorn houses in Old Havana where my mother grew up, where my
father grew up. I have walked through the rooms of our apartment and sat on the edge of the bed where my parents once made
love. I have sat on that bed with the striped bumpy spread that's
under a window looking toward the sea. I have stood again under
the brass lions of the Patronato Synagogue. I have stood on that
same spot where a picture was taken of me when I was four, a
Cuban flag half slipping out of my hand. I have gone as far as
the town whose sugar slopes cannot stop weeping for the Indians
and the slaves. I have gone as far as that town where my great-
grandfather brought the family from Poland, only to spend nights
of oblivion hunched before his account books, writing stories in
Yiddish of his childhood.

I don't understand anything.

My marriage has ended, but we're staying together because neither of us has the time or energy to do anything else. We have a
son who's more attached to his father than to me. Whenever he
needs anything, he calls out "Daddy!"—a wail as desperate as a

shofar* sounding in the desert. It's the price I've paid for being a professional woman. All of my son's friends are being raised by single mothers, divorced or never married, and they watch us like hawks. They flirt with my husband and wait for me to join them.

I'm going to Cuba for two weeks. I've lost weight, so I won't feel bad this time about looking fat while everyone else goes on a national Weight Watcher's program because of all the shortages. From the sale rack of the store that has all the rayon Javanese clothes, which I usually can't wear because it's too cold here, I've picked out a short dress with a drop waist. It has thin spaghetti straps that I'll need to tie into bows to keep them from falling off my shoulders. The dress is pale gray embedded with pale pink flowers. I don't know yet what shoes I'll wear with it. Everything I have is black and too heavy for that paper-thin dress with its little girl flounce. I need sandals. And I'll have to paint my toenails a shade of dusty rose.

I don't expect anything to happen in Cuba. I mean, a love affair or something like that. I'm too cautious. I won't let myself be used by some guy who needs a plane ticket to Miami. Politically, who knows what could happen? I've always suspected I'll end up there in the midst of the final chaos, during the last chapter of the Revolution. As the book is being closed. That's the price I imagine fate expects me to pay for returning after there's nothing left to find, nothing left to bring home.

He always said it didn't matter if I didn't love him. He had enough love for the two of us. More than enough for the two of us. I wanted him to prove it to me. I don't like false promises. That's why I held back. Gave little. I think he was lying. His love wasn't boundless. It ran out. Or maybe he just got tired. Men get tired, my mother always said. I guess I pushed too hard. But I won't blame myself. It's the cultural differences—what in the

---

*A shofar is a ram's horn, used in ancient times as a signaling trumpet, and still blown in synagogues on High Holy Days.

world could have brought together a Jewish Cuban woman carrying too much history on her back and a bashful guy from Texas who thrives on peanut butter and sliced banana glued together with mayonnaise? Pure madness, nothing but pure madness.

And yet I know our good-bye at the airport will be so tender that I'll believe I almost love him. I'll beg him to wish good things for me. As I step onto the plane, my heart will shatter like glass under my feet.

Just like last year, I'm going to Cuba on a Jewish humanitarian mission. It's one of the few ways to get into the country. All expenses paid in advance, staying at the best hotels. Bringing dried milk, powdered eggs, and potato flakes, stuff you eat in times of famine or war. For the last thousand Jews still living on the island. We're enchanted by the idea of helping the Jews who stayed behind, guarding over the palm trees. It makes us feel better about having left.

The first day in Cuba, it will be the same as always: we'll visit dead Jews first. In an air-conditioned bus they'll take us to the Jewish cemetery in Guanabacoa. I've gone many times, taken many pictures of the moldy graves and their salty Stars of David. But I will put on my new gray and pink dress and go again.

I'll leave a stone at the grave of my cousin, who died of leukemia.

I'll leave a stone at the grave of my great-uncle, who died of cancer.

I'll leave a stone at the site where they buried that sliver of soap made of sorrow and bitterness.

And before I wash my hands, I'll leave a stone by the gate.

For the losses I can't name. In case I don't return.

CRISTINA GARCÍA

(1 9 5 8 –   )

Cristina García was born in Havana but moved to New York City with her parents as a young child in 1961. Her first novel, *Dreaming in Cuban,* was nominated for the National Book Award in 1992. Her next novels, *The Agüero Sisters* and *Monkey Hunting,* earned García a reputation as one of the most prominent Cuban American writers. García grew up speaking Spanish in her home while living in an English-speaking society. She was raised far from Cuban American communities, and rather than rage against the past, she uses her essays and fiction to weave these fractured elements together; her writings depict relationships that span generations and countries and are developed with deftness and compassion. In her essay "Simple Life," García visits relatives in Cuba and learns about the Cuban talent for overcoming "all obstacles with inventiveness, spontaneity, and most important, humor."

SIMPLE LIFE

It was about four in the morning, and I was sitting on the porch of my aunt's house in Guanabo, a seaside town east of Havana, catching up on eleven years' worth of family news. The ocean breeze stirred the fronds of the coconut palms on her modest property as we swayed in our rocking chairs, keeping time with the rhythm of our stories, interrupting them with frequent bursts of laughter. Not fifty feet from us, the surf broke against an outcrop of rocks and a narrow lip of beach.

In the midst of one reminiscence or another, I heard a harsh buzzing sound, and then all was blackness.

"*Coño, otro apagón,*" my Tía Amada said, referring to the frequent blackouts of electricity that plague nearly every town on the island. But just as she was about to launch into her familiar litany of complaints against what is known as the "special period" in Cuba, a time of renewed sacrifice and deprivation, Tía Amada noticed my face. I was staring up at the sky, speechless with wonder. There was no moon that night, not even so much as a single bulb burning anywhere in the vicinity, but above us, the heavens looked as if they would collapse with stars. This was the unintentional gift from the apagón.

To me, that moment represents what I love most about Cuba. *No hay mal que por bien no venga.* This is a quintessential Cuban expression, a kind of mantra. Roughly translated, it means "good comes out of even the worst experiences." I heard it at least a dozen times a day.

Cubans are masters at making the best out of any difficult situation. *Resolver,* to resolve, is probably the most commonly used verb in the language on the island. "Resolver" can mean resuscitating a twenty-year-old Russian Lada for a ride to the beach or tracking down a single out-of-season sweet potato for a dessert offering to Yemayá, goddess of the seas.

One Saturday afternoon in Havana, I casually mentioned to my uncle, Tío Jorge, that I was yearning for a piece of cake. About four hours later a prim man appeared at our door carrying an enormous coconut layer cake topped with fluffy pink meringue. It turned out that the delivery man was, in fact, a heart surgeon who bakes cakes on weekends for extra cash. He is in high demand for weddings.

In Cuba, "resolver" means to survive, to overcome all obstacles with inventiveness, spontaneity, and most important, humor.

Recently my Tía Amada, who rents out part of her beach bungalow to foreign tourists, received a request from her guests, a demanding Canadian businessman and his wife, for a duck dinner.

My aunt, unfazed, assured the couple that they could expect their duck promptly at seven o'clock that evening. Need I add that my aunt had never cooked a duck in her life?

That day I accompanied Tía Amada to the farmer's market to track down a duck. There was only one available, scrawny and unsightly with half-plucked quills. She bargained hard and bought it for four dollars.

Back home, my aunt proceeded to wash the creature from her limited supply of fresh water (none was running from her faucets), and then shaved the duck from beak to claws with an antique razor that once belonged to her father.

No matter that Tía Amada's oven has not worked in years. No matter that her prerevolutionary pots and pans were now in advanced stages of disrepair. We schemed over how to best cook the beast on top of the stove. Finally, with a blunt knife and a hammer borrowed from a neighbor, we hacked the duck to pieces and opted for a fricassee.

The Canadian and his wife got their duck, savory and delicious, served with rice, fried plantains, and a fresh green salad. They said it was the best duck they had ever eaten.

My aunt and I laughed for a long time over that bird, reliving the small adventure, recounting it to relatives in ever more elaborate fashion. By the end of the telling, we might even say we'd gone to Warsaw to "resolve" that duck.

After a long day of such high-intensity resolving, my family would sit around and tell *chistes*, jokes. Cubans turn everything into chistes, most of which are aimed at themselves. There are no sacred cows on the island, including *El Jefe*, Fidel Castro. Neighbors might come by and join in on the fun, as the bottle of rum or *marasquino*, a sweet local liqueur, is passed around.

Often, someone would put a cassette in the tape deck, and the party would be on. Dancing is de rigueur. My uncle has taught me a decent cha-cha-chá, and I can almost make it through a *guaracha* without tripping over myself. Mambos, I'm afraid, the hot ones, the ones that scorch your shoes clear through to your arches, continue to elude me.

Last year I took my daughter with me to Cuba. She was two years old, the same age I was when my parents left the island for good. Over the years nostalgia clouded my parents' memories, bitterness the facts. It was impossible to get a true picture of what we had left behind. To me, Cuba was a beautiful daydream, colored by all that might have been but was not. In fact, I had no direct contact with my family on the island until I visited them for the first time at the age of twenty-five.

At Christmas I took my daughter for her second visit. My relatives continue to go crazy over her. Her great-grandmother Gloria accuses her of not being a girl at all but a *muñequita,* a little doll. Her great uncle Jorge, an industrial engineer, spends hours entertaining her with handkerchiefs he fashions into a gravelly voiced rabbit named Pepino. Her second cousin Estrella repeatedly demands *un beso rico,* and my daughter happily complies with a kiss.

I know now that I want to go back to Cuba as often as possible. My daughter will grow up knowing the island and her family there. For her, Cuba will not be an abstraction of lost hopes and misplaced longings, but a place of memories, good and bad mingling like any others. Whether my daughter will fall in love with Cuba the way I have, I cannot tell. But the opportunity to do so is one of the greatest gifts I can offer her.

CARLOS EIRE

(1 9 5 1 –   )

At the age of eleven, Carlos Eire, along with his older brother Tony, reached the shores of Florida as part of Operation Peter Pan. Between the years of 1960 and 1962, more than 14,000 children left Cuba for the United States, unaccompanied by their parents. Operation Peter Pan, sponsored by the Catholic Welfare Bureau and the U.S. Embassy in Havana, was a program that sought to airlift Catholic children out of a country where Marxist teachings were replacing religious education. People believed the revolution in Cuba would end soon, and then the children would return. Youth with family members in the States fared better than others, who were shuffled between foster care and orphanages. The Eire brothers lived in a group home for boys in Miami until they connected with an uncle outside of Chicago.

Eire's memoir, *Waiting for Snow in Havana: Confessions of a Cuban Boy,* centers on his eccentric family, including a father who believed he was King Louis XVI of France in a previous life. It captures a magical childhood: Eire recounts being chauffeured to private schools attended by the upper class of Havana, including the children of Fulgencio Batista. Neighbors who kept tigers and apes as pets and lavish birthday parties with giant movie screens projected over vast swimming pools are just a few of the extravagances that would be lost with the revolution in Cuba. Eire went on to study religion and is now the T. Lawrason Riggs Professor of History and Religious Studies at Yale University. *Waiting for Snow in Havana* won the National Book Award for nonfiction in 2003.

from WAITING FOR SNOW IN HAVANA: CONFESSIONS OF A CUBAN BOY
TRECE

Thirteen is a volatile number. Schizoid, highly charged, unstable, unpredictable.

If thirteen were a human being instead of a number, and it lived next door to you, what would you do? Could you live with the anxiety of not knowing how this neighbor might behave? Generous to a fault, this neighbor, capable of lending you lawn mowers with a full tank of gas, or murderous to the core, capable of skewering you with a fireplace poker and of sacrificing your children to Satan on your own kitchen table, slowly, with your dullest butter knife? Better to skirt thirteen, when possible, or to remove yourself from its presence.

If I can't avoid thirteen though, what then? Should I invoke the goddess Fortuna? Why not talk about luck? But not my own luck. No. That's like knocking on that unpredictable neighbor's door with an empty cup in my hand.

Better at this point, when speaking of luck and the lottery of existence, to reach back into the past. Better to deal with people and events that influenced me, but for which I bear no responsibility. And, after I make the briefest of appearances, exit quickly. Better to offer fragmentary sketches of luck, and odds, and improbable coincidences. Fragments of family history that mirror too much. Fragments of mirrors that hint at a carefully crafted plot.

Some of these fragments, I believe, have Fidel's face on them, mirrored endlessly.

Out of a very long list, I have chosen thirteen items. Thirteen, of course, to placate the ever-smoldering goddess. Do I have any choice, divine Fortuna?

1. One of my great-grandparents—the father of my father's

mother—won the top prize in the Spanish lottery three times. *El Premio Gordo.* The Fat Prize, literally. Lucky man, I think. Family tradition has it that someone tried to hack him to pieces with a machete for the money.

2. One of my great-great-grandmothers was chased out of Mexico in 1820, during the Mexican Revolution, and she and her family fled to Cuba on a boat. This boat apparently drifted aimlessly in the turquoise sea for a while, and they were all forced to drink their own urine. They lost everything they owned, too, which was a lot. According to my dad, whose facts can't really be trusted, she and her family, the Butrón-Múgicas, owned practically the entire city of Guanajuato. On some days, my dad said it was the whole state of Guanajuato. Unlucky woman. She won *El Premio Flaco,* the Thin Prize.

I had to hear this story endlessly as a child, along with that of Louis XVI and the guillotine. I'll spare you the details of what they ate on the boat, along with their urine cocktails.

3. After arriving in Cuba, Great-Great-Grandma Múgica, now bereft of her fortune and much skinnier, married a Spanish army officer named Nieto who had fought against the Mexicans for ten long years, only to lose the war. As a reward for his efforts, futile though they were, and possibly for his wounds, Captain Tomás Nieto was given some land in Cuba. So he gave up whatever waited for him back in Spain, married the thin woman who used to own Guanajuato, and the two of them raised a whole new branch of army officers, who were trained to ensure that Spain wouldn't lose Cuba too.

Spain lost Cuba anyway. And Guanajuato remained in the hands of others.

But I had another ancestor who had already beaten the Múgicas to the finish line in the lose-everything sweepstakes by three centuries.

4. There's a very good chance that the original Nieto, Alvaro, the first for whom there are written records, was a Jew. Or at least

the son of a Jew, forcibly converted into a Christian. Alvaro Nieto packed his bags and fled from Albuquerque, in hot, dry Extremadura, Spain, to seek a new life and a new identity in cool, green Galicia. Many converted Jews had to do this back in 1500, to escape prosecution for practicing Jewish rituals in their homes. Many of them fled to other places, and pretended not to be Jews, or the children of Jews. Many of them had all of their property confiscated by the Inquisition, or lost it, before fleeing.

Why do I suspect that Alvaro Nieto was a Jew, or the son of a Jew? Funny thing. We never ate pork at our house. Never ate clams, or lobster, or crabs. And it had been that way for generations. Cubans love pork and all that other stuff we never ate. It was unnatural for Cubans to observe Jewish dietary laws, especially without knowing why.

But that's not all. Another ancestor also lost everything for the sake of his faith.

5. On my mother's side of the family, one of my great-great-great-great-grandparents was chased out of Ireland in 1649 by Oliver Cromwell and his English Puritan army. Ultra-Great-Grandad Francis Eire and his Irish family fled to Spain, leaving everything they owned behind, so they could remain Catholic. And family tradition has it they owned a whole lot. Unlucky, I guess. But his son was lucky. He fell in love with a woman in Galicia whose family owned a lot of property and married her. Luck of the Irish?

Much of her property remained in my family's hands until my grandfather came along and fell in love with the wrong girl. Not wrong for him, mind you, only for his parents.

6. My mother's father and mother left Spain in 1920 because their parents didn't want them to get married. They eloped. Got on a ship, and crossed the ocean to Cuba. My grandfather left behind everything he owned and everything he hoped to inherit— which was a lot—just so he could marry the girl of his dreams. Lucky, lucky man, at least when it came to love. So lucky, he lived

with that girl, Josefa, for fifty-eight years, and they had three lovely children. Yes, of course, it was a lot that he gave up back in Galicia. I know this because I went there and saw it for myself. Everyone kept pointing out to me what would have belonged to my grandfather. *"Sabéis, esto debería ser vuestro."* You know, this ought to belong to you, they said. Orchards. Vineyards. Meadows. Houses. Stuff. Now, it all belongs to other relatives. One of them showed me a trunk full of fine china and silverware, tucked away in an attic, and said, "I shouldn't let you see this: it was supposed to go to your grandfather."

This same grandfather started to make his way in Cuba, but his house burned to the ground and his oldest daughter came down with polio. There was no insurance to cover either tragedy. He started all over again, and when the banks failed in 1929, he lost all his money once more. So he started over again, working as a truck driver. One day, shortly before I was born, he bought a lottery ticket, and it turned out to be the winning number. *El Premio Gordo.* The Fat Prize. But that very same night, right after he learned he was a wealthy man, his house burned down again. And inside the house was the winning ticket, which was devoured by flames. No ticket, no prize. Those were the rules of the Cuban lottery. He lost his house, his belongings, and the Fat Prize all in one night. So he started over again, driving his truck day after day, and saved enough money to buy a very nice house for his retirement years. And along came Fidel and Che Guevara, and one fine day Che seized all the money in the banks. And my grandfather lost all his savings in one day. Again. Lucky or not? I can't tell. He always seemed so happy. And he had nothing against lizards.

7. His name was Amador. In English this means "lover."

8. My other grandfather, my father's father, was named Amado. "Loved one," in English. What are the odds of having grandfathers named Lover and Loved One? A trillion to one? Probably much higher than that. Somewhere just short of infinity, I guess.

9. Amado, my father's father, met his wife, Lola, my grand-

mother, while watching Lola's house burn down. There she was, standing outside the house with her family, watching everything go up in smoke, and along came Amado, a previously unseen young neighbor, and they got to talking, and the next thing you know, they're getting married. Lucky pair.

By the way, the house they were watching burn down was the house owned by Lola's father, the man who had won the lottery Fat Prize in Spain three times, the man who was nearly murdered for money.

Amado chose not to follow a military career, like all of his male ancestors. He went to medical school for a while but dropped out because he didn't like the idea of having to find his own cadaver to dissect. (Back then, each medical student had to find their own cadaver, which meant that many of them stole corpses from cemeteries.) He finally ended up in the real estate business. He and Lola had four children, the youngest of whom was my dad.

Lola's sister, Uma, lived with them their entire married life. She was a musician and a very well-respected piano teacher. She never married. Family tradition has it that Uma had fallen in love with Amado the night of the fire, and had always remained in love with him. But he had fallen for her sister, and married her instead. Unlucky Uma. Was living under the same roof with her sister and the man she loved the seventh circle of hell, or could it have been just what she wanted, and a foretaste of heaven? Uma thought Amado was the funniest man in the world. Or at least in Havana. This is what she told my mother over and over again. No one was funnier than Amado, or nicer.

10. Amado is the only grandparent I never got to meet. Too bad. He died young, at the age of fifty-six. Killed by an envelope. Unlucky Amado. While licking an envelope, he nicked his tongue with its sharp edge. A small paper cut on the tongue. It was a tiny, ridiculous wound, but there were no antibiotics in 1927. His wound became infected and he died. Unlucky. Definitely. No doubt about it.

I never lick envelopes. And I yell at my children every time I see them do it, just like my father did to me. "Do you know my grandfather died from licking an envelope?"

They think I'm making it up.

Lola was widowed in her midfifties. She and Uma, and her unmarried daughter, Lucía, and my father, Antonio, moved to Miramar a few years after that. To a house on the very edge of civilization.

11. Then my dad met my mom. He met her through a psychic he used to visit regularly, a woman who claimed to have intimate connections with the spirit world. My mom and her family were not at all interested in psychic mediums or the spirit world, but they had a neighbor who knew someone who knew the medium, and somehow, in the weird way these things sometimes happen, my mom and dad were introduced to each other through her.

Louis XVI recognized Marie Antoinette the minute he laid eyes on her, and he began to court her furiously. She was not too interested at first. But slowly the persuasive woman was persuaded. Louis XVI wouldn't take no for an answer. This is what can happen when a man thinks he has met the woman who has been his soul mate for thousands and thousands of lifetimes.

He did outrageous things, such as stand outside her house with flowers in his hand for hours and hours. In the hot sun. In pouring rain. He used whatever intermediaries and advocates he could find. He sent letters. Presents. And he stood outside her door until she caved in. They started seeing each other, with chaperones of course, as was the Cuban custom, and before long, my mom fell in love with King Louis, in spite of the fact that she thought that all of this reincarnation stuff was utter nonsense. Non–Marie Antoinette she was to herself, Marie Antoinette to him. Non–Louis XVI he was to her, Louis XVI to himself. Dad was also twelve years older than Mom and not exactly the best-looking man in Havana. Whereas, if you had stood my mom next to Rita Hayworth in 1944, you would have been forced to say that Rita just didn't measure up. Although my mom did have one bad leg and Rita didn't. Still, in spite of every glaring difference between them, in spite of my mom's leg, and all the odds stacked up against this pairing, my parents got married.

King Louis brought Marie Antoinette to live in that house in Miramar. Brought her there to share the house with his mother, his aunt, and his sister. The neighbors took bets on how long the marriage would last. No one bet on more than one year. And no one won.

12. Sometime in the 1930s, a Jewish refugee fleeing from the Nazis landed in Havana. He had been wise enough to see what was looming on the horizon and had managed to escape with his whole family and several valuable works of art. Strapped for cash in a strange tropical land, this refugee sold off the art piece by piece. Much to his dismay, most of the items sold for a fraction of their real value. Havana during the Depression was not a good place in which to market works of art. Unlucky refugee.

One day, while scouring antique shops in Havana, trying to find more objects with which to fill up that house into which he would bring my mother, Louis XVI found a portrait he immediately recognized. A thrilling find. It was none other than Empress Maria Theresa of Austria. The painting was a bargain. A steal, practically. The shop owner had bought it from another dealer, who had bought it from the Jewish refugee for a pittance and was selling it for not much more than he himself had paid for it. About one hundred pesos. Nobody wanted that portrait. Such a dour-looking woman. Maybe she cussed out all potential buyers, telepathically, scaring them away.

Louis XVI purchased the portrait gleefully and hung it in a place of honor. The portrait of his mother-in-law.

Empress Maria Theresa of Austria, you see, was Marie Antoinette's mother.

Lucky Dad. Unlucky me.

Coño. Qué mierda.

What were the odds of a portrait of Empress Maria Theresa of Austria ending up in the hands of a man who claimed to have been her son-in-law in a former life? What were the odds that this strange man and the portrait would have crossed paths in Havana, of all places?

Only God could calculate those odds. Perhaps. Maybe not even He.

13. Finally, let me tell you more about *Abuela* Lola, from the luck angle. Houses that burn down, fortunes that are lost, tyrants and revolutions that force you into exile, these are all part of my family's luck. And so is the lizard-loathing gene. It was my luck to end up with it. She gave me that special gift.

How I wish Lola could tell you about this herself. I may have inherited the loathing from her, but have never fully fathomed it. I know for certain she understood it intimately.

Speak, Grandma. Please. *Llegó la hora.* The time has come. You, who loved speaking with the dead, speak now. You who were so superstitious, to you I offer the thirteenth place in chapter thirteen.

RICARDO PAU-LLOSA

(1 9 5 4 –)

Poet and fiction writer, art critic and curator, Ricardo Pau-Llosa left Cuba with his family at the age of six for Florida, where he now resides. Rich visual imagery and lively tempos keep the Cuba of the poet's youth alive in his work. Whether evoking the ripe tropical fruits *mameyes* and *caimitos,* or his relationship with the Santería deities, Pau-Llosa's poetry captures the flavors and textures of Cuba.

The poem "Charada China" comes from *Cuba,* Pau-Llosa's third book of poetry. Translated literally, the title means "Chinese Numbers" and is a popular approach to playing the lottery in Cuba based on Chinese lore. Two major waves of Chinese workers moved to Cuba, the first in 1847 to work the fields as inexpensive replacements for slaves. The second wave corresponded with the gold rush in the United States, from approximately 1860 to 1875, when Cuba became a stopover for future Chinese prospectors. Though the old Chinese neighborhood, the *barrio chino,* has greatly changed, the influence of the Chinese is still widespread in Cuba, from green medicine to martial arts. In particular the Chinese portents of luck—perhaps a legacy of those hopeful gold-seekers—have been solidly etched into Cuban culture via the Charada China.

CHARADA CHINA

Every image in every dream has a number.
Every digit from 1 to 100 corresponds
to several images. Thanks to us *chinos,*
the Cubans are now ready to win at lottery.
If last night you dreamt of a shark,

you must play 45, which is also
the number for President,
Suit, Streetcar, School, and Star,
and often comes up in June drawings.
You heard a phone ring in your dream?
Then play 70 as well, especially
if you also dreamt a coconut
a shot, a barrel, a rainbow, or a bullet.
A scorpion slid down the terrified leg
of a friend or a cow, play 43 in August.
Monkey, Family, Black Man, Supervisor,
and Dove are 34. And my favorite, 100
for Toilet, God, Broom, Automobile,
Bus Stop, and Collapsed Building.
It usually comes in January.
I know what you are thinking:
if these numbers work, why hasn't this *chino*
won the lottery a hundred times?
The wise are robed with poverty.
My dreams have been taken over
by the chart of the *Charada*.
You came to the *barrio chino* for advice
on how to play your dreams. Their free images
evoke a random series of lottery numbers.
Cockroach 48, Rabbit 39, Dark Sun 60, Beggar 91.
But last night I started dreaming
of train tracks and automatically
the other images of 72 came into focus:
an old ox, a saw, a necklace, a scepter
and thunder. Since we all have four dreams
each night, my mind divided 72 by 4 and all
the images of 18 came into focus: a small fish,
a church, a siren, a palm tree, men fishing
and a yellow cat. This last image grew larger

and bared huge teeth, and in came all the images for 92:
a lion, a high balloon, a suicide, Cuba, an anarchist.
All my dreams boil down to one number, 54,
the number for a dream you dreamt having,
You must never play this number!
There is no freedom in wisdom, only order,
and so my dreams are endless jugglings
which have long ago stopped meaning
the pathway to happiness, or riches.
That is why I don't sell the *Charada*
and all its listings. You need your dreams
as they are. You need them to terrify you
and to promise you kingdoms and lotteries.
Let them betray you and laugh at you.
Do not buy those charts on the street!
They are plagued with errors
and it would be a disaster to gamble with them.
I see the birth of a dream swirling in your pupils,
the dream you will have tonight and forget by morning.
No, my ethics prevent me from telling you what it is,
but here are its numbers: 6, 46, 82, 23, 17.

ROSA LOWINGER
(1 9 5 8 –)

Rosa Lowinger is a writer and art conservator who was born in Havana, left with her parents as a child, and now lives in Los Angeles. She visits Cuba regularly as an educator, as an architectural consultant, and as a Cuban American going back to her family's past. She has noted that "the history of Cuba can be read like a map by its buildings." The natural landscape, political upheavals, and cultural influences are reflected in the winding streets and high-rise buildings. Memory is also history of sorts, and her work deals in abstract maps of the past and the ways in which the past can be revisited, and at times even restored. Her book, *Tropicana Nights,* a history and memoir of the Tropicana Cabaret, is scheduled for publication by St. Martin's Press in 2004.

REPAIRING THINGS

Before I returned to Cuba in 1992, I had no idea what there was in the way of art, architecture, and museum collections, the basis of my work as an art conservator in the United States. For me, Cuba was a place left behind, a place of sadness and loss, a place once beautiful and full of promise that now languished in a rubble of despair. As an art conservator my job is to repair things; but Cuba was my parents' domain, part of a distant past they did not long for anymore.

In the mid-1980s I decided that I had to visit Cuba, to see the country for myself, to form an opinion of it based on my own observations and not the painful memories of my family. It took ten years, but finally my profession was the entry ticket. In 1992, I was invited to a professional conference on the preservation of cultural patrimony sponsored by Cuba's national art conservation laboratories—the Centro Nacional de Conservación, Restauración y Museología (CENCREM).

On the day I arrived in Havana, I took a taxi to Vedado, the stylish district where my parents lived when I was born. I wanted to walk down the streets my parents had loved, to photograph the apartment building my grandfather had built. The taxi left the hotel in Miramar and went along the Malecón—the sweeping seven-kilometer boulevard that arcs along the northern coast, demarcating the line between Cubans and Cuban exiles. Everyone who left Cuba speaks of the Malecón in rapturous tones. Over the years I had seen countless pictures of it in the still summer heat, or in winter, when waves spray high above the seawall. Now the same seawall was breaking up from corrosion of the iron rebar inside the mortar, and now hardly a car went past, due to the shortage of petroleum. The taxi dropped me off at the Hotel Riviera. Once the most glamorous casino-hotel ever built outside of Las Vegas, it was now missing portions of its tile facade and some of its oceanfront windows were boarded up.

I walked from the Riviera to my family's apartment building, not wishing to appear conspicuous. But there was no denying my foreignness. It was bright and windless and there were many people on this stretch of the Malecón—young lovers entwined while sitting on the seawall, a few intrepid children braving the rocks in the water. Everyone stared at me as I went past. Music blared from loudspeakers in an open plaza across from the hotel. The sound was metallic, grating to the ear. And my surroundings chafed at my eyes: I had expected to see some disrepair, but the extent of the destruction was dismal—everywhere I looked there was crumbling, peeling, rusting, spalling. Focused as I was on the corroded balconies and columns with cracks as thick as my thumbs, I failed to notice that the architecture was spectacular. On our street alone there were eclectic houses with Spanish tile facades, art deco high-rises, and apartment buildings from the 1940s and '50s with sweeping modernist staircases and marble entryways. My grandfather's building had had a number of its wide, square balconies enclosed in unsightly glass. Looking at it through my parents' eyes, not those of an art conservator, I failed to make note of the opalescent glass doors and black terrazzo hallway. I walked around for a few minutes, conspicuous with my camera, another exile disappointed by the rubble of loss.

The following day, before the conference began with an evening cocktail party, I went to the Jewish cemetery in Guanabacoa and laid a stone at the grave of my maternal grandmother. Jews eschew flowers on graves—I'm not sure why—but I have decided to believe that the stone on the grave has something to do with the perpetual exile's desire to be grounded, even in death. For conservators, stone is the most basic identifier of place: Knowing the origin of a stone, say in an ancient bracelet, sheds light on trade routes, economics, and artistic and social influences between cultures.

The same holds true for buildings. In Old Havana, most of the major eighteenth-century buildings are made of a porous limestone quarried on the island. The stone is full of tiny marine fossils that come into high relief as the stone sheds its matrix from the pummeling of wind and salt. On the way to the seventeenth-century Convento de Santa Clara, where the cocktail reception was held, I walked past block after block of these massive stone buildings. I was with a group of Venezuelan architects, but none of them were as nonplussed as I by the sheer size of the colonial district, and the magnitude of Cuba's architecture.

For example, I alone was ignorant of the fact that Havana lays claim to having both the oldest and the largest Spanish fortresses in the Americas. I also was unaware that the entire neighborhood where my mother was born was designated a World Heritage Site by UNESCO because of its architectural significance. Cuba is the only country in the Caribbean and one of very few in all of Latin America to have two World Heritage sites. The second one is

Trinidad de Cuba, an impossibly charming town of eighteenth-
and nineteenth-century buildings on the Caribbean coast that
once was the center of sugar production and the slave trade for
the island. But I did not know any of that then. I had worked for
fifteen years as a specialist in the preservation of sculpture and
monuments, but my knowledge of art history ended on this side
of the Malecón. The only thing I knew about Old Havana was
that my mother grew up on one of its streets, not far from the
Convento where the cocktail party was held and which now
houses the country's national conservation laboratories. She always
described this area as poor, run-down, and calamitous, some place
best forgotten. Her nostalgia was reserved entirely for the upscale
Vedado I had visited the day before, a place that now would surely
appall her.

Now, a decade since my first visit to Cuba, it seems odd that
throughout my childhood I never knew what there was to preserve in Cuba. I didn't know about the cobbled streets of Old
Havana, the wide paved plazas ringed by palatial houses with interior courtyards. I was ignorant of the fact that my mother had
grown up within a stone's throw of a grand baroque cathedral that
was both asymmetrical and so perfectly proportioned that the
architects I walked with that first day stood awed in front of it for
nearly half an hour. That day, my head buzzed with the sudden
recognition of a place that held something for me beyond memory. I turned wide circles in the plaza so I could absorb it all at
once, like in a panoramic photograph—broad buildings of coral
and limestone, stained glass as brilliant as the sky, the narrow,
noisy streets that fanned out from the cathedral plaza in all directions—poor and run-down, to be sure, but laden with historic
architectural treasures that link me to the people who live there
and to the architects, conservators, and historians who dedicate
their lives to making sure they don't fall down.

*   *   *

On my second visit to Cuba, later that year, I went to Trinidad. For architects, conservators, and students of Cuban history all roads eventually lead to Trinidad. Trinidad is a special place— notable for its exquisite location between the Escambray Moun- tains and the sea, for its historic importance as one of Cuba's centers of sugar production in the eighteenth and nineteenth cen- turies, for the magnificence of its period architecture, the vibrance of its African-rooted culture, and most important, at least to me, because it is a place where preservation of the past links everyone.

At the time of my visit, the conservation activity in Trinidad was coordinated by the department of restoration—a group of architects and conservators that worked out of the nineteenth- century mansion that once belonged to Don Mariano de Borrell, one of Trinidad's most illustrious former citizens, and one of its most infamous sugar barons. I climbed the steep hill to the office on a blazing August day in order to meet the head of the depart- ment, architect Roberto López Bastida. Nearly everyone in Trinidad knew Roberto López and everyone who did called him Macholo. He had lived in Trinidad his entire life. Macholo was a short, olive-skinned man with a thick shock of dark hair and a bristly mustache that bounced up and down against his lip when he spoke. He was articulate, kinetic, and passionate on many sub- jects, especially the preservation of Trinidad. On that first trip of mine to Trinidad we spent hours walking together through the scorching city, along cobbled streets lined with red-tile-roofed buildings, through house museums that had frescoed walls and collections of furniture, porcelain, and African artifacts that told the story of Trinidad and the surrounding Valle de los Ingenios— a valley of sugarcane fields and plantation houses that were also part of the UNESCO World Heritage designation.

Macholo peppered me with questions as we walked: "How can we get rid of these fungal stains on marble? What can be used to repair cloisonné or eradicate termites from the church archives?" Many of these issues were not complicated from a conservation point of view, but the sheer quantity left me nearly speechless. And then there was a problem of materials. As we toured, I became aware that Cuban conservators scraped by to find whatever they could to repair things.

At the Museo Romántico in Trinidad, the nineteenth-century home of the illustrious Brunet family that now served as a decorative arts museum, I had noticed a honeycomb drying out in the courtyard. When I prodded Macholo about the reason for this, he explained, candidly, that there was an infestation in one of the galleries, and the bees were being allowed to flourish so they could harvest the beeswax to make coatings for metals and linings for damaged paintings. It was an unorthodox solution, but at least it took care of one problem. But there were many others. A city's worth of conservation issues became evident as people stopped him on the street or in the seventeenth-century house that now served as a bar, where we had paused for a respite from the heat.

"Oye, Macholo, don't forget that my roof is leaking," said the bartender as he prepared us a potent local blend of aguardiente, lemon, and honey known as a canchanchara.

"My front door won't close properly," said someone else who spotted him from the street. "Did you get the cement you promised me?" "Did your office have a chance to review the plans for my new kitchen?" Even in the afternoon quiet of the bar, it was impossible to carry on a conversation.

"Every house around here is historic," Macholo explained. "Every major repair has to be approved or carried out by our department. We're responsible for museum collections, monuments, churches, and everyone's bathroom pipes."

At the end of my first day in Trinidad, Macholo led me up into the tower of a canary yellow mansion that had once belonged to the Cantero family. The rich in Trinidad used to compete with one another in the construction of their houses. They vied for the tallest towers, the most ornate frescoes, and opulent furnishings from Spain, Austria, and France. The tower of the Palacio Cantero, which now housed the history museum, affords one of the best views of the city, the blue-green hills that ring it, and the sparkling Caribbean to the south. Without even thinking, Macholo continued to point out the sights of the region he knew by heart, the place that he was never able to leave, no matter how many offers of work came in from Havana, or from international conservation centers in Rome and Spain that eventually began to discover Trinidad and Macholo's passion and talent. "That river in the distance was used by Hernán Cortés when he left Trinidad to conquer Mexico. And that one, further out, is where the sand for our mortar comes from." Earlier, in the courtyard of a ruined mansion, Macholo had shown me the great pits of aggregate and lime they used for making restoration mortar. The aggregate is a coarse mix of beach sand and river stones collected from a spot along the river. It is the same material used by the builders of the city. "At least we have enough of that material," he laughed, but I could tell that he was worried about his city, his country, in general.

He should have worried more about himself. In the summer of 2003, Macholo died suddenly at the age of forty-five from bacterial meningitis. It was a loss that was felt all over Cuba and in the international conservation community, where for weeks there was a flurry of e-mails from Spain, Italy, Peru, Mexico, and the United States expressing shock and sadness. Over the years Macholo and I had grown as close as siblings and I had watched him slowly bring the city that he loved back from near ruin. His work was his life, and it was in the throes of the daunting task of running a restoration department that had grown to three hundred employees that he failed to go to the doctor quickly enough when he developed bacterial meningitis. Macholo's wake was in the grand entry hall of the Palacio de Borrell. Hundreds followed his casket to the city's historic cemetery, where his friends and colleagues delivered tearful speeches, and a traditional Cuban band from the nearby

Valley of the Sugar Mills choked up while trying to sing his favorite songs. When I arrived, two days after his funeral, I had the taxi stop at the bridge that crosses the Guaurabo River before reaching the cemetery. I placed the smoothest brown river stone on his grave, beside the mounds of flowers.

JOSÉ BARREIRO

(1 9 4 8 –)

Scholar and writer José Barreiro has both Taíno and *guajiro* ancestry. The Taínos were the indigenous people who inhabited Cuba before the Spaniards arrived, and *guajiros* are the country people who farm the eastern provinces. Barreiro has dedicated his life's work to bringing the viewpoints of indigenous people throughout the Americas to light, currently by serving as the director of the American Indian Program at Cornell University, and as editor in chief of Akwe:kon Press's *Native Americas Journal*. In his novel, *The Indian Chronicles,* Barreiro draws on his scholarly knowledge of the Taíno people of Cuba to imagine the diary of Diego Colón, a captured Taíno boy who serves as Columbus's translator and adopted son, and through whose eyes we see the Spanish conquest of the Caribbean that will eventually decimate his people.

from THE INDIAN CHRONICLES

August 11, 1532

Thirty-one. *Sojourn in Cuba, along the northern coast, searching for the Great Khan, the curse of Old Guamax, days of early reverence.*

I still remember the Yunque of Baracoa, in Cuba—that wide, flat mountaintop that can be seen from the bay. I remember the Cuban coast, how thick and lush it was, how big the island felt that first time. The Admiral was very excited. A land more beautiful human eyes have never seen, he said, words I heard him repeat many times later in his discourses with nobles, bishops and powerful merchants of Spain.

In Cuba, we from Guanahani knew Cubanakán, a cacique from the center of the island whose fishermen made the journey, once a year, to Guanahani. And once a year our own men (my father and uncle Çibanakán among them) would reciprocate, visiting also on their shores. They traded woven jeniken ropes produced from maguey grass at Cubanakán for our good fish catchers, hookers and spear points made from the shells of our great caracol beach on the northeast corner of Guanahani. The great Cuban hemp twine, woven from tall savannah grass, was much requested, particularly their long, very fine ropes that made the best reinforcers of fishing nets. In good weather, it took the men six days to make the trip to Cubanakán; in my memory, they never lost anybody during those journeys.

Many times, encouraged by Rodrigo, I mentioned that cacique's name, Cubanakán, and the island's name, Cuba, to Don Christopherens, who wrote it down and had his secretary, Escobedo, write it down comparing the writings to my sounds. Carey, a man of my village and a cousin of mine, was forced on board as we left Guanahani. He was a guaxeri in the fishing with my father, and he guided Captain Pinzón and the Admiral. Carey had made the trip to Cuba for several years.

We sailed into Cuban waters on the thirteenth sun after leaving Guanahani, my home. By the Castilla calendar it was October 27, 1492. I remember it rained all night, drops pounding flat on the decks like frogs falling from trees; the ships hove to, drifting in the bay, and all night rain fell. The morning sky was so clean, the eyes drank from it—the kind of day my elders would have deemed, "swept by Coatriskie," the spirit cemí who, in our Taíno mind, ruled the heavy rains and assisted in the cleansing of the skies.

Cuba was different, from the beginning. The coastal caciques were not forthcoming. As he had done on four other islands, the Admiral landed the ship's boats. He liked the many small and large bays and took boats himself up the wide rivers, but for days the local Taínos fled from him. This excited him even more, as I could tell he had grown tired of the hundreds of people that had swarmed his ships in the smaller islands. When he found two very large and well-carved traveling canoes, one with capacity for over one hundred and fifty people, the Admiral paced and paced and many times showed me, Carey and others a bracelet and a chain made of fine gold. Rodrigo's agile hand signals interpreted for us: *The Guamikina wants to see other great guamikinas. The Guamikina wants to see them wear their gold.*

PERMISSIONS ACKNOWLEDGMENTS

Grateful acknowledgment is made to the following for permission to reprint previously published material:

Algonquin Books of Chapel Hill: Excerpt from *Cuba Diaries: An American Housewife in Havana* by Isadora Tattlin, copyright © 2002 by Isadora Tattlin. Reprinted by permission of Algonquin Books of Chapel Hill, a division of Workman Publishing.

Arte Público Press: Excerpt from *The Indian Chronicles* by José Barreiro, copyright © 1993 by José Barreiro (Houston: Arte Público Press—University of Houston). Reprinted by permission of Arte Público Press.

Basic Books: Excerpt from *Trading with the Enemy: A Yankee Travels Through Castro's Cuba* by Tom Miller, copyright © 1992 by Tom Miller. Reprinted by permission of Basic Books, a member of Perseus Books, LLC.

Ruth Behar: "In the Absence of Love" by Ruth Behar, copyright © 1999 by Ruth Behar. Originally published in *The House of Memory: Stories by Jewish Women Writers of Latin America,* edited by Marjorie Agosin (New York: Feminist Press, 1999). Reprinted by permission of Ruth Behar.

Carnegie Mellon University Press: "Charada China" from *Cuba* by Ricardo Pau-Llosa, copyright © 1993 by Ricardo Pau-Llosa. Reprinted by permission of Carnegie Mellon University Press.

Dell Publishing: Excerpt from *Cuba Libre* by Elmore Leonard, copyright © 1998 by Elmore Leonard, Inc. Reprinted by permission of Dell Publishing, a division of Random House, Inc.

Donadio & Olson, Inc.: "Havana Then and Now" by Robert Stone, copyright © 1992 by Robert Stone (*Harper's* magazine, March 1992). Reprinted by permission of Donadio & Olson, Inc.

Kimi Eisele: "The Flesh, the Bones, and the Beating Heart" by Kimi Eisele, copyright © 2004 by Kimi Eisele. Reprinted by permission of the author.

Farrar, Straus and Giroux, LLC: Excerpt from *The Mambo Kings Play Songs of Love* by Oscar Hijuelos, copyright © 1989 by Oscar Hijuelos. Reprinted by permission of Farrar, Straus and Giroux, LLC.

The Free Press: Excerpt from *Waiting for Snow in Havana: Confessions of a Cuban Boy* by Carlos Eire, copyright © 2003 by Carlos Eire. Reprinted by permission of The Free Press, a division of Simon & Schuster Adult Publishing Group.

Elizabeth Hanly: "Santería: An Alternative Pulse" by Elizabeth Hanly, copyright © 1995 by Elizabeth Hanly. Originally published in *Aperture* magazine, Fall 1995, edition 141. Reprinted by permission of the author.

David Higham Associates Ltd.: Excerpt from *Our Man in Havana* by Graham Greene, copyright © 1958 by William Heinemann Ltd., copyright renewed 1986 by Graham Greene (New York: Viking Press, 1958; London: William Heinemann Ltd., 1958). Reprinted by permission of David Higham Associates Ltd., London.

Hill and Wang: "Havana Nights" from *I Wonder as I Wander* by Langston Hughes, copyright © 1956 by Langston Hughes, copyright renewed 1984 by George Houston Bass. Reprinted by permission of Hill and Wang, a division of Farrar, Straus and Giroux, LLC.

Houghton Mifflin Company: Excerpt from *Ports of the Sun* by Eleanor Early, copyright © 1937, copyright renewed 1965 by Eleanor Early. All rights reserved. Reprinted by permission of Houghton Mifflin Company.

Alfred A. Knopf: Excerpt from *Cuba and the Night* by Pico Iyer, copyright © 1995 by Pico Iyer. "Batting Against Castro" from *Batting Against Castro* by Jim Shepard, copyright © 1996 by Jim Shepard. Reprinted by permission of Alfred A. Knopf, a division of Random House, Inc.

Ellen Levine Literary Agency/Trident Media Group: "Simple Life" by Cristina García, copyright © 1996 by Cristina García (*Islands* magazine, July/August 1996). "Repairing Things" by Rosa Lowinger, copyright © 1995 by Rosa Lowinger from *Bridges to Cuba,* edited by Ruth Behar (University of Michigan Press, 1995). Reprinted by permission of Ellen Levine Literary Agency/Trident Media Group.

Little, Brown and Company (Inc.): Excerpt from *A Naturalist in Cuba* by Thomas Barbour, copyright © 1945 by Little, Brown and Company (Inc.). Reprinted by permission of Little, Brown and Company (Inc.).

Holly Morris: "Adventure Divas" by Holly Morris, copyright © 2004 by Holly Morris. From *Divadom* by Holly Morris, to be published by Random House in 2005. Reprinted by arrangement with Random House, an imprint of Random House Publishing Group, a division of Random House, Inc.

Pantheon Books: Excerpt from *Looking for History: Dispatches from Latin America* by Alma Guillermoprieto, copyright © 2001 by Alma Guillermoprieto. Reprinted by permission of Pantheon Books, a division of Random House, Inc.

St. Martin's Press, LLC: Excerpt from *Ay, Cuba!* by Andrei Codrescu, copyright © 1999 by Andrei Codrescu. Reprinted by permission of St. Martin's Press, LLC.